I0777301

The Fate
of Our Years

a 509 Crime Story

by Colin Conway

What is the 509?

Separated by the Cascade Range, Washington State is divided into two distinctly different climates and cultures.

The western side of the Cascades is home to Seattle, its 34 inches of annual rainfall, and the incredibly weird and smelly Gum Wall. Most of the state's wealth and political power are concentrated in and around this enormous city. The residents of this area know the prosperity that has come from being the home of Microsoft, Amazon, Boeing, and Starbucks.

To the east of the Cascade Mountains lies nearly two-thirds of the entire state, a lot of which is used for agriculture. Washington State leads the nation in producing apples, it is the second-largest potato grower, and it's the fourth for providing wheat.

This eastern part of the state can enjoy more than 170 days of sunshine each year, which is important when there are more than 200 lakes nearby. However, the beautiful summers are offset by harsh winters, with average snowfall reaching 47 inches and the average high hovering around 37°.

While five telephone area codes provide service to the westside, only 509 covers everything east of the Cascades, a staggering twenty-one counties.

Of these, Spokane County is the largest with an estimated population of 506,000.

*"Whatever the universal nature assigns to any man at
any time is for the good of that man at that time."*

\- Marcus Aurelius,
Roman emperor/Stoic philosopher

The Fate
of Our Years

a 509 Crime Story

by Colin Conway

1

Marlene Anderson held a thick, white ceramic mug with both hands. It hovered in front of her lips. "That's really all you're going to eat?" She sipped her coffee.

I pulled a piece of croissant free and held it up for her to inspect. "What's wrong with it?"

We were seated in a booth at Madeline's Cafe & Patisserie in downtown Spokane. The French-themed restaurant was nearly full, and its customers seemed in a pleasant mood. I'd only eaten at the establishment once, and that was many years before with my wife. The suggestion to meet at the popular destination was Marlene's. She was waiting with her drink when I arrived.

She wore a silk burgundy top and black slacks. Marlene studied me from behind large wire-framed glasses. "You need more than a pastry and coffee for lunch."

"It's more than you've got." I shoved the piece of croissant into my mouth.

She set her mug on the table. "I had an energy bar back at the office."

"I'm not hungry."

"Big breakfast?"

I shrugged. "What are you doing downtown?"

She wiggled the cup handle back and forth. I wondered if she was considering my question or thinking about following up on my breakfast. "I met with an attorney."

"For?"

"The program." She waved off the rest of the explanation.

Marlene worked with Her Freedom, a women's advocacy group. We'd met last year while I was investigating a murder. We got together for coffee or the occasional meal, but we rarely talked shop when we did. It wasn't a hard-and-fast rule but one that developed naturally.

"You need to take better care of yourself," she said. Marlene was about ten years younger than I am. She often said things as if she considered me an older brother, but perhaps that's how female friends spoke.

I ripped another piece of croissant free. "I do fine."

"Sure you do." Her eyes softened. "I want you to do better, though."

"You sound like Dean."

"How is he, by the way?" She smiled. "Did they get back from their trip?"

"Last weekend." I stuffed the bite of pastry into my mouth and rolled my eyes. "I'm sure they'll want to show pictures."

"Don't be that way. The trip must have been amazing."

"I guess."

"Are you kidding? I would kill to go. Wouldn't you? You told me you've never been."

I hadn't.

"Florence, Rome, Venice. All that history." She shook her head in awe.

"It's just looking at someone else's pictures…" I let the thought trail off.

Marlene leaned in. "Take it from me. You should look forward to those moments. I don't have a brother—or a sister, for that matter—and with Dad gone…" It was her turn to let her thoughts drift away.

A silence overtook us. I stared into my coffee for several seconds.

"Hey."

I looked up and met her gaze.

Her long, auburn hair draped over her left shoulder. She tugged at it with a single hand. "Can I ask you something?"

My brow furrowed.

"It's been a while since we've talked about it." Marlene reached out and touched my hand. "When's the last time you heard it?"

I looked away.

The coffee machine behind the counter hissed. Off to my right, a table full of women laughed. Outside, a primer gray muscle car drove along Main Avenue; it sounded like it was missing its muffler.

Overhead, a sugary song played. I could make it out, but I tried not to focus on it. I didn't want to know what it was.

"Look at me, Dallas," she said softly. "Is that why you seem off?"

Off. That was one word for it.

Shortly after my wife's death, I began waking to snippets of music. At first, I wondered if Bobbie was trying to communicate from beyond the grave. Once I decided she wasn't, the music changed. The songs attacked my consciousness during the day. I felt on the verge of a breakdown. My work suffered, and the department ordered I see a therapist. He identified the music as auditory hallucinations. They went away not long after that.

I knew I wasn't crazy, but the diagnosis didn't make me feel better.

She squeezed my hand. "You can tell me."

"No, the music isn't back."

"Then what's wrong?"

I stared at her hand in mine. She had nice fingers. What a stupid observation, I thought. She squeezed my hand again.

Her voice was gentle. "You miss it, though. Don't you?"

Someone laughed in the kitchen. Outside, a car backfired.

"It's okay if you do." Marlene still didn't release my hand. "I understand."

I expected her to say something about addiction, but she didn't. I was glad she avoided the topic. We'd talked about it long ago, so we didn't need to rehash it. Marlene battled her monsters and won. I didn't want to admit the demons I wrestled with were due to a fragile psyche. There was too much pride in confessing I missed the music—doing so would make me sound nuts.

"I'm sort of thinking about retirement," I said.

"Yeah?" There was a lilt to her voice. "That's exciting."

I didn't respond.

"Don't you want to retire?"

"I don't know." My head bobbled from side to side. "Maybe it's time to move on and let someone else move up the ranks."

"Is that what you want to do?"

I hadn't thought about it until recently. After Bobbie's death, the job gave me something to hold on to—a touchstone for reality. Now it felt like a daily slog to the crime factory. The need to be in the fight against evil no longer felt important.

Unfortunately, I didn't know what else was out there. What waited for me in retirement? All the plans I had with Bobbie no longer existed. Fulfilling them alone seemed hollow.

Marlene and I sat that way for several seconds—her holding my hand and me staring at her fingers. Eventually, she let go and settled back into her side of the booth. She grabbed her coffee cup with both hands but didn't lift it from the table.

"That's still no reason not to eat," she said.

"I ate." As soon as I said the words, I regretted them.

"What did you eat?"

Marlene should have been a detective. I didn't have to reengage the subject, and I didn't want to dig myself any deeper with another lie. Besides, I liked her too much to do such a thing. So, I avoided answering the question.

"I'll eat dinner tonight."

"I know you will," she said. "You're coming over."

"Huh?"

"Make it six."

"You don't have to."

"I know I don't, but it's the only way I can make sure you'll eat a healthy meal."

I was about to argue when she added, "Besides, it's been a couple weeks since you've seen Sadie. She's been asking about you."

I forced a smile.

"Don't expect fancy. You know how I cook."

"You do great." My phone buzzed and the screen illuminated with the caller's name—DISPATCH. "Hold on." I swiped my thumb across the screen. "Nash."

"Hey, Dallas. It's Ed. Sorry to interrupt your seven."

I had notified dispatch I was out for lunch and off my radio. "It's fine." I shrugged apologetically to Marlene.

She watched me with mild curiosity. She wasn't a fan of the police department. We'd become friends despite her feelings about my employer.

"There's a body," Ed said.

"There usually is."

I pulled a notebook from the inside of my suit jacket as Ed continued. Marlene sipped her coffee while the phone conversation played out. When I got the particulars from Ed, I hung up.

"Duty calls," she muttered. She tried to hide her disdain for my employer, but it poked through in her tone.

"I need to go."

We both took a final sip of our drinks and slid out of the booth.

"About that dinner," I said. "I'll probably need to cancel."

Marlene shook her head. "Nonsense. Come by when you get done."

"It might be late."

"So? Spend the night." The words tumbled out, and she gasped as if surprised by their utterance. Her eyes widened, and she blushed. Now, Marlene spoke in a hurry. "I'm sorry. I shouldn't have said that."

"It's okay."

"Just stop by for a minute, and I'll make you a to-go plate." She kissed me on the side of the cheek, then backpedaled. "See you later, Dal."

I stood there as she rushed out of the restaurant. She never looked back.

***

The body lay balled up and crumpled in the middle of the living room floor like a discarded tissue from a bloody nose. I squatted next to a now bloating white male.

Longish silver hair fell across the side of his face. The skin nearest the floor was dark red—a result of pooling blood. The upper skin was waxy and pale. He'd been there for at least a few days.

Before entering the house, I'd put on a pair of latex gloves and shoe coverings. I also tapped a bit of Vick's VapoRub onto my upper lip in hopes of muting the stink of death.

I gently lifted the hair away from the man's face to confirm my suspicions. It took a little imagination to do such a thing. Age had changed him, as had the loss of life. Blood coagulated in the lower eye. I set the strands of hair back into place.

He wore a white T-shirt and underwear that had grown grayish and threadbare through the years. Blood had soaked the clothing and settled into the carpet. It appeared he'd been stabbed twice—perhaps more. We wouldn't know until we moved the body.

The fingers of his right hand were sliced—defensive wounds from fending off a knife attack. His left arm was pinned under his body. There would likely be wounds to that hand as well.

"Victor Bachman," Glenn Higgins said. "Sixty-seven."

My partner stood a few feet behind me with his notebook in hand. He'd beat me to the scene, gathered some preliminary information, and entered the house. It was only us inside now. Patrol officers and a couple of supervisors waited outside. The forensic team arrived a couple of minutes after I did and were preparing for their entry.

"I thought I knew the name," I said.

"How so?"

"A call from when I was on patrol." I stood.

"The homicide?"

My gaze shifted to Glenn.

"Radio pulled his history for me." Glenn motioned to the body. "Except for some recent traffic stops, the only thing the guy had in his jacket was a homicide almost twenty years ago. They said there was no arrest tied to it. What happened?"

I shrugged. "Self-defense."

"You don't see many of those."

There was more to the story, but it wasn't worth going into now. Besides, my recollection was shaky on the subject. Many cases had come and gone since that time, and I wasn't a detective then. My access to that investigation had been limited. I would like to read the file and acquaint myself with the detective's decision before forming an opinion.

"You think this could be linked to that?" Glenn asked.

I shrugged again. "Would be a long time for revenge."

"You know what they say about serving it cold."

"Cold is one thing; this would have freezer burn. Who found him?"

"The housekeeper." Glenn thumbed over his shoulder. "She's waiting outside with patrol."

I stood and considered the room. The couch and small recliners were dated. If I had to guess, I'd put them older than ten years. A framed sketch of a twin-engine World War II plane hung on the long wall. Models of other planes sat on the fireplace mantel.

Outside of the decaying body, everything else was in its place. I moved closer to the mantel and studied the models. There wasn't any dust. "How often does the housekeeper come in?"

"Only on Tuesdays. No telling how many days the guy's been here."

"Nobody missed him?"

"Guess not. He's been here a while, don't you think? Want to bet on how long?"

I didn't take Glenn up on his offer. Instead, I walked through the house.

The kitchen had linoleum floors, Formica counters, and metal cabinets. The appliances and utensils were also vintage, but none of them seemed purposeful. Bachman hadn't tried to make his kitchen appear retro. Everything was just old and tired.

There were two bedrooms. Both were tidy except for the bed in the first room. The covers were pulled back, and the mattress cover ruffled as if Bachman had been sleeping in it.

On top of the nightstand were his cell phone, car keys, a yellow highlighter, and a new study-version bible.

I activated the phone. There were a couple of missed phone calls but no text messages. The calls were from *Off the Lot*. I jotted the name and number into my notebook and then put the cell phone back where I found it. We'd have the evidence team log the phone onto property after they photographed the room.

There was a bookmark in the bible, and I flipped to the gospel of Mark. Chapter 8:36 was highlighted. *What good is it for someone to gain the whole world yet forfeit their soul?*

The study guide provided a brief note explaining the passage, but I didn't bother reading it. I got the text's gist and figured I didn't need more.

I opened the nightstand drawer. Inside was the detritus of most bedrooms. Nail clippers, lip balm, a pen, and an unused notepad. I had expected to find a gun, but none was there.

A pair of faded jeans lay in the gray wingback chair beside the bed. I patted the lump in the rear pocket before removing a wallet. Inside were several credit cards, Bachman's driver's license, and eighty-seven dollars. I tucked the billfold back into the pocket.

Had Victor Bachman awakened from his sleep to greet his murderer, or had he met them in the morning after he naturally awoke? If either of those were true, why hadn't he put on the pants in the nearby chair?

I returned to the living room. Blood spatter was in the doorway. Drops of blood led to where the body lay. Someone had stabbed Bachman and fled with the murder weapon. They didn't bother to burglarize the house or rob him.

Bachman likely stumbled into the living room and died. Why hadn't he tried to get to his phone? Why hadn't he gone into the front yard for help?

A bucket of cleaning supplies sat in the entryway near the front door.

"Well?" Glenn said. "What do you think?"

"Let's talk with the housekeeper."

***

Patrol cars lined Douglas Drive in front of Victor Bachman's blue and gray one-story rancher. Two vehicles were parked in the gravel driveway—a black convertible Ford Mustang with its top still down and a light green Kia Soul.

The forensic team's van was stopped in the middle of the street. A couple of sawhorses sat at opposite ends of the block to announce the closure of the thoroughfare. Only local residents would be let into their homes now.

Loma Vista Park sat to the south, and families gathered there to play in the sun. Some stood at its edge and tried to make out what was occurring where we were.

I removed my latex gloves and booties, then stuffed them into a jacket pocket. Then I used a napkin I had in another to wipe away the VapoRub from my upper lip. The menthol smell would linger for an hour. Better than the aroma of rotting flesh. As it was, I'd probably picked up the stink of Victor Bachman in my clothes for the rest of the day.

"I'll touch base with the techs," Glenn said. He headed off toward the boxy van.

Officer Lee Sheets leaned against the rear of his patrol car. The back door was open, and an attractive woman sat inside with her feet on the curb. She appeared to be in her late twenties. The woman wore a tight pink T-shirt, black mini-skirt, and clunky white tennis shoes. She smoked from a vape pen as Sheets chatted.

I lifted my chin in acknowledgment as I approached.

Sheets pushed off the car, and we shook hands. He motioned toward the housekeeper. "This is Dina Foust."

Sheets smiled at the woman. "Dina, this is Detective Nash."

Dina slipped out of the car. Her miniskirt rode up on her thighs and revealed she wasn't wearing panties. She hurriedly tugged it into place. I glanced back toward the house to convince myself I had indeed noticed a bucket of cleaning supplies in the entryway.

Sheets closed the rear door and stepped away.

"Tell me what happened," I said.

"I found Vic." She inhaled on the vape pen, held her breath for a moment, then exhaled a plume of mist that smelled like peppermint. "I didn't touch him or nothing. I swear to God. Once I saw the blood, and how he looked, I ran outside and called you guys." She nodded emphatically.

"Did you see anybody in the house when you arrived?"

"No one. I swear."

I hadn't expected anyone to be with the victim. Bachman had been on the floor for some time. It was likely the killer had fled days ago.

"And you only come by on Tuesdays?"

"That's right. Once a week. Always on Tuesdays."

"Was the house locked when you arrived?"

She shook her head. "But it never is. Vic's always here. I thought it weird he didn't open the door." Her voice caught on the last couple of words.

"How long have you been cleaning his house?"

"Six months." Another inhale on the vape pen followed by a quick head turn to exhale.

"Do you own the company, or do you work for someone?"

"It's mine. Dina's Clean and Go."

"How'd he find you?"

"Why's that matter?" Her face pinched. "Whatever. I bought a route he was part of." One more hit on the vape pen. "The former cleaner and her husband moved to someplace in New Mexico. Or maybe it was Arizona. One of those desert places. I don't remember the town."

I motioned toward her outfit. "Is that what you clean in?"

She blinked several times before answering. "What are you implying?"

"I'm trying to understand how things were."

Dina crossed her arms. The move pushed her breasts up, but it didn't seem intentional because her face soured. "I don't always clean in this—no. If you look in my car, my work clothes are in there."

"Why are they in there, and you're cleaning supplies inside the house?"

She put the vape pen in her mouth but didn't inhale. Dina looked away.

"You dressed that way for Vic."

"No shit."

"You two were intimate."

Her face soured further. "Oh, my God, no. He watched. That's all." She inhaled on the vape pen and held it longer than before. As she spoke, the mist escaped. "I don't normally do this." Her hand waved along her clothing. "I swear to God. Go look in my car for my work clothes. You'll find them, I promise. But Vic paid me extra to dress like this while I cleaned. That extra cash goes a long way to covering rent and food—"

I raised a hand to stop her. "Did you kill him?"

"No!" Her face reddened. "Vic was good to me. He never laid a finger on me. All he did was watch." She quickly added, "And he never... well, you know. I don't know if he ever did anything, but if he did, it happened after I left."

"All right."

"I swear to God." She lifted a hand into the air. "I'll take one of those lie detector tests if you don't believe me."

"Do you know if he had any family?"

She shook her head. "We never talked about stuff like that."

"What did you talk about?"

She shrugged a single shoulder. "Me and my stuff. He wanted me to talk about what I did. I promise. We never talked about him. He never talked about himself."

"He never mentioned any friends?"

"Like I said, I talked, and he listened. He wanted to know about old boyfriends and what we did. You know, sexual stuff. That's it. But I swear he never touched me, and I never touched him."

"Do you have a current boyfriend?"

The question seemed to give her pause. "Why?"

"A guy might get jealous of what you were doing here with Vic."

Her brow furrowed. "Oh, I see." She lowered her head. "No, no boyfriend. Not for some time. Nobody would care about what I was doing here except maybe my mom." She looked up instantly. "Don't tell her, okay?"

"I promise."

I confirmed the spelling of her name and got her address. I escorted her to the Kia Soul and explained I might have some follow-up questions. It was mostly an excuse to peer into the car.

On the backseat was a cleaning uniform—like she promised.

***

Glenn and I stood at the edge of the Bachman property with Lieutenant George Brand. It was customary for him to stop by a homicide scene. He'd never been a Major Crimes investigator, but he wanted to ensure we always had everything needed to fulfill our tasks.

"Things are going well?" Brand asked.

"As can be expected," I said.

The lieutenant pushed his glasses up his nose as he studied me. The examination seemed to go on a little longer than necessary. I was about to ask why when Glenn offered, "We're barely off the starting line, Lieutenant. When we know more, we'll loop you in."

Brand nodded but didn't take his eyes off me. He was a strange duck and prone to odd behaviors.

"Hey, Dallas," Geri Utley called. "Glenn!"

She stood in the doorway of the Bachman house and wore a white hazmat suit. A digital camera with a short zoom lens hung around her neck. Geri waved us closer.

The three of us crossed the lawn. When we were at the bottom of the entry stairs, she said, "We photographed the body. There was nothing in his other hand."

"The one underneath him?" Glenn asked.

Geri nodded.

I glanced over to the Ford Mustang convertible. If Vic Bachman had been dead for several days, it meant the top was down on the car for the whole time. Unless someone lowered it after, but I saw the car keys on his nightstand. "Do me a favor and dust the car."

Glenn cocked his head.

"Only one shot at a crime scene," I said, repeating an often-used homicide investigator mantra.

"All right," Geri said with a lack of enthusiasm. She returned inside the house.

Her spiritless response about the Mustang wasn't a critique of my request. Instead, it was a comment about printing a car in general. Cars were fingerprint magnets. Vehicles were touched throughout the day. Random people touched them in a parking lot. Of any personal item, they were most likely to be handled by a random person.

Lieutenant Brand studied Glenn and me. "If there's nothing else?"

"We're good," we said in unison.

"In that case." He wandered off toward his car.

2

I dropped into my chair and started my computer. As the hard drive whirred to life, Andrew Parker walked by. He seemed surprised to see me sitting there and stopped.

"Hey, man. Heard you guys caught one."

"Yeah. Glenn's still out there wrapping up the scene."

Parker was short and built like a tank. The mini-Schwarzenegger spent a considerable amount of time in the gym. I had no idea how a Major Crimes detective could do something like that. It seemed to me his priorities were out of whack. The sleeves of his white shirt were rolled up around his forearms. His black tie was loosened around his thick neck. He crossed his arms and leaned a shoulder against the cubicle. "Is it bad?"

I shrugged. "Single victim stabbing."

"Guy's dead. Bad enough, right?" Parker glanced nonchalantly around. When his gaze returned to me, he leaned in slightly and lowered his voice. "Let me ask you something."

"Fire away."

"Would you like to have dinner sometime?"

Surprised by his request, I pulled back slightly. "Excuse me?"

"I know." He smiled apologetically. Parker uncrossed his arms and held his hands up in a defensive posture. "We haven't been on the best terms since I rotated over here, but after working together on that pimp killing, I thought—" He set a hand down on the edge of the cubicle. "Well, my wife thought maybe you'd like to come over and meet our family."

"Your family?"

Parker's brow furrowed. "You don't have kids, right? Somebody told me that. I don't remember who."

I shook my head.

"I didn't think so." His face relaxed. "And even if you did, they'd be older than mine. You like kids, don't you?"

"They're fine."

"Okay, that's good. I have three girls."

"You do?" He never mentioned them. Although to be fair, I never gave the guy a chance to tell me much about his personal life. In fact, I don't think I even knew he was married until right then. Maybe he told me before, or someone had mentioned it, but I couldn't remember such a thing.

Now I was thinking about the guy's family, when did he have time to work out like a contestant for Mr. Universe? The guy still had cases to work.

Parker continued. "My wife is an excellent cook. Me, not so much." His fingers drummed along the top of my cubicle. "No pressure, but I thought it might be nice for us to get together, break some bread, tell some stories. Not work ones, though. I get enough of those around here. I hate talking about the job when I'm at home." He stopped drumming on the cubicle. "So, what do you think? Wanna work on setting something up?"

I nodded even though I didn't want to have dinner with the guy or his family. We'd had several dustups since he'd come to Major Crimes. Parker was an arrogant jerk who thought Glenn and I were too long in the tooth to matter. Now, he wanted to make nice? I shouldn't have agreed to the meal. I should have told him to shove the invitation up his—

"And hey." Parker glanced around once more. He lowered his voice even further. "I'm sorry."

"For?"

"For being a dick. It's just…" He let the thought drift off. "It's not important. Never mind. I'm sorry." He nodded several times. "Talk with you later."

I watched him walk off until he turned the corner and disappeared. I stayed facing that way for several seconds. When the shock of Parker's invitation and apology wore off, I turned back to my computer and logged into the network. I called up the National Crime Information Center and entered Victor Bachman's information. I wanted to reread the report I wrote so many years ago.

Once I found the corresponding case number, I jotted it on a scrap of paper and headed to Records. Had this been a newer report, I could have called it up and read it on my screen. That showed how long I'd been on the department.

The system for requesting old reports remained an antiquated process. I had to complete a form and turn it in, creating a paper trail which could be audited.

Stephanie Lesh walked over to the counter. Her long brown hair cascaded to her waist. She wore a printed beige shirt and brown slacks. Lesh was the head of the Records Division. Her office was down the hall, so she must have been in the area to check on her staff.

"Dallas, long time no see. How've you been?"

"Good, Steph. You?"

"Can't complain. No one would listen if I did. What are we looking for today?"

I passed her the Records Request form.

Her brow furrowed. "This should have been scanned into the system by now." I felt foolish then. If it had been scanned, I would have been able to pull it up on the system. "Gimme a minute, and I'll get it for you."

Lesh wandered back to her desk. Several clerks hustled around the section. The days of physical reports were mostly in the long ago past. Almost everything was filed digitally now. I was still in the patrol car when the department purchased report-writing software. Initially, some guys fought against it. There were still some things I balked at when it came to technology. Typing my report wasn't one of them.

Yet the controls around who could retrieve old reports still irked me. It seemed a draconian measure for which the department should have found a workaround by now.

"Dallas?"

I turned to see Chaplain Karen Roland.

She smiled kindly. "How are you?"

"Fine." I didn't return the smile. "Yourself?"

"I'm doing well. Thank you for asking."

When Gabriel Greene retired a few months back, Roland took over the department's chaplaincy program. Roland had been a volunteer in the program for many years, and Greene had groomed her for the leadership role—a full-time, paid position funded by donations from police officers.

"How's work?" she asked.

I glanced down the hallway. No one was coming. Chatting with a chaplain wasn't something I wanted to be seen doing. I kept my answer short. "Work's fine."

Her smile broadened. "Good. I'm glad to hear that. What do you say we grab a cup of coffee sometime and catch up?"

Chaplain Greene had kept a Keurig machine in his office and lured officers into conversations about their problems with a promise of a cup of quality coffee. I'd been ordered to talk with him shortly after Bobbie's death. No one knew then how the morning music affected my life. I wasn't going to fall for the coffee invitation trick again—not from a new chaplain.

I shook my head. "I appreciate the offer, but I'd rather not."

Roland's smile never faltered. "It doesn't have to be for anything other than to get to know each other better. You pick the place and time."

First Parker, now the new chaplain. What vibes was I giving off in my life?

Motion caught my eye. Stephanie Lesh moved toward a large printer/copier machine.

I turned back to the chaplain. "Listen, ma'am—"

"Karen is fine."

I paused.

She smiled again. "I only want to make sure you're doing well."

"I'm fine. Really."

"If you're certain."

I cocked my head. Her questioning seemed similar to Lieutenant Brand's at the morning's crime scene.

The chaplain nodded. "Well, if you want to talk, you know where to find me." Roland continued down the hallway.

Stephanie Lesh approached the counter then. "Here's the report. Although, there wasn't much to your narrative, was there?"

"What can I say?" I accepted the papers.

"Guess I expected to see something like your current work. Interesting to see what a Patrol Officer Dallas Nash report looked like."

"We all start somewhere."

I stepped away from the counter.

"Hey, Dal," she said. Her voice lowered. "Everything okay?"

"Why wouldn't it be?"

"I saw you talking with the chaplain."

***

Back at my desk, I reviewed the report that was filed eighteen years ago—another lifetime.

Kelsie Rockford had accused Victor Bachman of rape.

Victor was forty-nine at the time of the incident. Kelsie was twenty-one and a friend of Victor's daughter, Amanda Schoen. Victor and Kelsie knew each other through that relationship.

Amanda retained her mother's maiden name as her parents never married. Her parents lived together for several years and parted amicably shortly after Amanda's second birthday. Victor remained in Amanda's life with parental visitation rights.

The two girls had grown up friends on the South Hill. They lived within a couple of blocks of each other, attended the same schools, and went to Spokane Falls Community College for a semester before deciding higher education wasn't for them.

At the time of the incident, Kelsie worked as a receptionist at a real estate office. Amanda was employed by the Spokane Valley Parks Department.

Victor Bachman ran into Kelsie Rockford one evening at Ankeny's, a bar that once resided on top of the Ridpath Hotel. The club overlooked downtown and featured jazz music. Its relaxed vibe didn't attract the college crowd, which preferred high-energy nightclubs. Patrons who went to Ankeny's were there for different reasons—those often helped by dark corners, soft music, and views of city lights.

Kelsie had gone because her boyfriend, Randy Seaver, broke up with her earlier in the day for another girl. She'd never been to Ankeny's before but heard some of the older women in the office talk about the bar in hushed tones. Kelsie didn't want to see any of them, but she also didn't want to go to any of the bars she usually visited with her friends. She was hurt and angry and about to add alcohol—a dangerous mixture.

Victor was there because Ankeny's was the perfect place for a single guy pushing fifty. According to him, he rarely met women there and never had plans to do such a thing. He simply wanted to drink in peace and watch the city lights.

Both Victor and Kelsie admitted they remembered each other immediately.

"I used to think he was handsome," Kelsie had said. Her statement was recorded in the report. She rubbed her hands while she spoke. "Sort of in a hot dad sort of way. He had kind eyes, too. I never thought he would do what he did."

For his part, Victor stated, "I never considered Kelsie that way. Never once. Not until we started drinking, and then, well, she quit being my daughter's friend, and she became this beautiful woman who seemed really interested in the things I had to say. I guess we got over our skis the way men and women tend to do, and one thing led to another."

Victor bought them drinks for several hours. When the bar closed, he realized he was too drunk to drive. They took the elevator downstairs and rented a room at the hotel. At that time, the Ridpath Hotel was still operational. It would later close and get wrapped up in a legal quagmire, but that was still many years off.

Kelsie claimed she didn't remember anything about the evening after her second drink. She continued to rub her hands the whole time she spoke. "Maybe he put something in my drink," she said. "I don't know."

A toxicology report was in the file. By the time a blood sample was taken, a couple of days had passed since the incident. No chemical irregularities were found in Kelsie's system.

According to Victor Bachman, when he awoke the following day, he felt the shame a man his age likely would. "I couldn't believe I did such a thing," he stated. "I mean, yeah, if she weren't my daughter's friend, I would have hung around and maybe tried to spend the day with her. She was young and pretty, but she was Kelsie for crying out loud. I used to take her for ice cream. It messed with my head. I should never have done it. Sleep with her, I mean. But I didn't do what she's accusing me of."

Victor reported he hurriedly dressed and slipped out of the room. He left Kelsie sleeping alone in the bed. He hoped they would both forget the night ever happened.

Maybe they both could have, except Randy Seaver started a series of terrible events.

When Kelsie returned home, her boyfriend waited on the steps of her apartment. He was angry and demanded to know where she'd been. According to Kelsie, he'd been up through the night worrying about her.

"He had no right to ask me any questions," she reportedly said. "He broke up with me. I didn't break up with him."

Randy cried then and claimed he'd made a horrible mistake. He followed it up with professions of love and claimed that he didn't want to be with anyone else. He said he'd broken it off with the other girl and had come back to tell Kelsie what a fool he'd been.

That's when Randy Seaver demanded for a second time to know where she'd been.

Twisted up by her boyfriend's emotions, Kelsie admitted to getting drunk and having sex with a friend's father. Randy flew into a rage. He yelled and grabbed her by the arms. He shook her and questioned how she could do such a thing. I had asked how she felt, and Kelsie said, "I was scared but mostly ashamed of what had happened."

The latter was because Randy had backpedaled and claimed he never slept with the other woman. "He broke up with me in case something did happen between them," Kelsie had said, "because he didn't want to cheat on me, but then he realized he didn't like the girl and wanted to get back together."

That's when Kelsie told Randy her friend's father had raped her. She refused to tell me the name of her attacker. She only talked to me because Randy made her call the police.

I cringed when I read the initial report. The words I slipped into the narrative made me regretful. Simple word choices such as *claimed* versus *stated* can negatively impact a jury. Writing "She claimed she was raped" could create doubt, while writing "She stated she was raped" was unequivocal. I had made up my mind about Kelsie Rockford's accusation before submitting my report.

"What are you reading?" Glenn Higgins asked. He tossed his notepad onto his desk. He slipped his suit jacket off and hung it over the back of his chair.

"The homicide report related to our victim."

"The one you worked on while on patrol? Find anything?"

"The next of kin info. I'm going to contact her in a minute."

Glenn thumbed over his shoulder. "If you want, I'll go with you after I hit the head."

I waved him off. "I got it. Why don't you get started on the paperwork?"

"Deal." He walked off toward the restroom, and I returned to the report.

Investigators followed up on Kelsie's claim the next day. Upon their arrival, she told them Victor Bachman was her attacker. When they asked why she was now forthcoming with her attacker's name, she stated her boyfriend had forced the truth out of her. They dutifully listened to her story as she provided it.

Maybe my report set the detectives down the same path I had been on, but I doubted it. I was a lowly patrol officer. Yet, their narrative contained plenty of clues as to what they thought of her allegation.

"The victim claimed…"

"The lack of evidence and injury…"

"Inconsistencies in her story…"

The responding detectives filed their report and probably hoped they would never hear again from Kelsie Rockford.

Unfortunately, Randy Seaver used the phone book to look up the home address of his girlfriend's attacker. He drove to Victor Bachman's house, kicked in the front door, and confronted Kelsie's alleged rapist with a baseball bat.

Bachman shot him dead with the loaded .38 he kept in his nightstand.

***

Amanda Schoen leaned forward and flicked her cigarette into an ash tray. "How'd Vic die?"

"He was stabbed," I said.

"Just once?" She sniffed dismissively. "I'da figured it would have been more."

It seemed an odd comment from the man's daughter. The fact she called him by his given name was even more disconcerting.

"It was more than one," I said.

Amanda flopped back onto the couch and rested her hands on her knees. She sat crossed-legged. Smoke drifted up from the cigarette.

We were in the living room of her lower South Hill home. It was decorated nicely, but the house had seen considerable wear—the evidence of long-term residency with a family in tow. The house smelled of dog. Amanda had put an aging Golden Retriever into the backyard upon my arrival.

When I told her of her father's death, she didn't cry. She only asked if I cared if she smoked. It was her house, and she'd just been notified of her father's death, so I told her

27

I didn't mind. She found her purse, opened it, and pulled out a pack of Marlboro Lights. She inhaled and exhaled twice before asking how her father had died.

"Well?" she asked. "How many times?"

"Multiple."

"How many is that?"

"We can't confirm until the autopsy, but it looked like three."

She held the cigarette in her mouth and inhaled deeply. When she moved her hand away, it shook slightly—the first physical betrayal of emotion. Amanda lifted her face toward the ceiling. She stared upward for several seconds before blowing the smoke in that direction. "So, he suffered."

"It's likely."

Amanda lowered her head. She sucked her lips inward, then pushed them outward and side to side. It appeared as if she was searching for something to say. She settled on, "Vic was a terrible father."

"Because of the incident with Kelsie Rockford?"

"That's how the police refer to rape these days—the *incident*? Good to know in case it ever happens to me."

"He was cleared of—"

Amanda interrupted. "Vic raped my best friend and then killed her boyfriend." She frowned. "And if you can't figure out why she changed her story, Detective, let me help you. Kelsie did it to protect our friendship. She saw what happened to Randy. She didn't want that to happen to us."

I understood what she meant. After Randy Seaver's death, Kelsie Rockford held to her claim of rape for several days. Victor Bachman staunchly denied any forcible intercourse. Employees at Ankeny's had seen them drinking, smiling, and laughing together. They left arm-in-arm. The hotel clerk who completed Vic's registration stated Kelsie had been overly affectionate to Victor to the point of it being "uncomfortable" in a public setting.

The witness statements did not preclude that a rape occurred behind closed doors, but they did paint a picture of two people having a nice time. Kelsie had even stated she and Vic had enjoyed each other's company while at the bar. She only said things turned violent inside the hotel room.

Eventually, though, Kelsie recanted her claim. She admitted she told Randy she'd been raped to avoid his anger and get back together with him. That admission finally cleared Victor Bachman of any suspicion. The resulting homicide was determined to be the unfortunate outcome of a jealous boyfriend's overreaction and ruled as justifiable self-defense.

Nearly two decades had passed, yet Amanda Schoen refused to see the truth.

I asked, "How often did you visit your father?"

Amanda stuck the cigarette in her mouth. "When I had to," she said through clenched teeth. She inhaled and exhaled. Waved off the resulting smoke. "Birthdays. Holidays. That sort of thing."

"Nothing regularly?"

"No, thank God. I didn't want my family to be around Vic."

I glanced around the house. "Where *is* your family?"

"My husband took the boys to the gym. They're at that age." She inspected her cigarette. "I'm gonna catch holy hell for smoking in the house." She eyed me suspiciously. "He'll complain. That's all. It never goes any further."

I nodded. "Did your father have any friends?"

"None that I know of. Vic was never really the type to have deep connections. The only thing I know he does—" She waved a hand, and a small trail of smoke from the cigarette followed the motion. "—is play in some stupid dart league. Why he got involved with that, I'll never know."

"Where's he play?"

"All over, I guess. He wouldn't shut up about it whenever we talked. But you probably want to know what bar he played for. The Baseline on Monroe. You know the one? He'd been hanging there for years. Maybe he's got some friends. I don't know."

"Has your mother talked with him?"

Amanda scoffed, then smiled. "She hates his guts." Her grin quickly melted. "*Hated*. Anyway, she's back in the D.C. area. Gaithersburg. I can give you her number if you think it's important, but she hasn't talked with Vic in years. They were totally cool my whole childhood, but after the rape, she wouldn't have anything to do with him. Can you blame her? They didn't even talk at my wedding."

"Relatives?"

"He's got some cousins in California. What do they call them? Shirttail relatives? I can probably dig up their contact info if you need it."

"Not now, but it would be helpful." I jotted a note to follow up on the relative information. It likely wasn't germane to the investigation, but it was better to have some info and not need it than the other way around. "What happened to your father after he killed Randy Seaver?"

She leaned forward and crushed the cigarette into the ashtray. "Is this what a murder investigation is—picking old scabs? I never see them do that in those shows I watch."

I didn't answer. I let her work herself toward the answer.

Amanda grabbed the pack of cigarettes and leaned back. She opened the box. "I refused to talk with Vic for a long time after that. Might have been a year. Maybe even eighteen months. I didn't care to know him anymore. If he would have died, it would have made my life easier."

"What happened to get you back together?"

She smirked. "We never recovered from what he did. We talked is all. A little on the holidays, like I said. That was it."

"But what caused the ice to melt?"

Amanda tugged another cigarette free and tossed the pack to the coffee table. "My husband and I got sideways on our house after he lost his job. This was before the real estate crash. We were about to lose everything. His parents couldn't help. Neither could my mom. Believe it or not, she suggested I reach out to Vic. He pulled cash out of his retirement account. I guess he took a big hit for doing it, but he saved us."

She lit the cigarette and then gently set the lighter on the end table. She exhaled a plume of smoke. "I must sound like an ungrateful bitch, huh? Vic rides to our rescue, and I still resent him." She tapped her chest. "But I wasn't going to let him buy my forgiveness. He raped my friend and killed her boyfriend. It changed our lives. It ruined Kelsie's. It damaged our friendship. It ruined my relationship with my father. And I don't know what it did to him, but it certainly affected him. He sold his business after that. People don't want to do business with a rapist. I know that much."

"What did he do?"

"He was an insurance broker—home and auto stuff. My mom said he was pretty successful with it. When I reconnected with him, he was living off the proceeds of the sale. A few years back, he started working at a car lot to make ends meet."

"Would you be willing to come to his house and tell us if anything is missing?"

Amanda shrugged. "I could try, but I doubt I'd notice anything. It wasn't like I was taking an inventory of things when I visited."

"Do you know if he still owned a gun?"

"I don't think so. He tried to make up to me several times by saying he wished he had never bought the gun in the first place. That might have stopped him from killing Randy, but it sure wouldn't have stopped him from raping Kelsie, would it? You know, all those years, he kept saying he never did it. Didn't own up to it once. Yeah, he said, he wished they never hooked up, but he never said he was sorry for what he actually did to her." She flicked the cigarette ash into the tray. "I would have liked to hear the truth just once."

"Did he go to church?"

She laughed a quick derisive snort. "Not that I know of. Why would you ask?"

"He had a bible next to his bed."

"He did?"

"Maybe he had friends at church."

"And maybe he thought he can get—" Her brow furrowed. "What do the bible thumpers call it when their sins get magically washed away?"

"Absolution."

"That's it." She inhaled on the cigarette. "Vic probably thought he could get absolution for what he did. If there is a hell, I hope he's going." Her face relaxed. "That's a pretty shitty thing to say, isn't it?" She studied her cigarette. "When I was a little girl, he was a pretty good father. And he did save our home."

I closed my notebook and tucked it into my jacket pocket. "I'll call you in a day or two for us to walk through his house." I stood. "I'm sorry for your loss."

Amanda tapped the cigarette above the ash tray. "I lost him the moment he raped my friend." She looked up. "I can probably let that go now, huh?"

"Thank you for your time."

***

My phone buzzed while I waited for a red light at the intersection of 29th Avenue and Grand Boulevard. The screen read *Glenn*, so I answered.

"Hey," he said. "Where you at?"

"On the way back to the station? You?"

"Still at my desk. You got anything hot that needs to be checked now?"

"Nothing burning. Why?"

The light changed, and traffic moved.

"I got a date," Glenn said. "I'd like to keep it. I'd cancel it if we had something pressing."

"Do I know this girl?"

"The librarian."

"I thought you broke it off with her."

"I'm recycling. What can I say? So, we're good?"

There was no need for me to go back to the department now. I slowed and changed lanes.

"We're good," I said. "See you in the morning."

The call ended.

I was about to toss the phone into the passenger seat but looked up Marlene's contact info. I didn't call her. Instead, I drove for several blocks.

I'd like to say various reasons not to call her ran through my mind, but a strange silence reverberated through my skull. It wasn't peaceful, but it wasn't unsettling either. It was confusing.

When the lack of decision won out, I put the phone on the seat and ignored it. I'd go home, make something simple, and call it a night.

A minute later, I picked the phone up again and called her. She answered on the second ring.

"Hello?"

"It's Dallas. Things worked out differently than I thought."

"That's perfect." A young girl chattered in the background. "Sadie and I are making dinner right now."

"*Who's that?*" Sadie asked.

"Dallas," Marlene said away from the phone.

"*Hi, Dallas!*" the girl hollered.

"Did you hear that?"

"I did."

"Are you going to swing by?" Marlene asked.

"How much time do I have?"

"It's almost done."

"I'm still in my suit."

"That's okay. You look—" She didn't finish the statement. "Come as you are."

"I'll be there in about twenty."

"We'll wait for you."

"You don't have to," I said.

"I know, but we will. See you when you get here."

She hung up.

***

"And there's this bird," Sadie said.

"A bird?" I asked.

"That's right. A big talking bird."

"Like Big Bird?"

Sadie laughed. "No! Her name is Lady Bird."

I eyed Marlene. "I think Mrs. Johnson might have something to say about that."

Marlene cocked her head. "Who?"

"Lyndon Johnson's wife."

She shrugged. "I don't know him."

Sadie waved her hand. "Lady Bird rules the animal kingdom. She's the smartest of them all."

"And you wrote this?" I asked.

She nodded. "I'm drawing the pictures, too. Wanna see?"

Marlene covered her daughter's hand. "Next time, Sadie. Go upstairs and brush your teeth."

"But Dallas is still here."

"He needs to go. He's had a long day."

Sadie's expression flattened. "Fine." She slid off the chair and headed for the stairs. She turned excitedly. "When can we see your house?"

Marlene pointed up the stairs. "Go."

"Fine." She clomped up a couple of stairs and stopped. Sadie faced me once more. "Bye, Dallas."

"Bye, kiddo."

She ran noisily up the remaining stairs.

Marlene turned to me. "Thank you for staying."

"Thank you for the invitation."

"I didn't think you would come."

"We got lucky with how things worked out today."

She shook her head. "That's not how I meant."

I stared at her.

Her eyes softened. "I'm sorry for what I said at the restaurant."

"It's all right."

"I don't want things to be weird between us."

"They're not. Listen—"

She tapped the table near my hand. "It's okay. We don't have to talk about it. Actually, I'd prefer if we didn't."

I nodded.

"So." Marlene forced a smile. "What's this case you're working?"

"It's a homicide with an unknown assailant."

"Wow." She blinked a couple of times. "That was official."

I shrugged. "A guy was stabbed and died. He'd been there for several days before someone found him."

"Does it ever bother you—the dead bodies?"

"It's the job."

"Do you have any leads?"

"None yet."

"What happens if you never find any?"

"We put it on the back burner."

"But someone was murdered."

I shrugged again. "That's how it goes."

She studied me for several moments. "Does it bother you—"

"You already asked that."

"Not this one. Does it bother you if you don't get the bad guy?"

"Even when we get the bad guy, it weighs on me."

"All the death and hurt?"

I nodded.

"How do you deal with it?"

"We see a lot of the ugliness this life offers, but I can't imagine the things *you've* seen and lived through. I should be asking you for advice."

Marlene lowered her eyes at the mention of her past. She wouldn't have done that previously. She never wore her life on the street as a badge of honor, but she didn't shy away from it either. Right now, she seemed embarrassed by it.

"I'm sorry," I said. "I shouldn't have brought it up."

She waved off my apology. "It's fine. It's not a secret." But something had changed in her demeanor. The sweetness had left her eyes and was replaced by the mask of professionalism she wore at work. "You asked how I deal with the hurt. One day at a time like everyone else." She shrugged. "I'm glad you came for dinner."

"It was good. You're a great cook."

"You probably need to get some rest." Marlene stood and collected the plates. "You have a big day tomorrow. Bad guys to catch." She entered the kitchen.

I stood. "Thank you for everything," I called into the other room. "It was nice."

Marlene stepped out of the kitchen, but her face remained tight. "Sadie had fun."

We stared at each other for a couple of moments. I didn't need to ask what had made her upset. It was the reminder of her past.

"I'll call you later," I said.

She nodded once, then headed back into the kitchen.

***

I walked into my house and closed the door as gently as possible. I remained in the entryway.

My wife was somewhere in the quiet of my home. When I stopped looking for Bobbie in the music of my subconscious, I realized she was always with me in the stillness of our home.

A weight draped itself over my shoulders, and I lowered my head.

Her absence could be felt in the emptiness of my life.

I stayed with my head bowed until the stupid refrigerator started in the other room. Its motor whirred. It wasn't loud, but it made me question whether I needed to have the damn appliance so cold? Maybe it wouldn't come on so often if I turned the thermostat up.

A lawn mower started next door. My jaw flexed. The son of a bitch across the street just bought a riding one with a headlight. Now, he started his yard maintenance when the sun went down. It was as if he had to do things to irritate the neighborhood. If it wasn't the blinking Christmas lights, it was this. The incessant whine of that engine would go on for some time.

The silence was gone. So was my wife.

I left the entryway and entered the house.

3

"It's been a few days," I said.

Bobbie didn't respond. Even when the music greeted me daily, I never expected her to reply.

Her stone marker stared back at me—*Roberta "Bobbie" Ann Nash*. I squatted and brushed away errant grass clippings.

The cemetery was silent; it was always quiet at this time of day. The lawn crews came later in the morning hours after the grass was free of dew. Families tended to come in the afternoons.

An older man stood near a marker about fifty feet away. He noticed me, and we both lifted a hand in acknowledgment. This wasn't the place for friendly rejoinders.

"I'm thinking about retirement." I shoved my hands into my pockets. "At least, I've said the words out loud. I don't know if I really am." My foot skimmed over the grass. "It's probably dumb. What else have I got? It's not like I'm going to take up stamp collecting. I don't even know what they cost anymore." My chuckle was self-conscious. "They don't buy regular stamps, do they? The collectors, I mean. They buy rare ones. What's a stamp collector called? I read about it once, but I don't remember. It's something like a philanthropist, but that's not it."

The phone in my pocket buzzed once. I pulled it out to find a text message from Marlene—I'M SORRY FOR BEING WEIRD LAST NIGHT.

I looked at Bobbie's grave and immediately felt a surge of guilt. "It's from a friend."

Shame was an emotion I'd never felt with Bobbie. I'd never done anything inappropriate while we were married, so it was stupid to feel something like that now.

I slipped the phone back into my pocket. "I don't know why I started thinking about it." My head bobbled. "Retirement, I mean. The job's the only thing I've looked forward to since you've gone away."

Two foreign cars raced by the cemetery. I watched them go. When I faced Bobbie's headstone again, I studied it for a moment.

"The music made you being gone easier." I waved my hand in frustration. "That didn't come out right. I meant it distracted me. Gave me something to focus on besides your absence. You being gone isn't easy."

The old man at the other marker walked away. He shuffled with his head down. Is that how I moved after talking with Bobbie?

Probably.

What do you want?

It was a strange question and sounded like Bobbie's voice in my head. I knew it couldn't be. She was dead, and I wasn't crazy. No matter how much I wanted her back, that wouldn't happen. The more I thought about it, the more I became convinced the question was in my own voice.

Regardless, I was bothered because of the question's open-ended nature. Perhaps it was related to retirement. Or maybe it was linked to Marlene, but how would Bobbie know? I hadn't told her anything.

Either way, I didn't feel like answering it even if I had asked it of myself.

And what if she had asked the question? Then answering it would definitely mean I was crazy.

I looked at my watch. "I have to go." I squatted and touched the marker. "I love you."

***

"How was your night?" Glenn asked. He hung his suit jacket over the back of his chair and then flopped into it.

"Fine," I said.

I hadn't told him about any of my meetings with Marlene. It wasn't any of his business. When he first learned of her, it was regarding the case we were investigating. He wouldn't understand why I continued to see her. Besides, Glenn hadn't asked me how my night was so he could actually hear my response. It was to set up his story.

"How was yours?" I asked.

"Great." Glenn leaned forward and put his elbows on his knees. "Why I ever stopped seeing the librarian, I don't know. She has access to so many books. The things she knows." He grinned.

"I get it."

"Dirty things." He wriggled his eyebrows.

"Enough."

"She has this friend."

"I don't want to hear this."

"Not like that." He smirked. "For you."

"Then I really don't want to hear about it."

Glenn settled back in his chair. "Why not?"

"Because I'm not interested."

"You haven't even let me tell you about her."

"It doesn't matter."

Glenn grinned. "You should see her."

"I don't want to."

"She's a teacher, and she's smoking. Like wow." He blew on his hand and waved it as if putting out a fire.

I expected my subconscious to attack me then with Van Halen's "Hot for Teacher." Perhaps it would have been some of Eddie Van Halen's guitar noodling or Alex Van Halen's skipping drum intro. Hell, it might even have been David Lee Roth's infamous "I'm not tardy" line, but my brain remained quiet. I felt oddly alone with the silence inside my head.

Glenn continued. "You wouldn't believe how hot this one is. She could have been a centerfold." He ruefully shook his head. "So, what do you say?"

"To centerfolds?"

"To the teacher."

"No."

The phone on Glenn's desk rang, and he absently reached for it. "I'm telling you, Dallas, this is the one for you." He lifted the receiver. "Higgins. Uh-huh. But we just caught one." He eyed me. "I know. All right. What's the address?" He spun toward his desk, cradled the phone between his neck and shoulder, then jotted an address into his notebook. "Got it. We'll head out." He hung up and faced me. "This is bullshit."

"What is?"

"How understaffed we are."

"The whole department is."

"Yeah, but—"

I rolled my hand for Glenn to hurry up his complaint. It was the same one I'd heard before. He stopped talking, and his disposition soured.

"Don't be that way," I said. "What's the call?"

"A body under the Monroe Street Bridge."

"Did they fish it out of the water?"

"How should I know? You heard the call." Glenn stood and snatched his suit jacket. "This is bullshit." He shoved an arm into a sleeve. "Complete and utter." He shrugged the jacket over his shoulders and tugged on the lapels. "Why aren't you mad?"

"How's it going to help?"

Glenn looked away.

"We're still going to have the case," I said, "and we're going to handle it. Being mad isn't good for either of us. Probably not good for the victim either."

He sighed and lowered his head. The sourness vanished from his face.

I stood. "Two cases in a row have happened before. Who knows why things fall the way they do?"

"You sound like the Buddha."

"I don't think that's how he sounded."

Glenn smirked. "Probably not. You ready?"

I grabbed my notebook.

"So I'm clear," Glenn said. "You don't want to check the teacher for staple marks?"

My brow furrowed.

"You know—" He tapped his belly. "—from her centerfold?

He'd gotten over his anger at the assignment of another new case. That's one of the things I liked about Glenn— he didn't stay mad for long.

I shook my head. "What can I say?"

"You can say yes, Dal." He smirked. "Just once, you can say yes to the opportunities I bring you."

"Not this time." I patted his shoulder as I walked by.

4

The drive to the crime scene was less than five minutes. Most of the delay was spent sitting at a couple of red lights. Glenn drove and parked his Chevy Impala on West Summit Parkway Avenue. We exited the car and headed down the hillside.

Off to our right, the massive Monroe Street Bridge spanned the Spokane River. Across the water to the south stood city hall, the recently redeveloped Huntington Park, and a red brick building proudly displaying a Washington Water Power sign even though that company no longer existed.

We were within walking distance of downtown Spokane and the city's crown jewel, Riverfront Park. The planned community Kendall Yards was to the west, and the Spokane Arena was only a few blocks to the north.

Glenn and I dropped onto a concrete pathway known as the Centennial Trail. It ran east to Coeur d'Alene, Idaho. It also ran west through the Nine Mile Falls Recreation Area. The whole path was about forty miles long.

All that meant was a mass of people went through this area daily.

Looky-loos stood along the bridge's railing less than fifty feet above the pathway. The people seemed too close for comfort, but it was a perspective thing. It would have been a comfortable distance if they were that far away at ground level.

A cluster of onlookers gathered in Huntington Park. They were more than far enough away since the river rushed loudly between us.

It was still early, but the gondolas from Riverfront Park would soon swoop down along the river. Their occupants would get an eyeful of what we were doing.

"The mayor has gotta love this," Glenn said. "How far is she going to crawl up the chief's ass to get this wrapped up soon?"

I spotted Captain Gary Ackerman standing near the outer perimeter of the crime scene. "The brass is already on scene, so I'm thinking she's already there."

"Great," muttered Glenn.

Ackerman turned his attention to us as we approached the yellow DO NOT CROSS tape, which designated the crime scene's outer perimeter. A second string of tape was further down the path for the inner perimeter. The captain was dressed in a tailored blue suit. His silver hair was expertly trimmed, and he wore expensive-looking sunglasses. Every day, the man appeared ready to be photographed for the cover of an over-fifty spread for *GQ* magazine.

"Gentlemen," Ackerman said. He glanced at the watchers across the river. "How are we this morning?"

"Better than our victim," Glenn said.

The captain eyed me. "What about you, Nash?"

"I'm fine." His gaze lingered on me longer than I would have liked, so I added, "Thank you for asking."

He frowned and nodded at the same time. It wasn't a tough message to decipher. Ackerman was the one who requested I return to duty after Bobbie's death. He was also one of the few who knew about the troubles I experienced. In fact, it was he and the lieutenant who had insisted I see a therapist. He'd kept a careful eye out for me since then. His asking how I was doing on the heels of Lieutenant Brand's and Chaplain Roland's questioning yesterday seemed suspect.

"Is the lieutenant around?" I asked.

"On the other side of the path with the complainant." Ackerman motioned down the way. "It's a mess."

"The body?" Glenn asked.

"I don't know." The captain waved a hand. "I'm talking about the logistics. People coming from every direction. Views from all angles. It's a staffing suck to redirect traffic, stop walkers and runners, all of it. Plus, the press is already here, and we're barely set up."

Glenn chuckled. "Don't forget city hall has a sight line to the whole show."

Ackerman's eyes narrowed. "You think I forgot?"

Glenn's smile faded. "No, sir."

The captain resettled his sunglasses and looked up toward the bridge. "Let us know if you want a tent brought in or the partitions. The body's on a slope, so it's not going to be easy to hide." He scowled at us. "Understand?"

Glenn and I nodded.

"Good luck," the captain said and walked off.

When Ackerman was out of earshot, Glenn said, "Change your mind about that teacher yet?"

***

The body was wrapped in a dirty, blue sleeping bag. It lay in the bridge's shadow and was covered by scrub brush. Glenn and I took our time walking up to it. It wasn't far off the path, but we wanted to ensure we didn't disturb any potential evidence.

"Thank God, he's not a jumper," Glenn said. "I worried about that when I heard he was under the bridge."

An aroma of feces permeated the air. I wandered away from the body and the cover of the bridge. I found a mound of human waste and wadded toilet paper near a cluster of rocks.

"Gross," a woman yelled from the overpass above.

Her friend hollered, "Is that what we think it is?"

I ignored her question and headed back to the body.

"He'd been at this location long enough to defecate at least once," I said.

Glenn grunted an acknowledgment, then lifted the edge of the sleeping bag to allow us both to peer at the body. I stood over my partner's shoulder.

The victim was a white man in his late forties or early fifties. Dirt covered his cheeks and his hair appeared greasy.

"Guy took a beating." Glenn pointed at the victim's face.

I squatted for a better look.

His face was indeed swollen, and his left eye was blackened. Under his oily hair, there was blood. Not a lot, as if he had been clubbed or shot, but a wound of some sort had occurred.

Glenn looked up at me. "You good?"

We wouldn't disturb the crime scene any further until the techs photographed the scene, collected their samples, and took measurements.

"I'm good," I said.

Glenn lowered the corner of the sleeping bag to its original position.

****

"You found the body?" I asked.

Sabina Wrencher rubbed her hands together. "I did."

She wore fingerless gloves, and her nails were dirty and chipped. Sabina had short, unkempt hair. She wore several layers of clothes, and two bandannas were tied around her left wrist. Her right tennis shoe had a hole in the toe.

Sabina had yet to make eye contact with either Glenn or me. Her head constantly swiveled, and her eyes moved independently of that motion. I didn't know if the movements were related to a physical or mental condition, but she seemed coherent enough upon our introductions to continue the conversation.

We were on the west side of the bridge now. The tony development, Kendall Yards, was further in the distance, and its grocery store, My Fresh Basket, loomed above us. A small crowd gathered on West Summit Parkway. They stood almost overhead due to the elevation change of the Centennial Trail.

Lieutenant Brand remained a few feet away and watched Glenn and me closely.

"What were you doing under the bridge?" Glenn asked.

While he asked questions, I took notes.

"Looking for Ranger."

"Ranger?"

Sabina's head continued to swivel "That's where I heard he was sleeping." Sabina mashed her palms together. Her head stopped turning when she noticed the crowd. Her face pinched, and her cheeks reddened. "The fuck you looking at!"

"Sabina," Glenn said.

"Get a life!" Spittle flew as she shouted, and her arms waved in the air as if to chase curious wildlife.

"Sabina."

"Don't you losers have nothin' better to do!"

"Sabina!"

She spun to Glenn. "Stop calling me that!" As if surprised Glenn and I were there, she took a half step back. She powerfully cleared her throat and spat phlegm into the scrub brush. Her head began its swivel again, and her palms returned to their mashing.

"What's Ranger's real name?" Glenn asked.

"Stranger Danger Dick Ranger." Her head whirled back toward the crowd. "Get a fuckin' job!"

"Sabina," Glenn said sternly.

She faced him, but she never made eye contact. "Name's Gypsy." She blinked several times before pausing to look him in the eye. That only lasted a moment, and her head was on the move again. "People call me Gypsy."

"All right, Gypsy. Do you know Ranger's real name?"

"I already told you." She waved her hand. "Down here, that's as official as it gets."

Glenn looked at me, and I shrugged. We'd get Ranger's real name if an identification card was discovered in his belongings or when his fingerprints came back. Maybe Crime Analysis had him in the system under a Stranger Danger alias.

"When was the last time you saw Ranger?" he asked.

"Last night."

"When had he been assaulted?"

Her face pinched, but it didn't stop her head from swiveling.

"Who hit him?" Glenn asked.

Sabina's face relaxed. "Mango." As an afterthought, she shrugged and said, "I think. Maybe. That's what I heard. I might be wrong."

Glenn moved closer. "You heard Mango hit Ranger? What for?"

"Lots of stuff." Sabina kneaded her palm as her gaze continued to bounce about. She didn't make eye contact with Glenn either. "Spanging on his corner."

I looked at Glenn and raised an eyebrow.

"Begging for spare change," he said.

Sabina continued. "Which is totally messed up if you want my opinion. We're all out there, and Mango hadn't been on that corner in weeks. It's not like he owns the city. It's a free country."

"What corner are we talking about?" Glenn asked.

"That one near the freeway." She pointed toward downtown. "That guy—" Sabina noticed the people standing on top of the bridge now. "Why are you watching me? Go on!" She looked at us. "Can't you make them go away or something?"

"That guy, what?" Glenn said.

"Huh?"

"You started to say something about Mango."

Sabina closed her eyes and lifted her face to the sun like a lizard sunning itself on a rock. It was the first time she'd stopped moving, and she stayed frozen for several moments. Eventually, she said, "That guy thinks he owns everything out here."

Glenn crossed his arms. "Did Mango ever threaten Ranger?"

"Uh-huh." Sabina nodded even though her face remained pointed toward the sky. "Lots of times."

"Because of the spanging?"

"And other things."

"What other things?" Glenn asked.

"He wanted Ranger's pocket watch."

"Ranger had a pocket watch?"

Sabina lowered her head, but her attention didn't return to Glenn. It was on the move again. "Where do all these people come from?" She sounded genuinely confused. "How big is this town anyway?"

"Ranger," Glenn said. "He had a pocket watch?"

Sabina nodded. "A gold one. Mango talked about it all the time. He started saying Ranger stole it from him, but that's not true. It was Ranger's granddad's or something. Maybe even his great granddad's. I don't know for sure."

"How did Mango see it?"

"Ranger wore it on his belt. Real proud like. It told the time and everything."

Glenn smiled. "Do you know Mango's real name?"

"Mango the Magnificent." She cleared her throat once more. "But he ain't so magnificent," she said through a mouthful of mucus. She turned her head and spat. Sabina wiped her mouth with her fingers and left a trail of dirt smeared across her lips. "I'll tell you what. The guy is all talk. I've had better."

"Where can we find Mango?"

"I don't know where he's at now. He was staying at the camp, but they made him go."

Glenn cocked his head. "Which one?"

She pointed toward the east. "You know—the *camp*. The big one near the freeway."

"Camp Faith?"

"That's right." She nodded. "Mango doesn't get along well with others, so they forced him out." She turned to the crowd and spread her arms. "Take a picture!"

"Do you live at the camp?" Glenn asked.

"You're a bunch of vultures," Sabina yelled at the crowd. Several teenagers in the assembled mass seemed delighted by her outburst.

"Gypsy," Glenn said.

She faced him.

"Do you live at the camp?"

"Not anymore. They started making all those stupid rules." She frowned. "If I wanted to follow the rules, I would have stayed married."

"Where are you living now?"

"I got a place."

"Where's that?"

She eyed us with suspicion. "Why do you want to know?"

"In case we need to contact you."

"I'm down by the river, but I'm thinking about moving again. I don't like the people there. They think they're better than everybody else because they got a water view." Sabina shook her head. "I can get a water view any time I want. It's not that special."

"What's Mango look like?" I asked.

"You can't miss the bastard." She lifted her hand into the air. "He's taller than a building, and his hair is so orange it looks like the son of a bitch is wearing a basketball on his head."

***

Kyle Singleton cupped a digital camera in his hand. He was in his late twenties with perfectly cut dark hair, waxed eyebrows, and straight teeth. He was overly tanned and extremely fit. He was all wrong for the moment. The guy seemed more suited to hawking protein powder than documenting a crime scene.

The three of us moved into position.

Glenn hunkered next to the body and reached for the sleeping bag covering it.

I stood out of the way with my notebook at the ready. The last place I needed to be was next to the body and in the way of the shot. Glenn would announce anything of interest, Kyle would photograph it, then I could step up and look. It was a slow, methodical process, but that's how crime scene analysis worked.

"Ready when you are," Kyle said.

Glenn looked over his shoulder. His brow furrowed, and he cocked his head in a questioning manner.

Kyle lifted the camera for emphasis, and he smiled. "I mean it. Go ahead when you're ready."

"You sure?" Glenn asked. He didn't bother hiding his sarcasm.

"Oh, yeah. I'm totally set. I got my establishing shots, my close-ins. I'm super good to go." Kyle turned and grinned at me. "Let's do this."

Glenn's smirk morphed into a scowl.

"Where's Geri?" I asked.

"Court," Kyle said. "But we're all trained to take photos." He lifted the camera again. "Seriously, you can begin anytime you want. I've documented a scene before."

"Just one?" Glenn asked.

Kyle blinked a couple of times before saying, "Well, yeah, but I went to the school—"

Glenn grunted and cut off his explanation. He lifted the sleeping bag away from the body.

The technician hurriedly lifted the camera. "Got it," he announced.

"You did?" Glenn asked.

"Check it out." Kyle turned the camera for both of us to see the digital viewer. He beamed proudly. "The composition is great. We're lucky the sun is behind us and at this angle. It's gonna make for a fantastic series of—"

Glenn interrupted. "We don't need the commentary."

"But I thought you might like to know I got a good photograph without the sleeping bag."

"I would expect nothing less."

Kyle looked down and stared at the camera's monitor. His cheeks reddened, and in a moment, he muttered. "I understand."

"May we continue?" Glenn asked.

The tech nodded, and the rest of the search went efficiently.

Ranger wore dirty jeans, a zippered hoodie over a T-shirt, and no boots. He had eighty-seven cents in his left front pocket, a crumpled pack of unfiltered Camel cigarettes in the right, but no wallet or ID card.

Glenn lifted Ranger's shirt and noticed bruising on his stomach and sternum. "You see this?"

"Looks like a beat down."

"If what Gypsy said was right—" Glenn stood and dusted dirt from his knees that wasn't there. "—Mango put a hell of a beating on this guy. You think Ranger wandered back here, climbed into his bag, and died?"

"Let's see what the medical examiner has to say, but it's as good an explanation as any."

As far as crime scenes went, this one was simple. It was a sleeping bag in the middle of a mostly open area. It wasn't a house. There wasn't going to be much to wrap up.

Once the medical examiner's team arrived to collect the body, Ranger's effects and sleeping bag would be logged into the property room. That was it.

Kyle stared at Glenn.

"What?" Glenn asked.

"Am I needed any further?"

"After the body is collected," Glenn said, "we'll need the sleeping bag logged into evidence."

Kyle's face tightened. "I'll make sure to get on that." He removed the camera strap from around his neck. "Is that all?"

"Yeah," Glenn said.

The evidence tech walked away.

"Looks like you made a friend," I muttered.

Glenn twisted his lips. "I was probably a little rough on him."

"You think?"

He looked at me. "I'd have been in a better mood if you had said yes to the teacher."

"So, this is my fault?"

Glenn shook his head. "It's mine. I let the second case get to me." His shoulders slumped. "Shit."

***

Glenn and I headed to our respective cubicles when we returned to the department. He dropped heavily into his chair as I eased into mine. Now we had two fresh cases to investigate.

I considered the binders at the top of my desk. Besides the Bachman murder and Ranger's death, I had six open cases. They were in various stages of investigation—all were waiting on the work of others.

Three were waiting for DNA results, two had active Attempt to Locates on homicide suspects, and one was waiting for a ballistic analysis. There wasn't anything I could do about those except wait.

The best thing to do was focus energy on the latest cases while everything was still hot.

"Hey," Glenn said.

I leaned back and eyed him.

"I'll stay with Ranger," Glenn said, "if you run with the Bachman case. If either of us needs help with something, we sing out. Maybe we'll make some headway, and we can knock one of them down."

"Sounds like a plan."

My seat dropped back into position, and I opened my notes from the Bachman murder. There wasn't much to go on at this point.

No murder weapon was found at the scene. The forensics team had yet to send back a fingerprint report from their sweep of the house or the car.

The medical examiner also hadn't scheduled Bachman's autopsy. They'd likely confirm he'd died from the stabbing, and they would also reveal the length and width of the knife. That would help determine the murder weapon.

Yesterday, I interviewed Bachman's daughter. She provided information I could follow up on—the bar where her father drank.

There were two other avenues still to run down. The first was Bachman's employment. I wanted to get a better understanding of the man. Maybe he had some friends there. Also, his work might provide answers to what happened—a jealous co-worker perhaps, or a pissed-off customer. Without a viable suspect at this point, we had to consider anyone.

The second avenue to explore was Kelsie Rockford, who claimed Bachman raped her eighteen years ago. It was probably a waste of time to speak with her, but Glenn pointed out yesterday that revenge was a dish best served cold. Why would Kelsie have retaliated against Bachman? And would she have waited nearly two decades to do it?

I checked my watch. It was shortly after eleven. Too early to go to a bar.

When I stood, Glenn said, "That was quick."

"Going out for some interviews."

He glanced around the office before whispering, "It's Wednesday."

"So?"

"Are you still going to meet with your cousin?"

"I'm planning on it. Why?"

He took another furtive look around the office. "I like knowing you two get to spend time together."

"You've got nothing to worry about," I said.

"If you need me to handle anything so you can make the meeting, let me know."

"I'm fine, Mom." I walked off.

"That was unnecessary," he called after me.

5

"Vic? He was all right as far as employees go." Roger Fitzhugh rested both elbows along the edge of his desk. His gaze flicked briefly over my shoulder to the lobby. There were voices behind us as business continued without his involvement. Fitzhugh frowned, shook his head, and returned his attention to me. "Vic wasn't exactly a ball of fire, but it seems most of my guys aren't." Fitzhugh's expression tightened. "That's speaking ill of the dead, isn't it?"

I shrugged.

Before I could ask a follow-up question, Fitzhugh fell back into his chair and threw his hands into the air. "What can I say?"

He'd said a lot so far. Most of it had been about himself, his business, or how smart he was to start his own car lot before his thirtieth birthday. He had a clumsy way of turning every question into some chattering about himself.

Fitzhugh was thirty-eight years old but dressed like he was ready for the return of disco. His longish hair was parted down the middle and feathered. His collared shirt was unbuttoned to his tanned, hairless chest. The shirt was wrapped around his swollen biceps and was rolled up to the midpoint of his thick forearms. A gold chain with a cross hung around his neck.

We were in his office, which barely contained his desk and two metal chairs. My knees bumped against the back of the bulky piece of furniture. The room smelled like musky cologne, coffee, and past sex. On the walls were posters of bikini-clad women draped over exotic cars with names like Ferrari, Lamborghini, and Maserati, yet there wasn't a single fancy brand on the lot.

Several books stood against the wall at the edge of the desk—*Sell or Be Sold* by Grant Cardone, Jeffrey Gitomer's *Little Red Book of Selling*, and Zig Ziglar's *Secrets of Closing the Sale*.

"I tried to help Vic develop some sales mojo," Fitzhugh said, "but talk about a lost cause. Before I hired him, he gave me this song and dance about how he sold insurance when he was younger. Like back in the nineties or something. Came on strong about how good he was at it. Even sold his book of business to some other schmo." Fitzhugh mimed masturbating. "Blahdy-blahdy-blah. Don't tell me what you did yesterday. Tell me what you can do for me today. Am I right? I wonder if the guy shined me on to get hired. Isn't that a crime or something? Lying on an application?" He flicked his hand toward the lobby. "If it is, most of these mooks should be charged."

Fitzhugh owned Off the Lot Motors, a used car dealership at the intersection of Sprague Avenue and Altamont Street. Across the road was The Flame Bar & Grill. I could see the squat restaurant from where I sat.

A dilapidated Honda Accord sped northbound on Altamont toward the industrial complex that replaced the former greyhound track. Its muffler dragged behind it and created a trail of sparks.

"When was the last time Vic reported for work?" I asked.

Fitzhugh laughed. "Reported for work. I like that. You make it sound like the military or something." His expression grew serious. "You know, I almost joined the Navy out of high school. Were you in the military?"

"Vic," I said.

"Yeah, yeah." Fitzhugh looked out the window as if searching for something. "So, this recruiter came to my school. Checked us out like those guys scouting a football team. Said he liked what he saw and wanted me to join the SEALs. You've heard of them, right?" He cast a sideways glance in my direction. "I was in perfect shape back then. Like way better than I am now, and I'm still in great shape." He slapped his belly once. "The gym coach tested my body fat and told me I had zero percent. Can you believe that? And I ate burgers and fries all the time. Can't do that today. No, I gotta eat like I'm training for the Mr. Universe contest but we gotta do what we gotta do to keep the bunnies. Am I right? Anyway, I told that recruiter I wasn't interested in being a SEAL because I wanted to go to college."

I tapped my notepad. "When was the last time Vic came in for work?"

Fitzhugh frowned. "Vic. Right. I think his last day was Friday." He leaned forward and hollered through his office door, "Carly, when was Vic here last?"

A woman's voice came back, "Thursday."

Fitzhugh fell back in his chair. "There you go. Thursday. What do you think of Carly? She's pretty hot for a chick in her forties, right? I don't normally go for redheads, but she's super into me. Not that I'm going to get tied down by one woman."

"Was Vic here the whole day?"

Fitzhugh blinked several times before answering. "Yeah. Vic was good that way. He normally put in a full day. Didn't amount to much, but at least he was here."

"Did he mention any problems with anyone?"

"You know what I think?" Fitzhugh waved dismissively. "Selling is a diminishing skill. Like once you hit a certain age, your shit's no longer wired tight." He tapped the desk with two fingers. "Forty and done." He tapped the desk again. "Just like that. I mean, that's not going to happen to me because I keep myself sharp. I'm in the mix every day. Even got a health and strength regimen like Tom Brady. You know who he is? Sure, you do. Everyone does. TB twelve. Am I right? That's who I'm like. My days are about cashing checks and snapping necks. I'm gonna keep at it until I'm at least fifty, then I'll walk away from the game like Tom Terrific. How old are you?"

I repeated my question. "Did Vic mention any problems with anyone?"

"No, but who would he be a problem to?" Fitzhugh clicked his tongue against the back of his teeth. "Except me, maybe?" He laughed and lifted his hands in mock surrender. "I'm kidding, but the guy might as well not even come in. Took him six and a half hours to sell one dented Hyundai. There were plenty of better cars—" He winked. "You get what I'm saying? There were way nicer cars to put a customer in— Hell, we've got a cherry-ass Lexus out there. But, no, Vic lets a customer talk him into a cheap, dented bitch of a Hyundai. I always tell my guys you're either selling the customer or the customer is selling you. You get what I'm saying?"

My gaze drifted to the books on his desk.

Fitzhugh continued. "Vic's customer sold him on that Hyundai. Just like that." He snapped his fingers. "I'd never let anyone do that to me. They would have walked out of here with that Lexus. Mark my word. What about you?"

"I've got a car."

"No. The detecting thing. Is it a diminishing skill?" Fitzhugh waved his hand up and down my length. "Is there only so much stuff you guys can take?"

There was only so much of Roger Fitzhugh I could take. I tried to keep my expression blank. "Was there a customer who wanted to harm Vic? Maybe over a faulty car?"

Fitzhugh reared back as if he had smelled something offensive. "We stand behind our products if that's what you're asking."

"I was asking about customers."

"Because I'll tell you this." Fitzhugh pointed over my shoulder. "I have every one of my cars serviced by Mike over at Activate Auto before they ever hit the lot." He motioned to the west. "That's my pledge. All my cars get a stamp of approval." His fist pounded on the desk. "The ol' Off the Lot Pledge of Quality."

It was an act I'm sure he'd practiced. If I was buying a car, it might have made me happy to hand over my hard-earned money for one of his clunkers.

"I love selling cars. It's in my blood." Fitzhugh put his hand over his heart and did his best to appear sincere. "But I could have been a cop. I even thought about it when I was in high school. Yeah, there was this school resource officer who said I had a natural talent for sizing people up, reading them, you know? Is that something you do?"

"We're talking about Vic."

"I know. I am." Fitzhugh ran his fingers through the top of his feathered hair, then shook his head. His brow furrowed. "What was your question?"

"Were there any troubles with Vic?"

"Besides his lack of effort?"

"If he was so bad, why not fire him?"

Fitzhugh shrugged a single shoulder. "The guy sold an occasional car. What can I say? I guess the sun shines on a dog's ass every now and then. I add up all these mooks out there, and they don't beat my production. It's pitiful what the job market looks like right now. But I take what I can get. You ever get in any fights?"

"Was Vic friendly with the other guys?"

Fitzhugh lifted slightly in his chair to look over my shoulder into the lobby. He nodded, then dropped back into his seat. "You know, I treat my guys like my brothers. They love me, and I love them."

"Except Vic."

"What? No. He was all right. A middle-of-the-road sort. Never the best, never the worst. If it's anything, it's that he didn't join in our reindeer games. We'd go out, get beers, and cause a little trouble, but he wouldn't participate. Maybe it's an age thing. I'm never gonna be like that. So, no fights, huh? I used to get in them all the time. Not so much anymore because I got a business to protect, but I'd throw down if someone came at me now." He nodded appreciatively at the image of himself. "I could still go a full ten rounds if need be."

I closed my notebook. "Thank you for your time."

Fitzhugh smiled. "You bet. Anytime." He stood and stepped around the desk. He handed me his business card. "It's been a real pleasure talking to you. If you need anything else or are in the market for a car, call me. Or if you want to grab a beer sometime." He thumbed toward The Flame. "I'll buy you a cold one.

I'll tell you about some of those fights I used to have. You'd probably get a kick out of hearing them."

***

"How'd he die?"

Kelsie Rockford bounced the baby boy on her knee. She puffed her cheeks and crossed her eyes immediately after asking the question. The child giggled.

She wore a wrinkled white T-shirt and gray yoga pants. Her hair appeared unwashed and was pulled back with a red scrunchie. Her face was free of makeup and dark bags hung under her eyes. The baby wore a little blue shirt and a cloth diaper. A small blanket and several brightly colored toys sat next to her on the blue overstuffed couch.

"I figured Amanda would have told you what happened," I said.

Kelsie looked up from the child. "Is that why she texted for me to call?" Her attention returned to the baby. "Who's a good boy? You are. That's right."

She talked to the child like it was a dog. Maybe that's how parents spoke with little kids. I didn't have either, so I wouldn't know.

"He was stabbed," I said.

Kelsi spun the baby around and clutched him to her side. "Why are you here?"

I leaned forward so I could better see her eyes. I wanted to see her reaction. "Have you had contact with Victor Bachman?"

She bent and kissed the child's head. "Why on earth would I do that?"

I opened my palms.

Kelsie studied me for a moment before asking, "You think I had something to do with his death?"

So far, all she'd done was ask me questions. Kelsie hadn't given any information since our initial introductions. She recalled my name, and there was a moment of awkwardness that lasted until I told her Vic was dead.

We sat in the living room of her South Hill apartment. She lived behind the Target Superstore off Regal Street. It was a massive complex—the kind Spokane had suddenly grown accustomed to over recent years.

Two recliners matched the style of the couch, and the three were the only major pieces of furniture in the room. In the corner, a two-foot stone water feature gurgled loudly. A plethora of plants of all sizes filled the room and gave it a soft yet oddly wild feel. No art hung on the white walls, and there was no television present. The lamp behind the couch illuminated the room in a dull yellow glow.

The house was mostly clean and organized, but it smelled of dirt and baby poop.

"Here's the thing," Kelsie said. "I don't want anyone to die. Inviting that kind of junk into my life, my soul, it's bad karma. Understand?"

I nodded once, and the baby smiled at me.

She continued. "I haven't talked with Vic since that night. After everything that happened—" Kelsie stopped talking and inhaled deeply. She shook her head and let out one long, controlled breath. "I hoped I'd never hear about him again. I guess that wasn't going to happen if I lived in this town. Especially not if Amanda and I stayed in contact."

She spun the baby around and lifted him in the air. They touched noses.

"We haven't been the best of friends over the years," Kelsie said. "Amanda started a family and moved on with her life."

She bounced the baby on her knee again, but this time it was slower. Melancholy filled her eyes as she studied the child. "Amanda got a family, and I got counseling." A sad smile spread over her lips. "It worked out in the end, though. I finally got Elijah here." Kelsie looked up. "Her kids are almost out of the house, and I'm just starting. How's that for another disconnect in our lives?" She exhaled heavily. "That's how it goes, I guess."

"If I asked for an alibi, would you be able to provide one?"

Her brow furrowed. "I guess that depends on what you're asking. It's not like I have anyone to account for my nights." She tilted her head toward the baby. "His father isn't around, and Elijah's not going to make the best witness, now is he? But I'll tell you where I was if you give me a day and time."

Unfortunately, we couldn't pinpoint the time of death until the medical examiner gave us a window. Right now, I was doing preliminary legwork on the case. Sometimes they broke early due to interviews like this. Other times—more than we'd like to admit—interviews simply provided background on a victim. The information garnered would never make it into a court case or a final report.

She stared into the baby's eyes. "Vic never did anything wrong." Her voice was soft, and I couldn't tell if the admission was meant for the baby or me. "He told the truth."

The water feature bubbled in the corner.

Tears welled in Kelsie's eyes. She pulled the baby in tight to her, and her eyes challenged mine. "I'm sure you think I'm a terrible person because of what I did."

I shook my head.

Kelsie caressed the child's head as she looked toward the ceiling. "Karma's a terrible thing."

The words sounded heavy, as if they carried a lifetime of guilt. I stayed quiet and let her continue.

"I was scared, you know? My boyfriend said he didn't want to break up. That he'd screwed up royally. Of course, he did. He basically cheated on me, but we would never have gotten back together if I said I hooked up with Vic for a revenge—" She pulled the baby away from her chest and looked at him. "Mommy doesn't use those kinds of words anymore, does she? No, she doesn't."

She wiggled the child, and he giggled. Kelsie slowly pulled him back to her as several tears rolled down her cheeks.

"Maybe I was weak," she said. Her gaze returned to me. "There's no maybe about it, is there? I *was* weak. I've lived with the guilt for so long." Her hand stroked the baby's head. "Randy died because of what I said. When that whole thing happened, I couldn't back off my statement. Randy went after Vic because he thought I'd been…" She didn't finish the thought.

We listened to the water feature gurgle for several beats. I didn't feel the need to ask her any questions. She was doing a fine job of providing me with more than anything I had hoped to get.

Kelsie hugged the child. Her lips contorted, and she pinched her eyes closed. After a moment, she lowered the baby and refocused on me. The tears had stopped, but her eyes glistened. She ran the back of a finger underneath her nose. "At first, I thought I would stick to my story, but the more I thought about it, the less I wanted to continue the lie. I knew I'd eventually have to go to court and make the lie forever."

The lie was already eternal. Her boyfriend was dead, and Victor Bachman's life was irretrievably altered. Telling her such a thing wouldn't help at the moment, though.

She rubbed her cheek against the baby's. "Maybe that's why I'm telling you all this. I tried to tell Amanda years ago, but she wouldn't believe me. She thought I was saying it to protect our friendship, but I didn't try very hard to convince her of the truth. Once she said she wouldn't believe me, I let her believe what she wanted. As long as I didn't have to go to court, I figured Vic could go on with his life and me with mine."

Waiting nearly two decades for revenge wasn't out of the question, but I didn't think Kelsie Rockford killed Victor Bachman. Still, if I was proved wrong by evidence, I didn't want to have to eat those words. When we pinpointed the time frame of Vic's murder, I'd confirm an alibi with her or at least get an explanation of where she was.

I closed my notebook and tucked it inside my jacket. I started to stand when she said, "I cried wolf."

"Excuse me?"

"With Vic. I cried wolf, and karma made me pay."

Tears filled her eyes. She wasn't done confessing, so I returned to my seat.

Kelsie nodded several times before saying, "First, it took Randy, then it made me eat my words."

I stared at her, but she didn't look away.

Kelsie's lips trembled. "I've never told anyone this, not even my parents."

She shook her head when I reached for my notebook. "You won't need it. It's too long ago, and it no longer matters."

Her tears told me otherwise.

"Maybe I wanted it to happen," she said. "You know, like I put it out into the universe that I needed to be punished or something." Her words caught, and she inhaled sharply. "But I didn't think it would. Not in a million years. No one does." She gnawed on her lower lip and glanced at the water feature. "Afterward, I figured, who would believe me? Everybody thought I was a liar anyway. They would just believe I was doing it again."

"Nobody deserves to have that happen," I said.

Kelsie wiped the tears away with the tips of her fingers. "Yeah, well, I don't think those thoughts anymore. I don't wish bad things happen to me or anyone—not even Vic."

We stared at each other for several moments.

"You should be a priest," she said. She kissed the top of her baby's head. "You're good at listening to confessions."

"I'm sorry it happened." I stood once again.

"What now?" she asked.

"Nothing," I said. "You have a beautiful baby." I headed for the door.

***

Stephen Yoder settled into his maroon wingback chair. "You're looking better."

He wore an argyle sweater vest over a long-sleeved white collared shirt. His beard had grown grayer over the time we'd known each other. It remained neatly trimmed, though. I wondered if he touched it up every day.

Stephen seemed the fastidious type. Everything in the office was always in its place. Perhaps it only occurred at the office. I often wondered what his home life was like. Was he as orderly there, or was he as screwed up as the rest of us?

He cocked his head. "You're eating better, I presume?"

"Some."

His left hand rested on his notepad. A pen rolled back and forth between the fingers of the other hand. "You've put on some weight."

"I guess. I haven't checked."

"It looks good. Healthy."

Stephen's office was within walking distance of the Public Safety campus. That made it convenient for officers who wanted to visit the department's psychiatrist. Unfortunately, its proximity to the station was also a detriment. Mental health might have been a popular buzzword in the Human Resources community, but officers seeking to protect theirs were considered weak by fellow cops.

At first, I didn't want to speak with Stephen. The administration ordered my participation. I had no choice if I wanted to keep working. Once I realized Stephen's input positively impacted my life, I mostly stopped worrying about what other officers might think.

Mostly.

It also helped that I carried a detective's rank and was at the end of my career. I'm unsure if I would have felt the same way if I was still in a patrol car. So far, I'd been able to keep my visits a secret—only Glenn and the administration knew.

Marlene also knew, but I shared everything with her now; it was the kind of friendship we had built.

"What are we talking about today?"

I shrugged. "I don't have anything. I'm good."

Stephen smiled. "That's nice to hear."

My gaze flitted about his office. It had been almost six months since I started with Stephen. The black and white line drawings hanging on his wall were familiar now. They represented a variety of locations around town—the Riverfront Park Clock Tower, the Monroe Street Bridge, and the Spokane County Courthouse. The familiarity of the locations brought comfort when I looked at them. Is that why Stephen had them in the office? Did others experience the same thing by looking at local landmarks?

"How long have you been without the music?" Stephen asked.

It was as if he and Marlene were talking.

Stephen studied me as he waited for an answer.

"Seven weeks," I said. "Nothing in that time."

He stopped rolling the pen between his fingers and jotted a note. "I would assume you've had stressful moments in that period."

"Some. Sure."

"How did you deal with them?"

I furrowed my brow.

"Did anything else seem to become more heightened? Sight, sound, aroma?"

"Other sounds."

Stephen tapped his pen against his notepad. "I suppose that makes the most sense. Your subconscious isn't delivering what your mind is expecting, so the body searches for it. Does it often occur—the heightened sound?"

"Not much." I shrugged. "Now and then, I suppose."

"How often do you visit Bobbie?"

"I saw her this morning."

Stephen watched me but didn't comment.

"Not every day." I looked away. "A few times a week."

"There's nothing wrong with visiting her, Dallas."

"I know." My hands rubbed anxiously together. "I would have thought it got easier after a time."

"For some, it does." Stephen shifted in his chair. "For others, it takes considerably longer. You were with her since high school. She was integral in everything you did. Life without her isn't going to feel normal for quite some time."

"What if I don't want it to feel normal?"

Stephen's eyes dropped as if he were considering a response to that question. Before he could find one, I said, "I tried sleeping in our bed again."

His gaze returned to me. "Explain that," he said, but his attention immediately dropped to his notepad. His pen pranced across the page.

I hated when he did that because it's what I did with suspects. If they said something I could use against them, I recorded it. I waited for him to finish writing.

When he looked up, his face relaxed. "Is everything okay?"

"Sure."

He rolled the pen between his fingers again. "I thought you moved back into your bedroom shortly after we started."

"I thought I could act like nothing had changed, but it didn't hold."

"Why not?"

"She wasn't there."

"And where've you been sleeping?"

"On the living room couch."

"That's where you stayed after she died."

He said it bluntly. I don't remember if that's how he always referred to her death, but I noticed the frankness in how he spoke about her about three months ago. It didn't bother me. It was better than others who still danced around the subject.

Stephen grabbed his notepad but didn't write on it. "Anything else?"

My hands rubbed together. They were sweaty now. "I got rid of our music collection."

"When did that happen? This last week?"

I nodded.

"You had a big collection, if I remember correctly."

"I did."

"That's a significant change." Stephen leaned forward. "Why did you do that?"

"I haven't listened to anything in a long time. When the music stopped, I didn't want to trigger anything." I tapped the side of my head.

"But it's been seven weeks without."

"Getting rid of the CDs was a precaution."

"You don't even listen to music on your computer?"

"I don't have one at home anymore, and I wouldn't do that at work."

Stephen looked toward the ceiling. "But there's music everywhere—the bank, the grocery store, even at a gas pump."

"I try not to listen."

Concern filled his eyes. "That's got to be hard."

"Nearly impossible."

The clock on the wall ticked noisily. A truck drove by with a rumbling engine. The central air-conditioning whirred through the ducting.

"But you didn't have to get rid of the CDs. You could have kept them and not played them."

"I didn't want to be reminded of who I was."

"That radical of a change might not be necessary."

"Maybe it is."

"It also could be unhealthy."

I stared at him. "Too late now."

Stephen settled back into his chair and made another note. "How's work?"

"It's the job."

"Don't want to talk about it?"

"What's there to say? It's the same thing day after day. People hurt people. What I do doesn't make it stop."

Stephen craned his neck as he studied me. "Sure it does. What you do is very important."

I waved a dismissive hand. "Maybe I stop one guy, but it's like trying to drain the ocean with a bucket. What difference do I really make? None."

My face warmed, and I felt foolish for voicing those emotions. It was childish. Maybe my actions didn't matter to those victims who were already dead, but I knew full well they made a difference for the families left behind. My work meant something to those crime victims still alive. And my job helped others never become victims because we took a predator off the street.

Feeling sorry for myself felt righteous for a moment. Unfortunately, it quickly turned into embarrassment.

Stephen's tongue darted underneath his upper lip. "What do you do for fun, Dallas?"

"Fun?"

"You weren't listening to your music collection, so you got rid of it. Not so long ago, you got rid of your TV. Did you ever get a new one?"

I hadn't.

"Do you work out? Ride a bike? Go for walks?"

I shook my head.

"What about reading? Do you journal?"

More shakes of the head.

"You go home at the end of the day and do what?"

"Putter."

"What's that mean?"

I shrugged. "Nothing."

"Then what do you do?"

"Sleep, I guess."

Stephen scribbled again on his notepad. The guy was writing a novel today. He asked, "How are your relationships?" without looking up.

"They're fine."

He set his pen down. "When's the last time you did something with your brother?"

"He's been out of the country. Italy."

"You'll get together soon?"

"I can't wait to see his pictures."

Stephen smirked. "I've gotten good at reading your sarcasm. What about other friends?"

I thought about Marlene.

"You do have other friends, don't you?"

I'd never talked with Stephen about her. If I mentioned Marlene, I'm sure he'd ask if I ever brought her up to Bobbie. Then I'd feel stupid. I wasn't doing anything bad by having coffee or the occasional meal with her. I wasn't going to start a relationship with Marlene, so there was no need to bring her up to my wife.

"Well?"

My eyes met Stephen's. "I'll work on getting some friends."

6

Back at the department, I pulled my notebook from my jacket and tossed it onto my desk. Next, I removed my jacket and hung it on the hook attached to my cubicle.

Glenn leaned back in his chair. "Anything break loose with your interview?"

"Nothing."

He glanced around. "Everything good with your cousin?"

Glenn had found out about the music in my head when I admitted to it while working on a confession from a killer. It almost broke our partnership, but we came through it. He started referring to Stephen as my cousin so others wouldn't know what we were talking about.

I dropped into my chair. "He said to say hello."

Glenn chuckled but quickly cut it off. "Wait." He scooted his chair closer. "You talked about me?"

"He asked about my stresses, and I mentioned you. What can I say?"

Glenn glanced around for prying ears. He lowered his voice before speaking again. "What did you say?"

"Don't be surprised if you get a call to see him in the next couple of days."

His eyes narrowed. "You're messing with me."

I smiled.

"I hate you." Glenn pushed his chair back toward his desk. "You wanna give me a hand with something?"

"What is it?"

Lieutenant George Brand approached, and we both stopped talking. It was best not to speak or act around the lieutenant. He tended to offer his opinions on how to do our jobs even though he'd never been a Major Crimes detective. He carried several thick folders in one hand while the other carried a steel water bottle. "Gentlemen."

As far as leaders go, Brand inspired little confidence. Every profession has a bell curve—a graphical representation of normal probability distribution. Teachers had it. Even the Navy SEALS had it. There was no way to ignore the bell curve existed within the Spokane Police Department.

There were some truly excellent cops at the right end— that slim piece of pie reserved for high achievers. The rest of us were in the meaty middle. I wouldn't fool myself into thinking I could run and gun with the best of them. I liked to do those things early in my career, but now I worked a thinking person's job. Thankfully, the department had that type of posting. At the left side of the curve were men and women like Brand—the misfits who were somehow drawn to law enforcement but didn't fit the traditional mold.

George Brand was an effective administrator—the type of man happy to sit behind a desk and compose lengthy emails about policy and procedures. Rumor was Brand irritated our current chief of police, which landed him this assignment in Major Crimes. It seemed ridiculous for the chief to punish a lieutenant by giving him the choicest leadership assignment in the department.

However, Brand operated the section with competence. Since his arrival, the closure rate in all categories grew higher than the national average. If there were an administrator bell curve, he'd be at the top end of it. The guy was a natural.

Thinking of the lieutenant in those terms, perhaps that's why the chief assigned him the Major Crimes position. It had nothing to do with a rumored punishment and everything to do with expected results.

"After I get set up," Brand said, "come by my office and brief me on how your cases are progressing."

Glenn's face pinched. "Which ones?"

"All of them. We just had a senior staff meeting, and Chief Dillon asked for a status update on everyone's caseload. I didn't like the way the assistant chief followed up on my answers." Brand glanced between the two of us. "Now you and your cohorts are going to update me, then I will provide a written update to the chain. And since I saw you two first, we can get started now."

Glenn knocked his knuckles against his desk. "We're in the middle of two new cases. We don't have time for this."

Brand waggled his water bottle between us. "You either do it now, or you do it before you go home. Your choice, but none of us are leaving today without my briefing the command."

I reached for a notepad. "Let's get it done."

"This is bullshit," Glenn muttered.

The lieutenant smirked. "I appreciate your enthusiasm, Higgins."

Brand's sarcasm surprised me. By the look on Glenn's face, it caught him off guard, too.

"What about you, Nash?" the lieutenant asked.

"I'm fine."

"Five minutes," he said. "My office. Both of you." He walked off.

I eyed the row of binders at the top of my cubicle. Each had a label to identify the corresponding case it held. I wrote the name and number associated with the first binder onto the notepad. I wouldn't need any more detail than that. I knew where each case stood. I moved on to the second.

Glenn leaned over. "Doesn't this piss you off?"

"Why's it matter?"

"It's a circle jerk."

I moved on to the third binder. "We waste more time than this when you talk about union issues."

Glenn pulled back. "What're you talking about? That's productive."

"To you."

"You don't think the city and the administration are screwing us over?"

I continued writing but didn't look at him. "Get moving."

Reluctantly, Glenn turned and grabbed a notepad. "We should stand up to this type of intrusion into our workday."

"What was the thing you wanted help with?"

Glenn lifted out of his chair to consider his own binders. He dropped back into his seat and wrote something. "I found Ranger in the system." He stole a glance in my direction. "Richard Ranger. Forty-seven. He's got a lengthy record for misdemeanor crimes. Assault, open and consume, public urination, malicious mischief, you name it, but no felonies."

"Stranger Danger Dick Ranger."

Glenn stopped writing and faced me. "I checked his most recent reports and there was no permanent address given."

"News flash—he's homeless."

"I was thinking about relatives. Someone we could contact."

"What about Mango the Magnificent? Any luck with that moniker?"

"Nothing, and I talked to Crime Analysis about him. I figured I'd make the rounds at the shelters."

"And you want me to go with you?"

"You don't have to."

I stood. "Of course, I'll go." I smacked my notepad against his shoulder. "See you in there."

"You're not going to wait?"

"I said you were wasting time."

"Crap." He spun toward his desk and hurriedly wrote.

***

Glenn pulled curbside to Pacific Avenue and parked. As soon as we climbed out of the car, someone in a small cluster of homeless men called out, "Five-oh."

The House of Charity stood at the corner of Pacific Avenue and Browne Street. Roughly thirty men and women were present on the sidewalks. Several crossed in the middle of the roadway and ignored oncoming cars.

"This place," Glenn said.

He didn't need to finish the comment. I felt the same. We worked together long enough that we visited this shelter multiple times. This was our third stop on the Mango the Magnificent Discovery Tour.

We had already struck out at the Union Gospel Mission and a start-up near Habitat for Humanity. No one at either location had heard of the man or felt compelled to go out of their way to help us.

A woman in faded camouflaged pants and a black Metallica sweatshirt watched us from the sidewalk. She had a dirty face and watery eyes. Two men stood behind her. When we neared, she raised her hands. "I didn't do it." Her words slurred together.

The men with her raised their hands in solidarity and cackled. All three stunk like stale alcohol and body odor.

We entered the building and approached the admittance desk. The intake clerk looked up from whatever he was reading. Glenn pulled his jacket aside to show his badge.

"Detective Higgins. This is Detective Nash."

The intake clerk eyed us warily. He was bald, roughly fifty, and appeared tired. His shoulders slumped. "Crud. Who did what now?"

"We're investigating a murder," Glenn said. "A man we believe to be known as Richard Ranger was found this morning."

"Ranger?" The intake clerk sat back in his chair. "Hell, he was a good guy."

"He stay here?"

"We can't disclose that." The clerk picked up a pen. "Policy and such. You understand."

It was the same old story. Shelters acted like a magnet for crime, yet the providers rarely helped the police unless an act occurred on their property. Then they would go out of their way due to liability reasons. Until then, they would hide behind piousness and ignore the trouble lurking outside their doors. Drugs, alcohol, and rampant mental health issues created a volatile cocktail that many levels of society refused to address.

Glenn rested a hand on the edge of the intake desk. "We're also looking for a guy who goes by the name Mango the Magnificent. Have you ever heard of anyone using that moniker?"

The clerk made no move toward his computer. "Nope."

"You're not going to even check your system?"

"Do you have a warrant?"

"We think he killed Ranger, who you said was a good guy."

The clerk tapped his pen on the table. "It's policy, man. You know how it is."

Glenn shook his head. "Yeah, I know how it is. Thanks for nothing."

***

We drove east to Camp Faith, a makeshift settlement that sprang up in the aftermath of a homeless protest at city hall. After the mayor forced the protesters to move, they landed on some of the vacant land owned by the Washington State Department of Transportation along Interstate 90.

For more than sixty years, Spokane has had only a single freeway serving its populace—an east-west thoroughfare allowing travelers to zip through its city on their way to Seattle or east to Idaho and Montana. State planners dragged their feet on constructing a north-south corridor for Spokane locals because funds for such a project always seemed to find their way to more important road projects located on the west side of the Cascade Mountains where the state planners lived.

Eventually, the pressure became too much, and a Spokane north-south corridor had to be funded. WSDOT purchased a large swath of homes running along Interstate 90 as part of a long-term plan to connect a North-South Freeway someday.

Instead of renting out the hundreds of homes it purchased, WSDOT razed them and created a large belt of dirt—nearly twenty blocks long—from Helena Street to Florida Street. Most of that belt of scab land consisted of half blocks, but four were full city blocks.

On one of those full blocks—Ray Street and 2nd Avenue—the city hall protesters landed. They attracted media attention which brought more campers. A local tow company was even offering free services to destitute RV owners to drag their rigs to the WSDOT land.

Glenn pulled to the curb on Ray Street. His lip curled. "This place."

It was the same comment as the House of Charity. Like before, he didn't need to say anything further.

There were tents, cars, and broken-down RVs. Dirty men and women shuffled about. A large cardboard sign at the edge of the encampment identified the location with block letters in black spray paint—*Camp Faith*. Someone added in red paint—*less*.

"What are we doing here?" I asked. "Gypsy already said he wasn't here. He got kicked out." Trudging through the camp wasn't an ideal way to spend the rest of my day.

"I thought maybe he might have tried to come back. Plus, maybe someone knows his real name. This place seems to be ground zero for the homeless right now. Isn't there a group overseeing it?"

"It looks like Deadwood."

Glenn sniffed dismissively. "It looks like the end of days is what it looks like. You ever see anything like this when you were a kid?"

I shook my head. "Bigger cities, maybe."

"You know we're going in there sometime. If not today, tomorrow. The news is already running stories about an increase in neighborhood crime."

"Huh."

Glenn cast a sideways glance. "I forgot. You got rid of your TV. Well, mark my words. Someone is going to get killed in there, and somehow it will be our fault."

"Your kumbaya speeches always get me—" I tapped the top of my fist against my chest. "—right here."

He dropped the car into gear and accelerated from the curb.

"We're not going to wade into the great unwashed?"

Glenn shook his head. "Maybe one of the churches will help us. You know, the ones giving out free meals to those people."

"Be careful with that."

He turned right onto Second. "With what?"

"*Those people*. That's what you said."

"I didn't mean it that way."

"Doesn't matter. What you say today can come back and haunt you tomorrow."

Glenn's brow furrowed. "I'm not going to worry about the word police. You and I both know it isn't a lack of housing and job opportunities keeping those people on the street. That's the bullshit the bleeding hearts and the politicians want us to believe so they can continue to get their projects funded."

This subject felt dangerously close to a union rant, so I needed to change the subject. "Churches, huh? I don't know. I think we'll get the same stone wall as we did at the House of Charity."

We slowed for a traffic light, but it changed color before we completely stopped. Glenn accelerated. "Got another suggestion?"

"What about the NRO for this neighborhood?" It was a long shot that the Neighborhood Resource Officer would know who Mango the Magnificent was, but it was worth reaching out.

Glenn shrugged a single shoulder. "Yeah, maybe. I'll call whoever it is when we get back to the station."

Up ahead, a large blue and green bus stopped to pick up a passenger. On the sidewalk, an elderly man shuffled toward the now-opened door.

I turned to Glenn with a smile.

"The bus plaza," he said before I could speak. "You were going to suggest we go there, weren't you?"

* * *

Glenn parked in the spot designated *Police Vehicles Only*. We were next to the Spokane Police Department's recently opened downtown precinct which was housed in a former bank branch. We were the only law enforcement vehicle on the side of the building.

"You think we should stop in there?" he asked.

"What for? You gotta use the head?"

The downtown precinct was a publicity win. The city and police department claimed it as an operational success. A team of uniformed officers and some behavioral health resources were assigned there. However, the officers still spent most of their time in their cars and out on the street.

"Maybe they'll know something about Mango." Glenn shrugged. "Worth a shot."

"You check with them, and I'll check with STA."

"You're volunteering to take the freak show? Done." Glenn headed for the precinct.

I trotted across Riverside Avenue and avoided oncoming traffic.

The Spokane Transit Authority's downtown plaza is an overbuilt monstrosity. I'm not sure who the original architect was, but the design never made much sense. The quasi-governmental agency plucked a prime piece of downtown real estate to construct its bus hub. Then it built a two-story structure serving only a single purpose—people loitering until their buses arrived.

A group of smokers congregated on the east side of the building. The aroma of tobacco hung in the air. The plaza's managers erected several metal partitions to separate the smokers from the building further. It placed them in Spokane's seasonal elements and away from the structure's protective overhang.

The automatic doors hissed open as I entered the building. Some jazzy Muzak played overhead. The tune was hard to discern due to the number of loud voices inside. I had learned to appreciate the distraction of other sounds drowning out music I might know.

An interior renovation had recently occurred to modernize the space and reduce loitering within the plaza. The STA marketed that most folks used the bus system for its true purpose and didn't linger around the building. Perhaps it was true, but I looked at the building with the jaded eye of a cop. Maybe most customers rode a bus to or from their destinations. The plaza was merely a point on the way. Unfortunately, I tended to focus on the opposite.

Two white men walked by me in the opposite direction. They had longish hair, black T-shirts, and dirty jeans, and the slow gait of someone with nowhere to be. Both eyed me with distrust as they passed.

A group of teenagers huddled together over a single telephone. They laughed together in response to whatever they were viewing.

Many malcontents hung out in the plaza's wide-open spaces. To them, the plaza was simply a final destination. This element created problems for the STA and the surrounding businesses.

I passed the customer service counter and continued toward the security office. The plaza had an on-site team. Due to the level of crime occurring in and around the property, SPD once provided an on-site officer. This relationship eventually proved unfruitful, especially when most cops didn't want the assignment.

Before I could ring the bell, the security door opened. A heavy-set man appeared. He wore a security vest with a Velcro nametag—*Jenkins*. Various items were clipped on or stored in the vest pockets—security badge, radio with an earpiece, spiral bound notebook, ballpoint pen, handcuffs, telescoping baton. His eyebrows went up as he asked, "Sir?"

"Detective Nash." I pulled my coat to the side to reveal the badge on my belt. "I'm hoping you can help me find a subject."

Jenkins shoved the door open wider. "C'mon in."

I followed him as he lumbered down a corridor to a control room. Inside was a multitude of monitors positioned around a single computer.

Jenkins dropped into a chair, and it groaned its displeasure. He hooked a finger over the security vest and tugged it away from his neck. "Who we looking for?"

"Mango the Magnificent."

"The bad guy from the old *Flash Gordon* movie?"

I shrugged.

Jenkins spun in the chair to face me. "I checked it out on YouTube once. It was cheesy as hell, but it had the guy who played James Bond in it. Know which one I'm talking about?"

I stared at him.

"Right," Jenkins said. He turned back to the computer and rested his hands on the keyboard. "Mango the Magnificent, huh? Got any other descriptors?"

"He's supposedly tall with orange hair."

Jenkins looked over his shoulder.

"Possibly red. We're starting out in a hole with this one."

The security guard typed in *Mango*, clicked the "exact" button, and hit Enter. He was rewarded with zero responses. "Poop on a popsicle stick."

Jenkins then entered the first three letters of Mango's name and followed it with an asterisk—*Man**. He unclicked the "exact" button and tapped the Enter key and was rewarded with over three hundred entries.

Last names such as Manchester and Mancini were sprinkled in with first names like Mandy and Manfred. There were even monikers of Mandingo X and Manifest.

There was a single surname of Mangold tied to the first name of Vince.

"Mango," I said. "Try that one."

Jenkins clicked the entry. A picture came up of a red-haired man scowling at the camera. He was listed as 6'4. "Says here one of the night guys contacted him for smoking in the building. Couple weeks ago. He's been trespassed for ninety days."

"Do you have an address?"

Jenkins pointed at the screen. The address field read *none*.

"Would you print that for me?"

"Is this your guy?"

I shrugged. "No idea but call me if he comes by." I handed him my business card.

"Oh, we'll call. He's trespassed. He's getting arrested if he sets foot on the block."

***

Glenn stepped out of the downtown precinct and moved to the corner. He waited as I crossed the street.

"Tell me you got something," he said.

"Why? What'd you get?"

"Nothing but union scuttlebutt."

"Keep that stuff to yourself." I handed him the printout. "Score one for the STA security team."

We headed for the car.

"Vince Mangold," Glenn said. "Is this Mango?"

"Who knows, but they didn't have any Mango in the system. This guy sort of fit the profile so I had them print it off."

Glenn shook the paper. "Let's birddog Sabina Wrencher. If she says this is Mango, then we'll put out an Attempt to Locate on him."

"That'll only take one of us. Drop me off at the station. I'll pick up my car and do some follow-up on Victor Bachman's case."

7

Bradley Simpson pulled a Bud Light handle and filled a glass. He walked to the far end of the bar and set it on the glossy counter. A male customer handed him several bills and took the drink back to his table.

It was shortly after five, and The Baseline was already full. All the customers were over forty, white, and casually dressed. The Seattle Mariners game was on multiple televisions, and the team had a one-run lead over the Los Angeles Angels.

The volume was up on the main TV, and classic rock still played throughout the bar. I tried to focus on what the announcer was saying.

Baseball paraphernalia hung on the walls. Worn baseball gloves, broken bats, pennants, and batting helmets made for eclectic eye candy. There were framed photos of former Mariners that appeared to be autographed. I didn't follow the game closely enough to know any players beyond Ken Griffey Jr.

Simpson returned to where I stood and tapped a key on the register. It clattered open. "Sorry about that. You were saying?"

"Victor Bachman."

"Yeah, I know him. Decent storyteller. Never sloppy with his drink. Leaves a good tip before he leaves. Haven't seen him in a few days. Is that what you need to know?"

Simpson was in his early fifties with a shock of white hair and a pockmarked face. He was a stocky man as if he'd spent some time in the gym when he was younger. Much of that muscle had turned to fat now, but he walked with his shoulders pulled back, and his head held high. He wore a white Mariners jersey and a red Spokane Indians baseball cap.

"He was murdered," I said. "I'm trying to get some background on the guy."

Simpson's smile faded. "Aw, man, that fucking sucks."

"What was the last day he came in?"

"I don't know." He lowered his eyes and rubbed his chin. When he looked up, he searched the bar. "Gina," he called. "Hey, Gina!"

A woman at a far table looked in his direction. Simpson waved her over.

She grabbed her drink and headed our way. The woman seemed to be in her late forties with long salt-and-pepper hair. Dark brows and fake lashes highlighted her green eyes. She wore a blue Mariners T-shirt and white jeans, both of which were a size too tight for her frame.

Several men turned to watch her walk over. She smiled as if she knew they were watching.

When she neared, Simpson asked, "When's the last time you saw Vic?"

Gina lifted her drink to her lips but briefly paused to appraise me over the edge of her glass. She tipped the cocktail back and swallowed. "Who's your friend?"

I pulled my jacket to the side to reveal my badge. "Detective Nash."

"A working man."

"Leave him alone, Gina. Just answer the question."

Her eyes shifted to the bartender, but she didn't turn her head. "Vic? I saw him on Thursday at dart league."

"There you go," Simpson said. "Vic's on the team we sponsor."

Gina's gaze returned to me. "You're looking for Vic? What'd he do?"

"He was murdered," I said.

She was lifting the glass to her lips again but paused before taking a sip. "No shit."

I shook my head. "No, ma'am."

She tipped the glass, took a healthy swallow, and emptied it. "There's no tomorrow. Am I right?" Gina shook the tumbler and jingled the remaining ice before setting it on the counter. "Another, please."

The bartender headed off to the bottles.

"Where'd this game take place?" I asked.

"The Playground."

I pulled my notebook from the inside of my jacket. "How'd he seem that night?"

Gina leaned an elbow on the counter. "Like his normal self."

"How would you describe that?"

She shrugged. "Vic is Vic. Guy drank his Pabst, threw his darts, tried to score every now and then." Gina raised an eyebrow and smirked. "We never made it if you want to know. I don't give it away to just anyone."

"How did he act that night?"

Her smirk vanished, and the eyebrow returned to its normal position. "I told you. He acted like Vic. The guy is a regular Eeyore. You know? That donkey from *Winnie-the-Pooh.*"

I nodded as I wrote in my notebook.

Simpson returned with Gina's drink and set it on the counter beside her elbow.

She lifted her chin and said, "Tell this guy about Vic."

"What about him?"

"How he was a regular Eeyore."

"He wasn't that bad," the bartender said.

Gina laughed. "Oh, the hell he wasn't. What was that donkey's line?" She frowned and lowered her voice. "Nobody's gonna believe me anyway?"

I thought about Kelsie Rockford's statement, *Who would believe me?*

Simpson pointed at Gina. "That's right. He did say shit like that, didn't he?"

"That's Eeyore."

"Did anything happen at the game?"

Gina's brow furrowed. "Are you asking if we hooked up? I already said no." She faced Simpson. "Can you imagine me and Vic? I'd break his sorry ass." She laughed while Simpson looked apologetically at me.

"Why are you looking at him like that?" Gina said. "Don't make this about me." She sipped her drink. "Vic was a good enough sort. He got himself some now and then." She turned and looked at the group she had been drinking with. "Hell, even Shirley threw it his way a few times. I think she said she liked it, too, but Vic was sort of hopeless." Gina's face pinched. "No woman wants to come home to a long, mopey face every night. You get what I'm saying?"

I asked, "Did Vic have a confrontation with anyone?"

Gina cocked her head. "What?"

"Did Vic—"

"I heard you." She sipped her drink and then crunched a piece of ice. "No. We lost our match and went home. That's it. It's not like we're going to get into a—" She faced Simpson. "What do you call a fight?"

"A fight."

She waved him off and turned back to me. "It's not like we were going to fight over losing a game of darts." Gina quickly looked at the bartender. "Fracas!" she shouted. "That's the word I was looking for."

"It was?" Simpson asked.

"I think so." She frowned and repeated, "Fracas."

I motioned with my notepad. "I need your name and number for my report."

Gina's gaze returned to me, and she smiled drunkenly. "You want my number?"

"And name. Strictly official."

"Uh-huh." She moved a little closer to peer at my notepad.

"Cool it, Gina," the bartender said.

"Gina Ann Keibler." She spelled out her name, watching me write it down. "That's right." She then gave her address and phone number. "Do you need directions to my house?"

I stepped back to create some distance between us. "Who else was on the team?"

"What team?" She lifted the drink to her lips.

"The dart team," I said.

"Oh, right. Them." Gina waved her hand. "The Acostas."

Simpson leaned in. "They're a husband and wife duo. Joe and Mary. Super cool couple."

"Got their phone number?"

The bartender shook his head.

"I got it," Gina said. "Just a second. She pulled her cell phone from a back pocket. In a moment, she read off the number. "That's Mary's. She wouldn't let me have Joe's."

Her eyes narrowed, and she said throatily, "I can't imagine why."

"Knock it off, Gina," Simpson said, "or I'm gonna hose you down."

I closed my notebook and tucked it inside my jacket. "Thank you for your time—both of you."

Gina angled her head, and her eyes again traveled up and down my length. "Wanna show me your handcuffs before you go, Officer?"

Simpson smacked the bar. "That's enough, Gina. Put it back in your pants."

***

The Playground was on the corner of Crown Avenue and Market Street. It was in an area known as Hillyard. Since I was a kid, that part of town was maligned as Spokane's roughest neighborhood. When I grew older, I realized most of the reputation wasn't deserved. Hillyard was like the rest of Spokane—a mixture of haves and have-nots. Some homes were kept better than others, some cars were nicer than others, and some families were better fed than others.

The Hillyard Business District, however, was the face of the community and did its best to dissuade folks from the attitude that the neighborhood was rough. When I started the job, the stretch of old buildings along Market Street was a hodgepodge of vacancies and thrift stores. Now, the business district was home to various restaurants, bars, and retail businesses.

I entered The Playground and stopped to take in the scene. The bar was a Hillyard mainstay. It had survived the lean years to hang around for the prosperous ones. That didn't mean its clientele changed with the times.

Even though it was shortly after six, the bar was already full. The crowd slowly quieted as they realized I was standing in the doorway.

The customers might have assumed I was a cop, but the suit I wore could represent several other things—outsider, authority, or success. All of them were likely suspect in The Playground.

Customers filled the booths and tables. Dartboards lined the far wall. Two pool tables were in the same area. Pictures of rock bands and alcohol brands littered the walls. Several cameras hung from the ceiling.

I moved toward the bar, and the conversations restarted. A classic rock song played. It was hard to ignore, but I tried. I didn't want any music in my head.

The bartender was a moderately fit white male in his late thirties. His broad smile exposed bright teeth. He leaned against the back bar as he chatted up two men that might have been father and son. A medical walker sat behind the older man's stool.

"I'll be back," the bartender said to the two men. He languidly pushed off the bar and walked over to me. "What can I get you, chief?"

"Let's start with your name."

A confused look replaced his smile.

"Doesn't sound good," the older man seated nearby said. His gaze remained straight ahead, but he watched me in the reflection of the mirror behind the bar.

I opened my jacket to the bartender, and his eyes dropped to my waist. No one else in the bar could see my badge and gun except the bartender.

"Adam," he said. "Adam Jones."

The young man at the bar—the one I assumed to be the son—stood on the rail of his stool and looked in our direction. He wore a curled baseball cap, a faded Def Leppard T-shirt, blue jeans, and black Converse. "He flash a badge, Jonesy?"

"Sit down, you," Adam said.

The younger man dropped onto his stool and grabbed his bottle of Rainer. "Either that, or you must have liked his package."

The older man chuckled. "Good one."

I asked, "Were you working last Thursday night?"

Now the older man turned in my direction. "What happened Thursday?" He was closest to me and smelled of body odor. He sported a flat-top haircut and wore a buttoned-up shirt and slacks. The left side of his face drooped as if he had a stroke and his left hand sat in his lap.

Adam glared at him. "Mind your own business." To me, he said, "I was here. What's this about?"

"Ever see this man?"

I pulled Vic's picture from my pocket, and Adam leaned in to study it.

"I don't know." The bartender straightened. "I see a lot of people in here."

The older man leaned over to examine the picture.

The younger one stood on the rail of his stool to see the photograph. "What do you think?"

"I think your breath stinks," the father said. "Sit down."

The son smirked. "The guy doesn't make much of an impression."

"Unlike your mouth." The older man's voice sounded mushy, as if the stroke did a number on him. "Were you eating at that buffet again?"

Adam asked, "What was this guy doing?"

"Playing in a dart league," I said.

The younger man dropped heavily onto his stool and scooped his beer. "Dart league. Gimme a break."

The father tapped the bar. "My son here isn't athletically inclined."

"Phew. Phew. Phew." The son mimed throwing a dart three times. "Big whoop. Who cares?" He tilted his bottle and swallowed.

"His girlfriend left him for the dart league champion."

The son winced. "She wasn't my girlfriend, and he wasn't champion. The guy could barely count to five-oh-one? At least I got a job."

"Sure you do," the father said. "What are you doing again?"

Adam tapped the photograph. "Something happen to this guy?"

"He was murdered."

"After the league?"

Both Adam and the older man leaned in again to study Vic's photograph. The son stayed seated and took another swig of beer. "Dart league," he muttered. "Athletes, my ass."

"We believe he came here last Thursday night," I said. "We haven't been able to confirm that."

The father pointed to the corner of the ceiling. "Let him look at your camera system."

Adam glared at him. "Thank you for your suggestion."

"You're welcome. Otherwise, he's gonna keep asking you questions while we're trying to peacefully drink our troubles away."

The bartender looked at me and shrugged. "I wouldn't get your hopes up. The system's over ten years old."

"Probably still works," the older man said.

Adam scowled. "I'm gonna cut you off."

I asked, "Mind if I take a look?"

The bartender shook his head. "I shouldn't. Doris is a stickler when it comes to the cops."

The older man pulled his bottle to him. "Ah hell, let him look. What's it going to hurt?"

"Yeah," the son muttered. He didn't bother looking at us. Instead, he studied the label on his bottle. "Otherwise, he's gonna come back with more cops, and none of us want that."

Adam reconsidered me. "Is that true? You'll come back?"

"We'd come with a warrant."

"If you find this guy on the video, you're not going to shut us down or anything, are you?"

The son flashed a skeptical look at the bartender. "Listen to yourself."

The father patted the air in front of his son. "Relax." To Adam, he said, "He'll probably write a warrant or something." His gaze shifted to me. "Tell me I'm right."

I studied Adam. "Unless you want to give it to me."

The bartender cringed. "Doris isn't the biggest fan of cops. It would be better if you could write it and maybe come back when she's here?"

The son elbowed his father. "I'm gonna put some music on the jukebox. Wanna come?"

"I don't know any of that garbage you listen to."

"I figured we should give these two some privacy to work out their issues."

"Yeah, yeah. Hold on." The father faced Adam. "Let him look. I'll vouch for you with Doris."

"You barely know her."

"What do you mean? She has big eyes for me. I know her enough to get you out of trouble."

Adam exhaled heavily before shaking his head. "I don't know."

The father smiled, but only the right side of his face turned up. "I got a way with charming the ladies."

"He's right, you know," the younger man said. "Doris has a thing for lame ducks."

"Fuck you, son. I'll have you know—"

The younger man hopped off his stool. "Either let the cop see the tapes, or he's coming back again to bother Doris. Which do you think she'll be madder about?" He wandered off toward the jukebox.

The father raised his eyebrows. "The kid's got a point." He turned awkwardly on his stool and slid into his walker. The old man clanged slowly after his son.

"All right," Adam said. He motioned me toward the end of the bar.

I followed him into a backroom. He sat at a computer displaying nine black and white camera feeds. He slid a control panel box over near the keyboard.

"This is a nice set-up for a bar," I said. Even if the cameras were monochrome, I'd never seen anything like it inside a drinking establishment. Nine cameras was a crazy amount of coverage.

"Blame the insurance company," Adam said. "There were some incidents before I got here. Doris told me she was about to lose her coverage, and they made her jump through a bunch of hoops. This was one of them." He tapped the keyboard. "Big pain in the ass if you ask me."

I leaned to study the screen.

Adam pointed at a series of buttons on the control box. "This allows you to change the feed you want to look at." He pointed at the screen. "Each one is numbered. See? Just click the number you want, then enter the date and time to jump there."

He showed me how to manipulate the controls for the next couple of minutes. He called up an individual camera angle, picked a random time from last week, and moved forward and backward through the feed with the control knob. "The more you twist it left or right, the faster it will go in the direction you want. Got it?"

I nodded.

"Any questions?"

"When did the dart league start?" I asked. "The one that played last Thursday?"

"Seven."

"And how long is the data saved on your system?"

"One week."

Today was Wednesday. I needed to locate the footage with Vic Bachman and have him save it. Otherwise, everything would be written over tomorrow morning when the new week started.

"I've been in here too long," Adam said. "I need to get back on the floor. When you find the time you want, write it down. Note how long the section runs. Come and get me, and I'll save it for you."

He left, and I started my search.

***

Vic was already in the bar and in the dartboard section when I set the playback time for 7 p.m. on the previous Thursday. The dart league started a few minutes after that and ended at 9:12 pm.

Watching a living, breathing Victor Bachman laugh and joke with his friends was interesting. It appeared there were four players on each team and both sides were cordial.

The Baseline team sported red T-shirts with the bar's logo printed across the back. Along with Vic was Gina Keibler, the woman I met earlier. The other man and woman on his team should be Joe and Mary Acosta. Watching them play reminded me of the earlier comment about dart players thinking they were athletes. There was a lot of laughing, high-fiving, and fist-pumping. It would have been a regular day at the ballpark if they spat on the floor.

Not that it mattered, but I already knew the game's outcome since Gina said The Baseline team lost. I watched the video at four times its regular speed and hurried through the match. There didn't seem to be any confrontations, and nothing appeared out of the ordinary.

At the end of the match, all the players shook hands, and The Baseline team exited the bar.

Only one camera feed was dedicated to the parking lot. Vic and his team exited the building and walked to their cars. Most of the parking was out of sight, but Vic's convertible Mustang was in the frame. Vic walked to his car, got in, reversed from his spot, and drove away.

I leaned back in my chair and crossed my arms.

Had nothing happened at The Playground? Perhaps it was like Gina said.

But I wasn't ready to give up yet. First, I had nowhere to be except my empty house. Second, seeing Vic alive bothered me. Was he the best man in the world? No. Not after listening to a few people talk about him. Vic wasn't necessarily a bad guy, either. He made some mistakes, and maybe he had some kinks—I thought about the deal he made with his housecleaner. Being a weird guy didn't mean he should end up stabbed to death in his home.

No one deserved that.

I stayed on the parking lot feed and reset the start time to 6:50 p.m. Vic's convertible was already in its spot when the screen flashed to a new image. I changed the start time to 6:30. The feed flickered, and now his car wasn't there yet. With a turn of the knob, I sped the watch time up until Vic arrived at 6:46 pm.

He got out of the car and entered The Playground. He wandered through the bar—I learned this by watching him meander through several camera feeds. He didn't say hello to anyone, and no one paid him any notice. Vic was the first of his team to make it to the area reserved for the dart league.

Vic greeted a couple of players from the opposing team who were already there. The others involved with the match soon entered the area, and the game started. I had already watched this play out. There was no need to rewatch it.

I reset the start time on the camera system to 6:46 p.m. when Vic arrived. I watched all the feeds. Maybe something occurred elsewhere in the bar. There was so much going on all over the monitor that it was hard to track everything.

The best course of action seemed to be to select one feed and watch it. I started with the parking lot. After resetting the time once again, I sped up the playback speed. I doubted much would happen on this feed, but it was less congested with people.

It felt stupid to watch cars come and go, and people climb in and out of their vehicles, but that's a lot of what police work was—grinding. If I could eliminate a confrontation at the bar, I would feel somewhat confident nothing happened at The Playground that led to Vic Bachman's untimely demise.

My cell phone buzzed once—a text message. I paused the feed. The message was from Marlene. THANKS FOR COMING BY FOR DINNER LAST NIGHT. SADIE SAYS HI.

I considered responding but put the phone away. I restarted the video.

A couple of minutes passed before there was movement near Vic's car. I rolled back the video until I saw the motion again and restarted it. A man and woman walked near Vic's Mustang. The woman abruptly stepped away from the man and tossed something into the convertible's backseat. She then returned to her partner as the two continued out of the frame.

It was 9:08 p.m.

A few minutes later, Vic's league match ended. He walked outside with his friends, got into his car, and drove away.

I reversed the feed to look closely at the man and woman who had walked by Vic's car. They weren't in the dart league—I would have seen them before and memorized their appearance.

He was a white man with short, brown hair, and he appeared to be in his mid-fifties. He wore a green T-shirt and baggy jeans. The woman was also white, but she had long dark hair. She wore a yellow shirt and jeans. They walked arm-in-arm and leaned on each other as if they might have had too much to drink.

I turned the control panel knob and reversed the camera feed.

They walked backward by Vic's Mustang. The woman stepped over to the car, and her hand waved over the open rear seats. She then walked in reverse to her friend, and they continued their backward stroll into the bar.

It took a few seconds, but I found them on the third camera feed.

The two walked in reverse past a tall table, and the woman set down a cell phone. They continued their backward stroll until they arrived at another table and sat.

It was an odd experience watching them drink in reverse. Their glasses filled up, and the bartender arrived to replace them with empties.

At different times, the man and woman left to use the restroom—I saw that on other feeds.

Eventually, the two walked backward from the bar and out of the frame. It was 5:17 p.m.

I watched the couple again, forward this time, slowing it where I needed, zooming past chunks of lazy time wherein they simply talked and drank. In the end, I learned something important.

The couple drank for almost four hours and never had a confrontation with anyone in the bar. As they walked out of the establishment, the woman swiped a cell phone from the edge of a table. When the couple made it into the parking lot, she tossed the phone into the back of Vic Bachman's convertible.

Next, I checked the feed which included the table that held the stolen cell phone. Another couple sat there—a white man and a white woman. He wore a black T-shirt. She wore a red summer dress. Both were heavily covered in tattoos.

This couple was significantly younger than the other—possibly late twenties and they seemed to enjoy each other's company. They smiled and often interlaced their fingers across the table. They had several drinks in the span of their evening.

The cell phone sat near the man's forearm. When the woman left to use the restroom, the man checked it. He never did it when she was around.

Shortly after nine, she went to the restroom a second time. The man left their table, approached the bar, and said something to Adam.

That's when the first couple walked by the table, and the woman swiped the cell phone.

I opened the office door and yelled for the bartender.

***

I drove by Victor Bachman's house and stopped.

A sense of foreboding hung over the neighborhood. The crime scene tape strung across his front lawn didn't help.

It had been less than forty-eight hours since we found his body.

I slipped under the tape and headed toward the convertible still parked in the driveway. We hadn't towed it for safekeeping or further evidence collection. There hadn't been any need.

The techs had dusted the car for fingerprints, so putting my hands on it now wouldn't be a concern except for transferring some of the graphite dust to myself. That stuff was miserable to get off clothing.

The car door was locked. I imagined the techs dusted the interior and then secured the car before leaving the scene. The convertible rooftop was up. Someone had lifted it before securing the car keys.

I shone my flashlight into the car, but I couldn't see anything.

"Get away from there," a man hollered. The voice came from across the street. "I'm calling the cops."

"Detective Nash," I said and moved away from the Mustang.

An elderly man walked down his sidewalk. He wore a white T-shirt, khaki pants, and slippers. He walked with a pronounced limp. "What were you doing over there?"

"Investigating your neighbor's murder."

"You haven't caught the bastard who did that yet?"

"No, sir." Patrol officers had contacted the neighbors, but none had claimed to have seen anything. "You spoke with an officer about Vic's death?"

When the neighbor neared, he put his hands on his hips, and his shoulders slumped. "Yeah, I spoke to that kid. He didn't look old enough to even be outta high school, but I'll tell you what I told him. I didn't see nothing because I was too busy watching my shows. Isn't that the most girlie thing you ever heard?"

"But you saw me tonight."

"You bet I did. I started paying attention after Vic's death. Damn thing got me all worked up about what could happen in our neighborhood. Fat lot of good that's going to do for Vic."

Unfortunately, that seems to be how it is for a lot of us. We ignore things until it's too late.

He continued. "But it ain't gonna happen to me or anybody else if I have my druthers. I got my eyes out for prowlers and bandits now. Once it gets dark—" He snapped his fingers. "—the TV is going off, and my antennae are going up."

"If you see anything," I said, "please call it in."

"You bet your ass." He pointed across the street. "Never again. Not on my watch."

I left him standing at the sidewalk's edge and headed to my car.

****

I remained in the entryway for several minutes. The refrigerator remained silent tonight, and my neighbor's lawn was already cut. The silence of my home embraced me. I closed my eyes and felt its warmth. She'd been gone almost two years.

I didn't want any more noise in the house, so I gave away the stereo and our music collection. I donated the television after I broke the remote. The living room only had a couch and a couple of matching end tables; it didn't need more.

When hunger motivated me to leave the entry, I moved to the kitchen. I pulled out several cold cuts and a piece of cheese from the fridge. I didn't want to start the microwave, the stove, or anything else that might make unnecessary noise. The meat and cheese were good enough. Besides, nothing else sounded good.

I set a couple of pieces of bread into the toaster and quietly made a sandwich.

A car drove down the street with its stereo blasting. Its heavy bass thumped throughout my house. A second car followed with its radio blaring the same kind of music. In the distance, a train rumbled.

I bit into my sandwich and pulled my phone from my pocket. Marlene's text remained unanswered.

THANKS FOR COMING BY FOR DINNER LAST NIGHT. SADIE SAYS HI.

I never had a problem responding to her in the past. We had shared meals before but yesterday felt different. It didn't take a genius to figure out why—it was because of what she let slip at the restaurant.

Nothing romantic had ever occurred between us. I replayed our moments together and couldn't determine where I might have sent the wrong signals. Did stopping by for dinner last night send an erroneous signal after what was said at the restaurant?

I shouldn't have gone. I realized that now.

Would I have felt differently with another woman? Most men would have trouble getting over Marlene's past—the addiction and the prostitution. However, she was different now. She was a leader, a care provider, and a caring mother.

No, it wouldn't be different with another woman. Bobbie had been my only love—from high school until her death. No one could take her place.

I set the unfinished sandwich on the counter with my cell phone and walked into the living room. I sat quietly on the couch and leaned back with my eyes closed.

The silence returned to the house, and I searched for Bobbie. She was gone, I reminded myself. It wasn't crazy to look for her in the quiet moments. I was only remembering her. It was to keep her close.

I didn't want a replacement.

I didn't need a lover.

I only wanted a friend who wouldn't take away the silence.

8

"You're here early," Glenn said. He dropped into his chair. "What's got you all bright eyed and bushy-tailed?"

"A warrant." My fingers stopped dancing across the keyboard, but I didn't look his way.

I'd been at the department for an hour already and had completed most of the work on the warrant for The Playground's security camera.

"A warrant for what?" he asked.

I handed him a disk. "We got something in the Bachman killing."

Glenn stared at the CD. "What's this?"

"Last night, I stopped by The Playground."

"Up in Hillyard?"

"Vic's dart team played there on Thursday."

"When did you learn this?"

"Last night after we left."

Glenn cocked his head. "You worked some overtime?"

I shook my head. "Did it on my own time."

My partner frowned. "That's a violation of the collective bargaining agreement, Dal. You need to charge these ungrateful bastards for your time."

"I didn't have anything else to do."

Glenn waved off my explanation. "Doesn't matter. What you do affects others. If the department can get one detective to work for free after hours, it can expect others to do it. We gotta stick together."

There was no use arguing with him. Glenn and I saw the union differently. I considered them a necessary evil. He believed them to be the tip of the spear and that they should lead the way in every decision we made.

My fingers returned to bouncing across the keyboard.

After a moment, Glenn scooted his chair closer. "So, what did you see?"

"Bachman tossing darts and having a nice time."

He wiggled the CD. "Had to be more than that for you to get an early start on a warrant."

"A couple in the bar at the same time walked by his car and threw a cell phone into the backseat."

Glenn's eyebrows went up. "The convertible?"

"The top was down that night."

"Wait." Glenn stood. "Did you see a phone in there yesterday?"

I shook my head. "I wasn't searching for a cell phone. I was checking if anything was disturbed. Nothing was."

Glenn scrunched his face. "Yeah. Even if you saw the cell phone in the back, we wouldn't have thought it odd. Maybe we would have put it on property for safekeeping."

I handed him a still shot from the camera. "That's the couple who stole the phone. The woman, anyway. I'm not sure if the guy knew what she did."

"Get any names?"

"The bartender said they're regulars, and they pay in cash. He only knows them as O.J. and Spritzer. The guy always orders a rum and orange juice. She orders a white wine spritzer."

"What about the guy whose cell phone got swiped?"

I handed Glenn a second photograph. "Ever seen those two?"

He shook his head. "Don't they look pretty with all those tattoos?"

"The bartender didn't know them either. He said they've never drank there before. After the guy's cell phone was stolen, he and his girlfriend checked around the table. You know, as if he might have accidentally knocked it off."

"But it was stolen."

"Right." I nodded. "I thought the guy would have made a helluva stink about the theft, maybe gone to the bartender and complained—"

"That's what I would have done."

"Me, too," I said. "Maybe I would have walked through the bar and checked out the various tables. In case someone picked it up and put it on a different table."

"What did our guy do?"

"Nothing. I think his girl tried to call his number. When they didn't find the phone, they left."

Glenn nodded thoughtfully. "You'd think the guy whose car the phone was in would have heard it and called them back."

"You'd think."

"Maybe the phone was on vibrate or silenced. I do that sometimes."

"Yeah. Me, too."

Glenn set the CD on his desk. "What's the warrant for?"

"I promised the bar owner I'd get this done first thing. The bartender was afraid to give me a copy of the video until I got approval from his boss. She was nice enough on the phone but wanted a warrant for her records."

"Everybody wants a warrant."

I shrugged a single shoulder. "So here I am, holding up my end of the bargain."

"What can I do to help?"

"Write a warrant for Bachman's convertible. We need to officially search it now."

***

Glenn offered to run the warrants over to Judge Whitaker for his signature. He had a positive relationship with the judge extending back to Whitaker's days as a prosecutor. The two always shared some easy laughs whenever they got together. Had I gone, it would simply have been a transactional moment.

I took The Playground's security film clip and accompanying photographs to Crime Analysis.

Debbie Wallette sat at the team's conference table. She hunkered over a mess of documents with a red pen clutched in her hand. When I dropped into the chair next to her, she looked displeased. "This better be important."

I set the two photographs and CD on top of her documents.

Her face scrunched as if she just smelled something bad. "What's that?"

"I need to know who those people are."

"You think we're magicians or something?"

"Yes."

"Hardly." She pulled the photos and the compact disc off her documents. "A CD? You're lucky we keep a portable reader around. None of our computers even have them anymore."

Debbie sounded perturbed.

I looked around and didn't notice any snacks. I should have brought something. Bribery was illegal, but donuts or bagels were always appreciated in Crime Analysis. Anyone who wanted to hop to the front of the line knew to come bearing gifts. The best I could do was force a lopsided smile. "Don't you even want to know why Glenn and I need to know who those folks are?"

Debbie sighed. "You see I'm in the middle of something, right?"

"This is important."

"And this isn't?"

I craned my neck to check out what she was examining. It appeared to be financial ledgers. "What are you doing?"

"Accounting."

"You're doing your taxes?"

"Funny. No. I'm trying to help with an embezzlement case and making some real headway. We're going to get this guy."

I pointed at the photographs and the CD. "That is related to a homicide. You can knock it out of the park without breaking a mental sweat."

"This—" Debbie waved her hands over the stack of documents. "—caused a company to lose several millions of dollars and shut down. A dozen people lost their jobs because of this."

"Somebody's dead because of this," I said.

"Lots of families can't make their mortgage payments this month and beyond because one self-entitled asshole thought he was more important than everyone else he worked with. I think that's pretty important, don't you?"

We stared at each other for several seconds.

When I worked in the general detectives' pool, I hated working cases that impacted businesses. Not because they didn't feel like true crimes but because there never felt like an immediacy of results. Officers and detectives could chase a financial crime but getting it to stick felt like throwing a clump of spaghetti at the wall.

Twelve people losing their jobs would result in a significant impact on a multitude of lives. If Debbie thought she could make a difference there, I shouldn't try to stop her. Besides, she didn't work for me or the Major Crimes office. She worked for the department.

I needed to wait my turn in line, especially since I didn't bring any goodies.

"Message received," I said.

Debbie rested her hand on the photographs. "I'll work on it when I get done here. Shouldn't be too much longer. I promise."

I patted the table. "Thank you."

***

I met Glenn at Victor Bachman's house. He was parked curbside in his own Chevy Impala. When I pulled up behind his car, Glenn's door popped open, and he climbed out.

A small paper sack sat in the passenger seat of my car. I opened it and removed a set of keys. I climbed out.

"Stopped for a donut?" Glenn said. "I hope you brought me one."

"You and Crime Analysis both."

"What's that?"

I waved off explaining my comment and wriggled the keys. "I stopped by Property to get these."

Across the street, the neighbor stepped out onto his doorstep. He lifted a hand in acknowledgment.

"Friend of yours?" Glenn asked.

"We met last night."

I returned the wave, and the old man went inside his house. The door closed behind him.

"Here you go." Glenn handed me two warrants—one for the Mustang and the other for the video taken from the Playground. "Whitaker said to say hi."

"That's nice of him." I folded the paperwork and tucked it inside my suit jacket.

"He said you haven't been by in a while to kiss the ring."

"He said that?"

Glenn cocked his head and smirked at the same time. "You know how he is."

We walked over to the Mustang. I approached the driver's door, and Glenn took the passenger side.

"He was joking," Glenn said.

"I know."

Using the fob on the key ring, I unlocked the car. I opened the driver's door and squatted.

"He doesn't think he's the pope," Glenn said as he searched underneath the passenger's seat.

"I know." I folded the driver's seat forward and peered into the back.

Glenn followed my action on the other side. "That would be unethical if he made everyone actually kiss the ring."

I reached underneath the driver's seat and felt about. Glenn did the same on the passenger side. He pulled out a small first-aid kit and set it on top of the backseat.

"Besides," Glenn said, "he doesn't even wear a ring. Although he probably got one from Gonzaga, don't you think?

I stopped searching. "What's wrong?"

"Nothing."

"Then why all this chatter about Whitaker and his lack of a ring?"

Glenn stared at me.

"Well?"

"He asked how you were doing."

I rolled back onto my heels but remained in my squat. "Huh?"

Glenn opened his palm. "He mentioned he heard some things."

"What things?"

"That you had a breakdown."

I furrowed my brow. "I never had a breakdown."

"I know. That's what I said." Glenn's lips twisted. "I told him that exactly."

"Wait. What happened?"

"Whitaker said he heard the department forced you into psychiatric care."

My face warmed. I stood and slammed the driver's seat back into position. "He heard that?"

Glenn stared at me over the car. "That's what he said."

"You're fucking kidding."

"I wouldn't joke about this. I told him he was wrong."

"But there's a rumor in the courthouse I'm—"

"Yeah," Glenn interrupted. "Cuckoo for Cocoa Puffs."

My jaw tightened. "Not helpful."

"I know. Listen. I'm sorry." Glenn waved a hand. "Whitaker's a good dude as far as judges go. More than anything, I think he was giving us a heads-up."

I felt sick. My career hinged on credibility. A rumor I had a breakdown followed by department-ordered psychiatric visits was terrible. If that gossip made it to the courthouse, my problems were clearly at another level. Attorneys and judges would look at me differently. They couldn't help but do so. It was human nature.

Several years ago, a prosecuting attorney broke down in his office. It hadn't happened in open court or occurred because of a case. It transpired because of issues in his personal life. The attorney openly wept and made comments full of despair. His coworkers worried he might harm himself. The man agreed to a voluntary committal in Sacred Heart's psychiatric ward. Forty-eight hours later, he was released. His career never recovered. Everyone—including me—looked at the guy differently after that. He eventually left the prosecutor's office to practice real estate law.

Was this rumor why Brand acted strangely toward me at the Bachman crime scene? If so, was he checking on my health so he could pass it up the chain of command? Brand was an effective administrator, but he wasn't the type of leader to go to the mat for one of his troops. Efficiency was his top goal.

If I developed a weakness that held the team back or would prove a detriment to getting convictions, Brand would find a way to remove me from Major Crimes. He hadn't done it yet to anyone on our team, but he'd done it to others he'd run.

I didn't want to be the first Major Crimes detective in recent history to be removed against his wishes.

"It's going to be okay," Glenn said. "I'm telling you because the judge brought it up. He likes us."

Captain Ackerman had looked at me strangely at the Richard Ranger crime scene. Did everyone know about this rumor? Was Chief Dillon aware, too?

"Let's finish the car," I said mechanically.

I squatted and searched the areas I'd already done. I knew the cell phone wasn't there, but I didn't care. I needed to pretend to be busy.

***

In the parking lot of The Playground, I sent a text message.

WOULD YOU HAVE TIME TO MEET TODAY? REALLY NEED TO TALK.

While I waited for her reply, I checked my emails. There was one from IDENT regarding the fingerprints pulled from Vic Bachman's house.

On the exterior front door handle, they discovered only Dina Foust's. That was strange. Typically, there would be a variety of prints, mostly smudged due to the twisting and turning nature of a knob and the variety of hands touching it. If only Dina's came through clearly, it likely meant someone wiped down the knob before she touched it.

No other unexplained prints were found inside the house.

The car also had no prints on it. That could be explained away by the cleanliness of the vehicle. Vic had likely washed his car either the day of his murder or in the preceding days. It was doubtful additional fingerprints would find their way to the vehicle if it was parked in his driveway.

If the killer was careful enough to wipe the knob before leaving the Bachman house, they would be cautious enough not to leave a print on the car door had they gone into it.

I closed that email and checked another sent out by Crime Analysis. It was labeled *Hot Sheet Update—Persons of Interest in Murder Case*. Debbie's email included photographs of the two couples from The Playground—the ones who stole the wallet and the victim of the theft. They were better than the printouts I'd given her, so she had pulled them from the video on the CD. Debbie asked anyone with information on the persons to contact Glenn or me.

My phone hadn't buzzed to announce the arrival of a text message which soured my mood further. Glenn's revelation of a rumor worming its way through the courthouse ate at me. I slipped out of my car.

Doris Nordhagen stood behind the bar, counting money. No one else was inside the establishment. No music played. It felt odd to walk into a closed bar. Life should have been occurring there, but it had been put on hold. It was almost like walking into a cemetery.

Almost.

"Ninety-eight," Doris whispered, "ninety-nine, two hundred." She set the final bill in place and tucked the various stacks into a cash register.

She was in her sixties with short, silver hair. Doris had a round, pleasant face with blossoms of rosacea on her cheeks.

"Pretty trusting that no one will walk in and not rob you," I said.

"You're on camera, and I got a gun under the counter." She set her hands on the bar. "Besides, you don't seem the type to worry about, Detective."

I opened my jacket and removed the warrant. "This is for the video. Thank you for letting me have it last night."

She unfolded the paperwork and smoothed it out on the bar. Her gaze flitted over the header, but she didn't bother reading the document. "You catch the bastards who did it?"

"No. Did your bartender show you who we're looking for?"

Doris nodded. "They didn't look familiar, but that don't mean much. I only work a couple hours each day now. I open up, putter around until the opening bartender comes on, then I slink on home."

I glanced around, trying to envision where the two couples sat when the place was full, but it wasn't easy to concentrate. The thought of my credibility being jeopardized because of rampant gossip bothered me. This was precisely why I didn't want to start seeing the therapist in the first place. It's why I didn't want to talk with a chaplain after Bobbie's death.

Cops aren't allowed to show weakness within those halls. Doing so only puts blood in the water, bringing the other sharks out for a feeding frenzy. Is that why Parker invited me to dinner—because he smelled blood? If so, it was the weirdest attack ever. Sharks weren't known for subtlety.

"You okay?" Doris asked.

"Yeah, I'm fine. Why do you ask?"

"I've been in the business a long time. If there's one thing I've learned to do, it's read people. You look like you could use a drink."

I forced a smile. "I appreciate the offer, but that's probably the last thing I need."

9

"Want something to drink?" Mary Acosta asked. She handed a can of Rainier to her husband, who sat on a beige fabric couch. She held a beer for herself.

"No, thank you," I said.

Anger bubbled within me and left me jumpy. I longed to lash out at fate for taking Bobbie and leaving me in this fucking situation. I didn't want to be left behind. If I could have skipped this interview, I would have, but that wouldn't have been fair to Glenn.

It wouldn't have been fair to Vic Bachman, either. However, I didn't care about him. He was some dead body as far as I was concerned. My career as a detective was littered with them, and he wasn't any more special than the others.

The movies could keep their bullshit about cops caring about all of their victims. That was make-believe pressure I didn't need. I just wanted to go home and wallow in worry and self-pity.

"In that case—" Mary dropped onto the couch next to her husband. "—you don't mind if we have one, do you?"

Joe Acosta wore an untucked red flannel shirt and blue jeans. His feet were bare, and his dark hair was uncombed. Mary's blond hair was brushed, but it looked in need of a cut and color. She wore a sleeveless white shirt, red jeans, and white sandals.

"O' course, he don't mind." Joe's words slurred together as he cracked open his beer. "It ain't his home."

On the coffee table were several empty cans and two plates. Some uneaten eggs were on the one in front of Mary. An aroma of bacon hung in the air.

The Acostas lived on Wellesley Avenue—kitty corner from the Walmart Supercenter and directly across from the Shadle Park Library. Behind the library was the massive complex of the local high school. A paved alley ran along the east side of the Acosta home.

"Vic was a good sort," Joe said. He wiped the back of his hand across his mouth.

I sat in a recliner with my notepad on my knee. "How'd you hear about his death?"

"Gina called me," Mary said.

Joe patted his wife's leg. "That woman is in e'rybody's business. She loves to call with news like that." He chuckled. "She coulda been a town crier back in the day."

Mary toasted me with her beer.

A car turned into the alley. It revved its engine before racing northbound.

"Sons a bitches," Joe said. He eyed me. "Can't you do something to stop them?"

"I'll let the traffic department know."

"We already have. Ain't done nothing about it."

The Acostas shared a withering glance.

Mary turned to me. "They come from the high school. Even in the summer, the racing never ends."

My pen hovered over my notepad. I'd yet to write anything worthwhile. "How did Vic seem that night?"

"Like hisself," Joe said. "He's not the life of the party, but he's known to toss out a good one every now and then."

Mary chuckled. "What are you talking about? I thought he was on fire."

I cocked my head. "He was funny that night?"

She mimed throwing a dart. "At the line."

Joe clucked his tongue. "Vic wasn't that good."

Mary smirked. "What game were you playing?"

"The same game as you."

"Vic hit that triple twenty pretty damn good."

"You think that's hard?" Joe tilted back his can of beer and swallowed.

"I do."

Joe lowered his head, and started to speak, but burped. "Try hitting the seventeen. That takes some skill. I'll tell you what."

"Tell yourself what." Mary turned to me, raised her eyebrows, and smiled. "He played good, is all I'm saying." Her hands cupped her beer can.

"You always come to his defense," Joe muttered. His eyes narrowed. "I better not find out you two—"

"Don't be a moron."

"Oh, I'm a moron? Is what happened with you and that fella from your old job make me a moron, too?"

Mary's smile faltered. She sipped her beer.

"I didn't think so," Joe said. He faced me. "What were you saying?"

"Did Vic have any altercations with anyone?"

"He was trying to hook up with Gina," Joe said. "Is that the kind of altercation you want to know about?"

Mary rolled her eyes. "No, it's not."

Joe waved Mary's comment off. "Vic was always tryin' to stick it to Gina, but she wasn't having nothing to do with it. I can't blame the guy. She's decent looking for a woman her age."

"I'm the same age as her."

I raised my hand to interrupt.

Joe furrowed his brow, ignoring me to stare at his wife. "So?"

"You're the same age, too."

"Hey," I said. My face warmed. The last thing I wanted to do this morning was to interview two drunks.

Joe shifted on the couch. "What're you saying?"

"You said you didn't like her."

"I don't."

"Hey," I said more firmly, but neither Acosta looked my way.

Mary's lips pursed. "You couldn't blame Vic for tryin', huh?"

Joe pulled back and tried his best to appear innocent. "The guy never had a woman."

"But it's Gina. She's had all the guys."

My cell phone buzzed once. A signal for a text message. I hoped it would be Marlene and reached for it. The interview with the Acostas wasn't setting any records for helpfulness.

Joe leaned toward Mary. "Why are you getting so upset about Vic?"

"I'm not." She bent toward her husband. "You're pushing Gina pretty hard on the detective. Why is that?"

"I'm not pushing no one on nobody." Joe pulled back. "Vic was lonely, and she's Gina."

Mary relaxed a little. "What's that mean?"

The text message was from Sergeant Trevor Hackworth, the leader of SPD's Special Investigation Unit.

CALL ME. WE KNOW THE GUY IN THE EMAIL.

Joe waved a hand about. "It's gotta drive a man crazy seeing a woman like that around and not be able to get at her."

Mary cocked her head. "A woman like that?"

"Slutty."

I stared at the phone. SIU was the department's gang unit. Hackworth and I crossed paths whenever a violent crime occurred involving gang members. His team usually had reliable and up-to-date information on who the players were. His text must be about the email Crime Analysis sent out earlier.

Mary set her Rainier on the table. "You always said you didn't like sluts."

"I don't." Joe sipped his beer and then waggled the empty can. "But if I couldn't get any—"

"I give it to you plenty," Mary interrupted.

"I know you do." Joe's smile was sloppy. "And I appreciate it."

"You appreciate it?"

"What I'm saying—"

"You're saying that if I didn't give you the sex, you'd be interested in Gina? That's what you're saying?"

"That's not it at all." Joe vigorously shook his head and tried to drink from the empty beer can. "We're talking about Vic." He faced me. "Vic is who we're talking about, right?"

I stood and pulled out my business card. Interviewing these two wasn't going anywhere. There was enough on The Playground cameras to make me reasonably sure no altercation occurred at the establishment. Besides, Gina had also confirmed nothing went down there. "If you remember anything about that night—"

"He remembers Gina," Mary said. "I know that."

Joe set his empty can on the coffee table. "Now, why would you go and say something stupid like that?"

"Because that's all you been talking about. Gina this, Gina that."

"We've been talking about Vic," Joe said. "Ask the detective."

I backpedaled for the door.

"Maybe I should call Gina over," Mary said. "See if she'd like to do your cooking and cleaning." She waved her hand over the breakfast plates before motioning toward the house.

"Don't do that." Joe reached for his wife. "We've been to her house. We already know she can't clean like you."

Mary screamed at her husband before running down the hall. A door slammed.

Joe fell back onto the couch. "Don't worry about her. She'll calm down and be back in a bit. She forgot to take a beer with her."

***

"Roman McCurdy." Sergeant Trevor Hackworth set a file on the edge of his desk. "That's the maggot you're looking for." He tapped the folder for emphasis. "Guaranteed."

I grabbed the folder and leaned back in my chair. The picture in the file closely matched the man whose phone was stolen from The Playground.

We were seated in Hackworth's office in the Gardner Building. The structure was part of the Public Safety campus but sat a block from the main building. Many of the department's more essential functions have moved over here. There was talk that Major Crimes would transition over as well, but it seemed the upper echelon liked having us around the corner from their offices.

With rumors of my mental health being bandied about in the halls of superior court, I wondered how long I would remain in any of the buildings. A headache formed at the back of my skull.

"Is he your murder suspect?" Hackworth asked.

I looked up from the file. I hadn't read any of it yet as I'd gotten lost in my thoughts.

"McCurdy," Hackworth clarified. He leaned back in his chair and put his feet up on the edge of his desk. He tossed his brown felt tip pen down and picked up his coffee mug. The sergeant was a bald, intense man with prying eyes. He'd been a hard charger his entire career, and the head of SIU seemed a natural landing point for him. Hackworth wore a black Polo shirt, khaki cargo pants, and combat boots. "Is he your murder suspect? It didn't say who did what in the email. It just gave some pictures."

"He had his cell phone stolen."

Hackworth choked on his coffee. He sat quickly forward and set his mug down. "You're kidding."

I shook my head.

He wiped his hand over his mouth. "We busted our asses to assemble this file so you could return this little shit's phone?"

"It's part of a homicide investigation."

"It better damn well be, Dallas." Hackworth pointed at the folder. "If you're doing this kid a solid, it'll be the last favor we ever do for you."

I waggled the file. "What's he done worse than the other turds you come in contact with?"

Hackworth waved away my question. "It's nothing. Forget it. Tell me something. How did your victim die?"

"He was stabbed."

"Yeah?" Hackworth smiled. "Roman carries a knife. Right here." He patted his right hip. "It's his thing. Word on the street is he's trying to get the nickname Gladiator to stick. No one is buying it."

"Gladiator, huh?"

The sergeant nodded. "Roman. Knife. Gladiator. Get it?"

"It wasn't hard to connect the dots."

"That's Roman." Hackworth sneered. "About as simple as they come."

"What about a gun? Does he carry one?"

"He's a felon." The sergeant's face pinched. "Carrying a gun wouldn't be smart, and I'll give the little bastard credit there. He at least figured that out."

"This guy got under your skin, huh?"

"He didn't get under my skin. He's a low-level piece of shit—simple as that."

"Right."

The sergeant frowned. *He's not under my skin.* He emphasized each word more than was necessary. Hackworth looked away and rolled his lips into his mouth. His left hand absently spun the coffee mug for several moments. Abruptly, he stood, walked around his desk, and shut the door to his office. "What I'm about to tell you, you can't tell anyone." He returned to his chair but didn't sit. "Well?"

"You know I can't promise that. Not at least until I hear what you've got to say."

He looked away again.

I took the opportunity to glance at McCurdy's file. Roman Branson McCurdy was twenty-seven years old. He had an extensive history of assault and drug distribution charges. McCurdy had multiple convictions and spent many years in jail and prison. He was not currently under community corrections supervision. He had a suspended driver's license.

Hackworth dropped into his chair and put his hand on his coffee mug. "Roman and my daughter—" He didn't elaborate, but the guy didn't need to.

I closed the file. "Are they still together?"

"Fuck no." His face pinched. "And he's lucky they're not. If he was—"

"How'd they meet?"

The sergeant rolled his eyes. "At some house party, I guess. Amber was in that rebellious stage. It started in high school. It's a little less now, but it's still there. I wonder if it will ever stop. When she told me who she was with—" Hackworth glanced over my shoulder. His expression softened, and his gaze became unfocused. "She had to go to a clinic. She couldn't tell her mother because of the church. It would have crushed my wife. It would have ruined their relationship. It's already strained as it is."

I tapped the file on the end of my knee and remained silent. It seemed there was more that Hackworth wanted to add, so I waited him out.

"You asked about guns," he said. "He has guns but never carries them. He made my daughter carry his. She carried his drugs, too."

Gang members often have their girlfriends carry their weapons or other contraband. That way, if the police stopped them, they were clean. The women were rarely the targets of law enforcement and usually didn't have warrants or other good reasons for getting searched. But if the girlfriends were checked, they took the fall for illegal weapons or drug possession. While their female counterparts lingered in jail, the gang members could find new girlfriends to participate in their criminal activity willingly.

"So, yeah," the sergeant said, "maybe he did get under my skin."

"Did you contact McCurdy?"

The sergeant's eyes refocused, and his face hardened, but he still didn't look at me. He remained silent.

"Nobody on the team knows about your daughter?"

Hackworth furrowed his brow, and his expression shifted to me. "Of course, my team knows. They couldn't do their jobs if they didn't, but no one else does, and it better stay that way."

"Why tell me then?"

"Because I figure I can trust you."

"How do you know?"

Hackworth leaned in. "You know how to keep a secret."

The judge's words to Glenn came to me. My ears warmed, and I wanted to yell how much I hated this game.

"What secret are we talking about?" I asked.

"Come on, Dallas, do I really need to explain it?"

"Consider me stupid."

We stared at each for several seconds before Hackworth said, "You're Major Crimes, man. You guys know all sorts of shit you can't talk about. Over there, you're considered the vault."

I didn't know whether I could believe him. I wanted to get up and leave right then. Maybe yelling at him would make me feel better. But it was the whole system I hated. In the end, I only asked, "What's your secret?"

The sergeant's gaze drifted toward the ceiling. "Roman might make a stink about our altercation."

"Whose altercation?"

Hackworth's eyes met mine. "I cornered him one night."

"Under the color of the badge?"

He turned up his palms. "It was an abortion. She was nineteen. The punk needed the fear of God put into him."

I wanted to tell him that his daughter was legally an adult and responsible for her own choices as well as the ramifications of her mistakes. However, I wasn't a parent. Maybe I couldn't fully comprehend the emotional baggage that came with this profession as it related to a cop's children.

"If he makes any comments about it," I said, "they won't make it into my report. I'll keep them to myself."

Hackworth pointed at the folder. "My guys will scoop him up if you want."

I studied him.

The sergeant raised his hands in deference. "I'll keep away from the guy. I don't want anything in my file I can't defend." His head bobbled. "I wouldn't do anything to jeopardize your case. Fair?"

"If your guys know where McCurdy's at, I'd appreciate it if they would stop him so I can interview him. Right now, I don't have enough to bring him in." I stood. "Thank you for the heads up."

"You bet." Hackworth picked up his brown felt tip pen and leaned back in his chair. "You doing okay?"

"I'm doing fantastic," I lied. "Thanks for asking."

***

"Is Marlene in?" I asked.

The dark-haired woman behind the Plexiglas shield smiled. "Can I get a name?"

"Dallas."

The volunteer stared expectantly. Her pen hovered over a pink notepad.

"She'll know."

The woman nodded curtly and picked up the phone.

I turned away to survey the small lobby of Her Freedom. Except for the woman at the receptionist's desk, nothing had changed since the last time I was there.

Five beige fabric chairs lined the walls. The chrome wrapping had peeled from several of their legs to reveal a black metal underneath.

Old magazines with the address labels cut away were lined up on the coffee table. Titles included *US*, *People*, and *Entertainment Weekly*. They were periodicals likely read by the staff of volunteers and brought in for visitors too young to care about their content.

The carpet showed heavy wear near the locked door leading to the rear of the building where the volunteers worked.

Posters hung on the walls. Most dealt with the victimization of women through rape, sex trafficking, or domestic violence. One had a Native American woman with a red hand over her face and the tagline *You Are Not Forgotten.*

But a small sticker placed surreptitiously near a chair always caught my eye on previous visits. It was a drawing of a woman stabbing a man in the head. It read *Dead Men*

Don't Rape. Every time I visited Marlene, I looked for it and wondered who had put it there.

The door to the back opened, and Marlene stepped out. She let the door close and latch behind her. The message wasn't subtle—I wasn't invited to sit in her office today. She forced a smile.

"Hey," I said. "Have you eaten lunch?"

"I ate a protein bar. What are you doing here?"

"I was hoping we could talk."

Marlene eyed the receptionist as she said, "This isn't a good time."

"Maybe I could come over later—"

She shook her head. "I don't think so."

"Did I do something wrong?"

Marlene opened her mouth to respond but stopped. Once again, she looked toward the receptionist.

The dark-haired woman stood and moved away from the Plexiglas partition.

"What do you want from me?" Marlene asked.

"Nothing."

"Then why are you here?"

"To talk."

"Right." Marlene's face reddened. "You want to talk. I texted it was nice to spend time with you, and you ignored it. Then you show up here unannounced to talk, and I'm supposed to drop everything and be grateful?"

"No."

"Then what is it?"

"What is what?"

"You don't want to see me anymore? Is that what you came by to tell me? Because you could have texted that. I'd have been fine with it."

"I—"

"Come on, Dallas. Spit it out."

I waited.

She leaned into the Plexiglas partition to make sure the receptionist wasn't standing around the corner.

"We can go back to your office," I said.

"No, you can't."

"Want to step outside?"

"You step outside. This is my office. I'm not leaving."

I lowered my head. "I'm sorry I didn't text back. I got…"

"Got what?"

"Scared, I guess."

"You? Scared." She barked a single, insulting laugh. "You're a cop. Don't feed me that bullshit."

"It's not bullshit. I don't want to lose you."

Marlene reared back slightly, and she blinked several times. "Why would you lose me?"

We stood in the lobby's silence for several seconds.

Her face relaxed. "Because of what I said."

I shrugged.

"But you came by for dinner."

"I probably shouldn't have."

"Because you think it will give me the wrong signals?" Marlene's smile was small. It contained some hurt but less than I expected. "I can handle that truth, Dallas." She reached out and touched my fingers with hers. "Is that what you came by to tell me?"

"Mostly. Yeah."

"What else?"

I inhaled deeply. "The department knows."

"About?"

"My therapist."

"So?"

"There are rumors floating around."

"What did you expect from that cesspool? Toxic macho bullshit."

"It's made it to the courthouse."

Marlene's fingers slipped from mine. Even she understood the ramifications of the rumors leaving the sanctity of the Public Safety Building. Officers saw therapists all the time, especially regarding an on-the-job shooting. It was unlikely my credibility would be questioned simply because of speaking with a counselor.

But rumors take on a life of their own. They can create a legend, or they can make a toxic environment. I'd certainly had enough odd behavior over the past two years. Were officers combining the rumor with those moments? Were they attributing my rapid weight loss to the visits?

Cops are suspicious to begin with. They create their own truths in a vacuum of information, especially if it makes for good locker-room gossip.

Would the rumor make it to the prosecutors' office? How would they respond? Would they issue a *Brady* notice—those letters prosecutors write to alert departments their officers are no longer deemed trustworthy to testify on a stand? I didn't think so since those were rare and resulted from blatant dishonesty. Would they question my work the way an adult child does an aging parent? Defense attorneys would openly doubt my work if given a chance. If the diagnosis of auditory hallucinations ever got out, I was sunk. Just the term hallucination might get me on a Brady list. Not as a liar but as unreliable.

Unstable.

"What are you going to do?" Marlene asked.

"I don't know. Maybe I'm overthinking it."

"Is that why you said you were thinking about retiring?"

I raised my hand in frustration. "No, I just found out, but I don't want to be forced to go. I wanted to leave on my own."

"Nobody's forcing you out."

"Not yet. If this is true, they will."

Marlene touched the side of my face. "Relax, Dallas. People talk. You're never going to stop that."

I looked at the poster of the Native American woman. *You Are Not Forgotten.*

"Just do your job," she said. "Screw them and their insecure bullshit."

"I'm sorry."

Marlene dropped her hand. "For what."

"For freaking out."

"You're human. It happens." She stepped toward the door but didn't open it. "If you want to grab lunch tomorrow, I'd like that."

"That would be nice."

The door buzzed, and she yanked it open. "And that other stuff, I said. Don't worry about it. We're cool."

I waited for the door to latch before leaving the lobby.

10

My cell phone buzzed. I answered it on the third ring.

"Where you at?" Glenn asked.

"Almost downtown."

I was stuck in a line of cars at Second Avenue and Division Street. The 7-Eleven was off to my right. A couple of deadbeats stood in the parking lot, staring at me. The dark-haired one with the Britney Spears T-shirt waved at me like a kid at a parade. His friend wore a white T-shirt with the logo turned outside in. His sunglasses sat cockeyed on his face as if they might be missing an arm. A cigarette dangled from his lip.

"Meet me at Erie and MLK," Glenn said.

"For?"

The deadbeats hadn't moved. The dark-haired guy continued to wave as he pulled the cigarette from his buddy's lip. The other's mouth gaped further open.

"I found Vince Mangold," Glenn said. "Looks like he's packing up camp. I need someone to watch my six."

"I'll head your way in a few minutes, tops."

He hung up.

The deadbeats lost interest in me and moved on. The dark-haired one animatedly talked. He held the cigarette between his teeth as he spoke, and his hands moved excitedly. The other guy shuffled beside him. His eyes widened, and his jaw hung limply. The high leading the high.

Behind me, someone honked. The light had changed, and the cars ahead of me had moved on.

I turned northbound on Division. A couple of blocks later, I hung a right on East Martin Luther King Jr. Way. It only took a couple of minutes to arrive at Glenn's position. His blue Impala was parked in the lot of Brown Building Supply with its nose pointed toward the viaduct running over Erie Street.

Several tents were set up in the shadow of that short expanse.

I pulled into the parking lot and stopped alongside his driver's side. We faced each other as I rolled down the window.

"He's walking off," Glenn said.

My gaze shifted to the rearview mirror. A tall man slung a green pack over his shoulder. A dirty, orange sleeping bag hung underneath. He walked southbound toward East First Avenue. A white dog trotted alongside him.

"You're sure it's him?"

Glenn reached into the passenger seat and then held up a pair of binoculars and an old booking photo. "Want to verify for yourself?"

"No, I'm good. Let me know when you're ready."

He set the items back into the other seat. "The guy's not going anywhere in a hurry. Let's wait for him to clear the camp. Then we'll grab him."

I nodded.

"Also, Mangold's got a warrant for failing to appear on a fourth assault charge. Radio's confirmed it."

"Will jail hold him?"

The county jail was overstaffed. Usually, a misdemeanor assault wouldn't warrant a stay behind bars.

"Already called," Glenn said. "They'll hold."

"How'd you find him? Sabina Wrencher?"

"I couldn't find Gypsy. I put out the word for her but struck out. No, one of the guys we talked to earlier called and said he heard Mangold camped down here. Let's get this started." He grabbed his microphone. "Ida-26."

His call sign blasted through my car. I turned down my radio.

Dispatch responded, *"Twenty-six, go ahead."*

"I'm out with Ida-25. We're at Erie and MLK Way. Continued."

"Go ahead."

"We're contacting Vince Mangold. He's got an outstanding warrant. Start a unit for transport."

"Copy. Any unit to back?"

"David-215," Officer Pauleen Sherman responded. *"I'll back. From downtown."*

Pauleen and I had worked together before. She was a good officer, if somewhat on the abrasive side. She'd likely be perfect for dealing with the Mangold-types of the world.

"Two-fifteen, copy," the dispatcher acknowledged.

"Show us out with him," Glenn said, then hung up the microphone. He turned to me. "Any luck with the Bachman case?"

I nodded. "Couple leads."

His attention returned to Mangold. "That's good. Maybe we can close both of these." He reached for the gearshift.

"Hey," I said.

"Yeah?" Glenn didn't look in my direction. His gaze was still down the road.

"Whitaker."

"What about him?"

"When he said that stuff about me, how did he seem?"

Glenn's brow furrowed, and he glanced at me. "He seemed fine. I told you. You all right?"

"I'm good."

"Then let's go." His attention returned to Vince Mangold, and he dropped his car into gear.

"Hold on. Do you think—"

Glenn drove off.

"Shit."

I spun the car around and followed him. The emergency lights of his Impala flashed.

Members of the small homeless camp watched us drive by. They didn't seem afraid of our presence. Quite the opposite. We were interlopers in their world—pests to be dealt with until they could return to their lives.

We passed under the trestle and continued to First Avenue. Vince Mangold looked over his shoulder, but he didn't hurry. He didn't stop walking either.

Everything about the tall man was dirty. His orange hair was clumped with mud, yet it hadn't rained in days. He wore a greasy camouflaged jacket, an Oakland Raiders jersey, and black cargo pants.

We pulled ahead of him and stopped. Glenn hopped out as if he expected the man to run. I exited my car a moment later, ready to join the chase if needed.

Mangold stopped walking, but he didn't turn. He faced eastward like a petulant child and clutched the pack's shoulder strap with both hands. His Nike tennis shoes had holes in the toes, which revealed different colored socks— white and black.

The well-mannered dog sat next to Mangold and looked up. It wasn't on a leash and didn't appear anxious by our arrival. The medium-sized animal was white with black spots. Its head was blocky, as if it might have some pit bull in its lineage. I often wondered how the homeless kept and fed animals like this.

"Vince Mangold?" Glenn asked.

"No." The tall man looked back toward the encampment. "Why you stopping me? What'd I do?"

"Drop the pack."

Mangold turned back to Glenn as he let the pack slide to the ground. The dog jumped out of the way to avoid getting hit. "I didn't do nothing," Mangold said. "Whatever you think I did, I ain't the guy."

"You're definitely the guy," Glenn said. "What do you think, partner?"

He handed me the old booking photo he'd had in his car. It was Mangold all right—a little older and a lot dirtier, but it was definitely him. I showed Mangold the picture, and he looked away.

"What do you want?" the tall man asked.

"We hear you're Mango the Magnificent," Glenn said. "Is that true?"

This brought a hint of a smile. "You heard that, huh? Word is getting around."

"It's true?"

Mango rolled his lower lip down and bounced his head from side to side. "If you wanna call me magnificent, why would I stop you?"

A black and white Ford Interceptor rounded the corner of Martin Luther King Junior Way and Erie Street. The small SUV headed toward our location.

Mango frowned at the arriving officer. "What's going on?" He stepped back and lifted his hands in mock surrender. "I didn't do nothing."

"Relax, Mango," Glenn said.

"I've been on my best behavior," the tall man said. "I promise. Ask anybody."

The patrol car pulled to a stop near us, and a female officer climbed out. Pauleen Sherman walked over and slid her side-handle baton into the O-ring on her duty belt. She wore the black jumpsuit most of the patrol officers donned now. Pauleen grabbed the top of her ballistic vest and yanked it down to resettle it. In her free hand, she carried a pair of black leather gloves.

"Somebody call for a transport?" she asked.

Mango turned to Glenn as worry creased his face. "What'd I do?"

"We'd like for you to come downtown with us."

"Why for?"

"To talk."

"Can't we do it here?" Mango glanced around. "I'll talk but I don't wanna go anywhere."

"We'd prefer to do this at the station," Glenn said.

Mango turned his palms up like a man begging for his life. "But I didn't do nothing. I promise."

"What do you want to do with the mutt?" Pauleen asked brusquely.

The tall man glanced down at his dog. "What do you mean?"

"He can't come with," Pauleen said. She tugged on the leather gloves. "I'll call animal control unless you got a friend he can stay with."

Mango looked pleading to Glenn. "Bocephus is my service dog."

Pauleen rolled her eyes. "Don't start with that."

"But I got trauma." Mango turned to me. He interlaced his fingers like he was praying. "I need him. He keeps me level."

"All right, Mango," Glenn said. "Why don't you step over here? We'll talk next to my car. Let's see how that goes. Maybe we don't need to go downtown."

I eyed my partner, but he kept his attention on the tall man. Maybe it was a ruse to get the man to think about something other than his dog. Or perhaps Glenn was serious, and we'd conduct the interview out here in the field. Both could be true in this instance. We wanted the man to be as cooperative as possible, especially since we didn't have any witnesses to the murder of Richard Ranger.

Mango stepped over his green pack as he moved toward Glenn. Bocephus started to follow along, but the tall man made a sound and the dog stopped. "I'll tell you whatever you wanna know."

"What's in the bag?" Pauleen asked.

He looked toward the pack and then over to her. "My stuff. Why?"

"Mind if I look?"

Mango's brow furrowed. "Do I have to let you?"

"No."

"If I let you, do I still have to go downtown?"

She pointed to Glenn. "Ask him."

"You don't have to let us search the bag," Glenn said, "but we'd appreciate it. Going downtown will depend completely on our conversation."

Mango's shoulders slumped. "I got nothing to hide."

Pauleen hefted the bag onto the hood of her car and flipped up the top flap. "There's nothing in here that'll stab or hurt me, right?"

"No." Mango dismissively waved at the bag. "You got nothing to worry about."

"Why don't you sit on the curb?" Glenn said. "You can call your dog over if you want."

When Mango settled onto the sidewalk's edge, he clicked his tongue, and the dog ambled over. It sat next to the man, and Mango wrapped his arm around it.

Glenn pulled out his notebook and removed a Miranda Warning card. "If we're not going to the station, I'm going to read this to you."

"What's that?"

"Your rights."

Mango flicked his hand. "Don't bother. I know them."

"You have the right to remain silent," Glenn read, "anything you say can and will be used against you in a court of law."

The tall man groaned.

When Glenn finished reading the card, he asked Mango if he understood his rights.

"Yeah, of course. I already told you I did."

Glenn handed Mango the card and a pen. "Sign and date it."

Mango scrawled his signature across the bottom of the card and handed it back. "I don't know the date."

Glenn tucked the card back into his notebook. "Where were you on Tuesday night/ Wednesday morning?"

"I don't know." He cocked his head. "What day is it?"

"Today is Thursday."

Mango's lips twisted. "Shit, man. I have no idea. I was around. But if I knew where I was, I would tell you. I got nothing to hide."

"Let's try the question this way. Where were you staying yesterday morning—Wednesday morning?"

"Under the bridge." He pointed to the camp he had walked away from.

"And you were there all night?"

Mango nodded. "I think so. Yeah."

"What time did you get there?"

"What time is it now?"

Glenn cocked his head. "What's that got to do with anything?"

Mango turned his free palm up while his other hand petted the dog. "I don't know." He sounded frustrated. "I got there when I got there. Ask one of them. Maybe they remember the time."

Pauleen pulled several items of clothing from the pack and set them on the car's hood. They all looked dirty. She crinkled her nose and shook her head as if the items smelled.

"Where did you stay the day before?" Glenn asked.

"What day would that be?"

"Tuesday."

"Same spot." Mango pointed at the trestle again.

"When did you arrive?"

"How should I know? It was dark. Same as every night."

It was getting dark around nine now.

"Did you know Rick Ranger?"

"Stranger Danger?" Mango nodded several times. "Everybody knew him." He smirked. "It's a shame what happened to him."

"You heard?"

"We all heard. He got himself killed across the river. Somewhere near the courthouse, right?"

"What do you think happened?"

Mango shrugged. "How would I know? You think maybe it could be a serial killer or something?"

Glenn stared at him.

"Maybe it was those teenagers again. Remember when they did that a couple years back? Those guys didn't get out already, did they? Maybe it's an initiation thing."

"How well did you know Ranger?"

Mango waggled his free hand. "He seemed okay, I guess. Lots of people liked him."

"But you fought with the man."

"That doesn't mean I have to think he's a bad person."

"You attacked him for spanging on your corner," Glenn said. "Is that correct?"

"What about it?" Mango's eyes narrowed. "He shoulda known better, but he was fine the last I seen him."

"He had multiple bruises."

"Ranger gave as good as he got." Mango lifted his shirt and revealed several bruises on his stomach. "I got plenty on my back from him, too. Fighting isn't killing. We all have bruises down here, Detective. It's the life. Nobody gets out of here without some dings."

Pauleen removed a rumpled brown sock from a side pocket on the pack. She held it by the toe, and a gold pocket watch slid out from the open end. Pauleen caught it before it hit the hood of the SUV. She set both items down and continued searching the bag.

I eyed Glenn. He noticed what Pauleen had found, too.

"Where'd you get the pocket watch?" he asked.

Mango looked toward the patrol car. "You want it? It doesn't work."

"That's not what I asked."

Pauleen finished her search and announced, "No weapons. No drugs."

"Great," Mangold said. He petted the dog with two loud thumps on its side. "Can I go now?"

Glenn pointed at the SUV. "Tell me about the pocket watch."

"I got it from a friend." Mango started to stand.

"Stay on the curb," Glenn ordered.

The tall man returned to his seated position. "Shit. What'd I do?"

"Tell me about the friend who gave it to you."

"Did somebody report it missing or something?" Mango pulled Bocephus closer to him. "I don't want to get her in trouble."

Pauleen grabbed the watch and popped it open. She turned it so I could see there was no inscription.

"I think it's time we move this down to the station," Glenn said.

"But you said we didn't have to go." Mango interlaced his fingers around the dog's chest. Bocephus licked the man's face.

Glenn shook his head. "I never said that. Stand up."

Mango pushed his head against the dog's. "Gypsy gave it to me." Tears welled in his eyes. "She said it was worth something, and she'd split the money with me if I kept it safe." He looked up. "Don't take my dog. He's all I got."

"Call a corporal," I told Pauleen. "We want photos of the bag and the watch."

She reached for her shoulder microphone and announced her call sign.

"Where'd the watch come from?" Glenn asked.

"I told you—Gypsy."

"You didn't steal it?"

"Why would I take it? I don't care what time it is."

Pauleen released her radio mike. "A corporal is on the way." She stepped over to us.

Glenn said, "We believe that pocket watch belonged to Rick Ranger."

Mango's mouth opened and closed like a fish out of water. It looked as if he was trying to form a thought but struggled to latch onto one.

"You took the watch after you killed him," Glenn said. "Didn't you?"

"No." Mango closed his eyes. "I didn't. I wouldn't." He buried his head into the side of his dog. "I couldn't."

"Stand up," Glenn ordered. He flashed three fingers at Pauleen and me. It was a silent signal that officers used for an arrest. We both nodded our understanding.

"Gypsy made me do it." Mango looked up pleadingly. "I beat Ranger for her."

"Not for spanging?" Glenn asked.

Tears streamed down Mango's cheeks. "That's what I told everyone, but I did it for her. I swear to Christ, he was fine when I left him. He walked away even!"

"Let go of the dog," Pauleen said, "and stand up."

"No!" Mango hugged Bocephus. "I didn't steal that watch! I didn't kill Ranger!"

Pauleen stepped back and put her hand on her Taser. "Here's what's going to happen. If you refuse to stand up, I will Tase you because I will not put my hand next to that dog."

Mango lifted his head.

Pauleen continued. "If that dog lunges at me, one of these detectives is going to shoot and kill it. Do you understand?"

"But Gypsy—"

She removed her Taser from its holster and pointed it at Mango. "Do you understand?"

Mango relaxed his grip around the dog. "Bocephus won't hurt you. He won't hurt nobody."

"I don't care," Pauleen said.

"He's a lover. That's how I traint him."

"Stand up."

The tall man stood; it was a slow, awkward unfolding. "Call one of my friends over to watch him?"

"Turn around," Pauleen ordered.

"Please."

"Turn around—*now*."

Mango faced away and put his hands behind his back.

I stepped forward and ratcheted my handcuffs around Mango's wrists. Pauleen secured her Taser back into its holster.

"Who do you want the dog to stay with?" Glenn asked.

"Anyone." Mango shrugged. "No, wait. Ask for Shaman. He'll do it."

Glenn said, "C'mon, Bocephus. Let's go."

The dog trotted alongside Glenn as he headed toward the trestle.

Pauleen moved Mango to the rear of her car and patted him down. She pulled a large plastic bag from the side pocket of her pants and handed it to me. I opened it and held it as she searched Mango. From one pocket, she removed thirty-seven cents, three ketchup packets, two screws, and a set of nail clippers.

When she finished her search, Pauleen guided Mango into the backseat of her car. She put her hand on his head so he wouldn't bang it as he dropped inside. She shut the door and turned to me.

"What am I booking him on?"

"Book him on the warrant he's got. Jail has already approved the holding. Write an additional on what you heard and saw here."

Pauleen nodded and headed for the driver's door.

***

I met Glenn in Peaceful Valley, a small community in the shadow of downtown. We both parked our cars along Water Avenue and got out.

The Spokane River ran lazily to the north as the winter runoff had since subsided, and the dam once again limited its flow. The Maple Street Bridge ran overhead. The rhythmic whizzing of traffic covered the soft gurgling of the river.

Trees and bushes lined the waterline. It was thicker along the area where we parked. It thinned out once it reached a line of homes but became denser beyond that. This was a well-known area for the homeless to camp in.

"This is like searching for a needle in a haystack," Glenn said.

My suit and dress shoes weren't the best attire for clomping through the bushes and along the rocky shoreline. My clothing was an excuse to avoid the effort, and I knew it. "She could also be camping along the other side of the river."

Glenn's attention went north, but we couldn't see the bank through the cluster of trees lining the water.

"And don't forget," I said, "Gypsy said she was going to move."

"We need to find her and either confirm or deny Mango's story." Glenn stuck his tongue under his bottom lip as he slowly shook his head. "Right now, what are we looking at for him?"

"He admitted to a fight on a corner which might have caused internal bleeding."

Glenn frowned. "What are you thinking? That Ranger went back to his campsite and died in his sleep? We'll have to wait for the autopsy to confirm that."

"We need to nail down Gypsy's involvement."

"We've got to find her first," Glenn said.

I checked my watch. "It's almost four. Tomorrow's Friday. Let's call a prosecutor and see if they can convince the jail to hold on to Mango for a few days. I'd hate for him to go before a judge and get released on his own recognizance."

Glenn didn't say anything. Instead, he kicked a stone and then headed back to his car.

I felt his frustration. Weak cases were better than no cases, but not by much.

11

Before dropping into my desk chair, I reached for the Roman McCurdy folder Sergeant Trevor Hackworth had given me. It contained reports from the Washington Department of Licensing and the National Crime Information Center. The file also had SIU's synopsis on McCurdy.

I reviewed the DOL report first as it contained the man's basics—his height, weight, eye and hair color, and date of birth. The two-page document also showed a lengthy history of traffic violations. He might have been a crappy driver, but it could have also been due to a reputation he had built among the patrol teams. Once a subject becomes known to law enforcement, the more aggressive officers will look for his vehicle. Even a decent driver makes mistakes, and I was sure McCurdy provided patrol with no shortage of reasons to stop him.

McCurdy had been cited for speeding multiple times, having no vehicle insurance, illegal lane changes, inoperable equipment, and no driver's license on person. Surprisingly, though, his driving status remained active. I would have assumed his license had been suspended.

The smile McCurdy flashed for his driver's license photo revealed an arrogance I'm sure he carried on the street. I flicked his picture with my finger. With that expression, it was a face I wouldn't forget.

Next, I flipped to the NCIC report. The National Crime Information Center was an FBI clearinghouse for tracking criminal history, warrants, stolen property, and missing persons.

According to this report, Roman McCurdy had an extensive history of minor crimes: misdemeanor thefts and assaults, malicious mischief, criminal trespass, and second-degree burglary. There wasn't one felony on the man's record and, curiously, nothing drug related. Three things could have been at work in this record.

Perhaps he had a sharp legal mind and understood the ramifications of certain crimes. Therefore, he avoided doing anything that would jam him up for a significant amount of prison time. McCurdy didn't strike me as the smart kind.

Or maybe he was too scared to do anything heinous and thereby avoided large chunks of jail time. There were no major crimes in his past—murder, robbery, or felonious assault, for example—so this argument might hold some weight. Could McCurdy be scared and involved in a gang? It was possible but unlikely.

If he wasn't scared, could he be smart? I already dismissed him from being book-smart, but what about street-smart? Perhaps the man got others to do his dirty work. Sergeant Hackworth said his daughter carried McCurdy's guns and drugs on occasion. Yet, if he was so street-smart, why did he have such a track record of misdemeanor crimes?

Perhaps the man was lucky. Maybe he committed all sorts of felonies but was only nabbed by the law when he got involved with a misdemeanor. I wanted to believe that no one was that lucky, but strange things happened in the world. There were tales about a legendary getaway driver that made me believe it possible.

Andrew Parker walked by then. He stopped when he noticed me. "Hey, man."

I looked up from the NCIC report and leaned back in my chair.

He rested a hand upon the edge of my cubicle. "Where's your partner?"

"In the head. He'll be back in a minute if you need him."

Parker waved off my comment. "We good for Saturday?"

"You don't have to."

"You don't know Brooke."

I imagined Parker's wife to be like him—a fitness junkie. Maybe she was one of those CrossFit instructors—a sinewy type with hardened muscles and a joyless, angular face. They probably lived an intense existence with motivational posters hung throughout the house with sayings like *No Pain, No Gain*, or *Pain is Weakness Leaving the Body*.

"C'mon, man. She's excited to meet you. You can't let me down. She thinks I only have one friend around here." He thumbed over his shoulder. "She loves Jessie and his wife, but she wants to cook for someone new."

And what would dinner with the Parkers be like? White chicken and steamed vegetables? Amino acid supplements for dessert? If there was ever a time to back out politely, it was now.

"I promise it won't be anything crazy," Parker said. "Not your first time over, at least." He smiled. "Brooke wants to try out this Hawaiian burger recipe. She'll do up some sweet potato fries. You'll love it. And wait until you try her dessert." He patted the top of the cubicle and pointed at me. "So, we're on?"

The guy seemed earnest, and at least he didn't throw a "bro" into the question.

Maybe it wouldn't be so bad. With the recent revelation about a rumor floating around the courthouse, what would I do this weekend besides worry? It's not like I had the most exciting home life. If my brother asked me to look at his Italy trip pictures on Saturday, I had a reason to decline and delay the inevitable.

"Sounds like a plan," I said.

"I was serious about what I said yesterday if you want to bring a date." His smile faded and was replaced by a look of care. "But no pressure, Dallas. If it's only you, Brooke and I would be super happy. We only want to get to know you better. I'll send you an email with our address. Say seven?"

With a final tap of the cubicle, he walked away.

A bad feeling washed over me. Perhaps this was Parker's attempt to convert me to his religion or to get me to join a multi-level marketing scheme selling protein powder. I watched him until he turned down a corner.

The guy didn't strike me as the religious type, and he had the sales skills of a Mack truck with its brakes out. I grunted at my stupidity and turned back to my desk.

Sensing I would get nothing further from McCurdy's NCIC report, I moved on to the SIU work-up. Even though it was a typed document, it appeared someone had put it together in a hurry. There were several misspelled words, fragmented sentences, and abbreviations.

McCurdy was affiliated with the Dog Town Titans, a gang localized to Spokane's north side. Its members were primarily white males who couldn't join the likes of the Dead Boys or the Giants, black gangs with origins outside the region. The Titans made little noise in Spokane County, and most members held low-level jobs to supplement their income.

He drove a burgundy Chrysler 300 and was often seen in the company of Leon Harding, his cousin.

McCurdy was unemployed and lived in a mobile home owned by his mother. The address was in the Park Estates trailer park, just off Trent Avenue in the Spokane Valley.

The social media analysis for McCurdy simply said "none."

Glenn dropped into his chair. "That the file Hackworth gave you?"

I nodded.

"Anything of value in it?"

"We'll see." I closed the file and extended it toward him. "Wanna look?"

He lifted his hand as if to say no. "I'll get it later. I'm working on the Ranger case."

I tapped the keyboard on my computer to call it to life. There was only one email of importance. Victor Bachman's autopsy was scheduled for tomorrow morning at 8:30 a.m. A detective didn't need to attend, but it was strongly encouraged.

"Bachman's autopsy is set for tomorrow morning," I said.

"And they're just telling us now?"

"Don't worry about it. I'll handle it."

He nodded his appreciation. "I'll take care of Ranger's."

I powered down my computer and stood.

"Done for the day?" Glenn asked.

"I'm gonna stop by The Playground later, see if I can find the couple who took McCurdy's phone."

"Want me to come with?"

"Don't you have a date?"

"Yeah, but—"

"I got it." I patted his shoulder. "Enjoy your night."

"You, too," he said. As I walked away, he called, "You know what I mean."

***

I pushed open the door and entered The Playground. Shortly after five, the bar already felt alive with the post-work crowd. Most of the tables were full so I found a spot at the bar.

A song overhead played. I knew it well but didn't want to focus on it. I was still concerned enjoying music might trigger something in my subconscious to start sending me the snippets again. My psyche and I were getting along, albeit on tenuous circumstances. I didn't want to feel crazy again. I wondered if this was how alcoholics felt.

I spun my chair and surveyed the bar's patrons. It took a few moments for me to categorize them.

All the customers were white. Perhaps that shouldn't be any significant revelation in a city still eighty-nine percent Caucasian. Statistically, a bar full of white patrons was more likely than not. Since classic rock & roll emanated from the jukebox, the probability of the bar being predominately pale should be higher than the city's demographics.

Rough hands, dusty shirts, and dirt-covered boots were at most of the tables in this establishment. The

Playground was a working man's bar, which also shouldn't have been a surprise due to its Hillyard location.

In the gaming area, a younger couple threw darts. A lone man worked a rack of balls around a pool table. Two men in mechanics' shirts played a pinball machine.

"You're back," a male voice said.

I looked over my shoulder.

Adam, the bartender, stood behind the counter. He reached for a napkin but paused. "Business or pleasure?"

"I'm looking for O.J. and Spritzer."

He peered deeper into the establishment. "They aren't in tonight."

"Do they come in most nights?"

"Most, not all."

"You still got my card?"

"Doris took it."

I pulled another from inside my suit jacket and set it on the bar. "If they come in, please call."

***

I entered the house and paused.

I searched the stillness for Bobbie. All the things we no longer were hung in the emptiness. Shattered dreams lingered in the quiet.

There wasn't a desire to speak, to ruin the moment. I held on to the quiet as long as possible. After being gone for some time, arriving home always felt the most—

My phone buzzed, and my body tensed. It rang a second time, and I reluctantly pulled it from my pocket. The ID screen showed *Marlene*.

I stared at her name as my face warmed. It rang a third time.

The stillness was destroyed, and I didn't want to talk with her. Not right then, at least.

It rang a fourth time before the phone quieted.

I looked deeper into the house, but the quiet was gone. The buzzing echoed in my ears.

A dog barked somewhere in the neighborhood. A second and third joined in to form a chorus.

The phone buzzed once in my hand—a text message. WE'RE AT THE HOSPITAL. SADIE FELL. PLEASE CALL.

***

Marlene met me in Sacred Heart Hospital's waiting room.

"How's she doing?" I asked.

"They're taking X-rays right now. We can go back when they're done."

"What happened? You said she fell."

I'd spoken briefly with Marlene on the phone, but she had to end the call because Sadie was admitted. I hurried to the hospital.

Marlene looked toward the emergency room doors as if hoping they would suddenly burst open, and a doctor would appear with some news. "She was supposed to be getting ready for bed. Instead, she came running down the stairs to tell me something. She must have tripped because I heard a crash." Tears welled in her eyes. "She was unconscious when I found her, and her arm was broken." Marlene covered her mouth.

"Did she regain consciousness?"

She nodded. "It scared me so bad." Tears streaked down her cheeks.

I stepped forward and hugged her. "She's going to be fine."

Marlene wrapped her arms around my waist and wept into my chest. "I didn't know who else to call."

"It's okay," I said. A few seconds passed before I added a second, "It's okay."

We stayed that way for several minutes. At one point, she hugged me tighter as the tears increased. When she cried herself out, she gently pushed herself away and wiped her eyes. "I'm sorry."

"Nothing to be sorry about."

"But you don't want to be here."

I pulled her to me, and she stopped talking. The tears returned, and she wrapped her arms around me.

"Everything will be fine," I said.

It didn't feel like a lie, but it didn't quite feel like the truth, either.

***

I waited on the sidewalk with Marlene's purse and car keys. She helped Sadie from the car. The child's left arm was in a cast, and her head lolled from exhaustion.

Finishing at the hospital took some time. It was past midnight now. A doctor examined Sadie and confirmed she didn't have a concussion. However, she had a broken ulna, which would take four to six weeks to heal.

When Marlene got Sadie free of the car, I closed the door. I trotted up to the house and unlocked it. Marlene carried Sadie past me.

"Don't leave yet," she whispered. "Let me put her down in my bed."

The two disappeared down the hallway.

I closed the door and put the purse and keys on a nearby table. From the other room came Marlene's soothing tone. I couldn't make out anything other than some cooing words.

Several moments passed before Marlene appeared. She rubbed her face with both hands before running her fingers through her hair. The woman seemed rung out.

"I don't know how to thank you," she said.

I shrugged. "I didn't do anything."

"But you came."

Marlene moved closer and slipped her arms around me. She put her head on my chest. I wrapped my arms around her.

"Dallas?"

"Hmm?"

"It's okay if you don't feel what I do." She held me tighter. Several quiet moments drifted away before she added, "I hope you'll always be my friend."

"I will."

Marlene relaxed her hold, but she didn't let go. After a moment, she looked up. Her eyes were red. "If you ever change your mind—"

She pulled me down and kissed my forehead. When she moved back, her eyes were closed. Marlene turned away without looking at me. She walked down the hallway and shut off the light.

I let myself out.

12

"There's this woman," I said. "Nothing's going on. She's a friend, I promise. But I probably should have told you about her sooner." I squatted and brushed some grass clippings away from the marble headstone. "Her kid was hurt last night. Broke her arm. She's going to be fine."

My fingers lingered on the flat rock. I no longer remember what it felt like to touch Bobbie's skin. This is the only thing I recalled now—that Goddamned gray stone.

I stood and shoved my hands into my pockets. "She likes me. The woman, I mean. The kid, too, I guess."

A lone runner jogged slowly through the cemetery. She must have been in her seventies. The woman wore a long-sleeved T-shirt and shorts. Her baseball hat was pushed back on her head, the way people do when they're wearing it more for style than function. Her pace slowed, and she stepped into a grassy section. She knelt and touched a headstone. It appeared she prayed before standing once more. She shuffled off the grass before trotting away.

I hadn't seen the runner before. Was her husband a new addition to the cemetery?

And why did it have to be her spouse? Could it have been a child, a sibling, or perhaps a lover? My own bias was showing.

I returned my attention to Bobbie's headstone. "I'm sorry. There was this lady who ran through— Never mind. Doesn't matter."

I looked into the morning sky. There were a few clouds, but it was mostly blue.

"I'd like to believe the three of us would have been friends, but I don't think so. Marlene's different than you. You probably wouldn't have liked her. I'm not sure if you could have understood her past. And besides, I wouldn't see her if you were around." My head bobbled from side to side. "I'm talking to you now, but you get my point."

I shrugged. For what reason, I didn't know. Probably because I was embarrassed to be talking about the subject with my wife, so I changed it.

"There's been some talk about me around the department. About me seeing a therapist."

Is that why you won't get involved with Marlene?

I'm not sure why the thought came to me in that fashion, but it sounded like Bobbie. I'm not crazy. I know she didn't ask the question. It was my mind playing tricks on me. I ignored the question. Answering it might make me crazy.

"The rumor even made it over to the courthouse. Judge Whitaker told Glenn he heard about it."

Are you afraid of what the guys might say?

It sounded kind of like Bobbie again. Maybe more so this time. I inhaled deeply and stared at the headstone.

If I answered the voice, would that make me crazy? It felt like it would. I didn't want to find out.

Well?

"It's time for me to go."

I headed back to my car.

***

"What's wrong?" Rima Sepulveda asked.

I waved a single hand. "I never like this part."

"You don't have to hang around." Rima dug her hands into Victor Bachman's chest, removed his heart, and set it on a scale. "If there are questions about my report, you can call."

Rima had been the Spokane County Medical Examiner for several years now, and we became friends over time. Her light olive skin revealed the mixture of Spanish and Arabic lineage she once revealed during a casual conversation. We both wore light blue medical scrubs, but she donned a face shield which I didn't need since I was only there to observe, not to participate, in the autopsy.

We were in the basement of Holy Family Hospital. The room was brightly lit and slightly cold. Exhaust fans hummed somewhere beyond the walls. When I first arrived that morning, the room smelled of bleach. Now, it stunk of Bachman's insides.

The body lay naked on a stainless-steel gurney. Bachman wasn't covered with a sheet like they do in the movies. Modesty at an autopsy is like chastity at an orgy— it doesn't belong.

After our perfunctory exchanges, Rima had gotten to work. She started the required recording, announced who was present, then described Bachman by his full legal name and provided his race, height and weight, hair, and eye color. Afterward, she walked slowly around the gurney, documenting the locations of the three stab wounds, the lacerations to his hands, and the bruising Bachman sustained from his falling to the floor.

I remained quiet as she studied the body.

"We're lucky there are three," Rima had said absently. She squatted until she was at eye level with Bachman's abdomen and one of the wounds. "They'll give us a spectrum to work with. Depending on the angle of entries and exits—" She motioned her hand like a knife stabbing Bachman's body. "—the killer might actually have widened the wounds. Also, one thrust might have gone deeper than the others, depending on the reaction of the victim and the suspect. But with three wounds, I should get a pretty good idea of what you're dealing with."

Rima had told me something similar once before about another homicide caused by a knife, but I didn't interrupt her today. I couldn't imagine how many detectives stood where I was now and needed this same information.

"Two wounds are located in the abdomen, and one entered the left rib cage between what feels like the eighth and ninth ribs. Based upon the locations of these wounds, any number of organs could have been hit. We'll know for sure when we get inside." Rima stood. "Okay, Victor, let's find your secrets."

She went to work then and started measuring the wounds. Every time she got a new reading, Rima tapped a foot pedal and announced her findings into a hanging microphone. She would also jot notes onto a nearby pad of paper.

Eventually, she faced me. "You're looking for a blade roughly an inch and a half wide and about four inches long. There is no serrated portion to it."

I wrote that in my own notepad. From my previous contacts with Rima, I knew her estimations would be precise to within an eighth of an inch either way.

"Got to be a million of those out there." She tossed her notes onto a nearby counter. "You can get something like that everywhere, huh?"

Without hesitation, Rima picked up a scalpel and made a Y-incision in Bachman's chest. After tearing the skin away, she used a battery-powered saw to cut various bones. Rima then removed the entire frontal ribcage and set it to the side.

She leaned in and studied Bachman's organs. She poked and prodded around with her fingers for a while. I didn't know how long it took, but it seemed like several minutes passed before she announced, "I don't see any lacerations of the major organs. His intestines, on the other hand. Sorry for the smell."

Rima opened a trash bag and set it on the table between Bachman's legs. She then cut his intestines and carefully slid them out of the body and into the sack. After that, she moved to the top of his chest.

She worked for several moments before lifting an organ from the cavity. I couldn't tell what it was and didn't bother asking. Rima walked over to a scale and placed the organ on it. She tapped another foot pedal and announced the weight. When she removed her foot, she said to me, "If I haven't said it, you're looking better."

"Me?"

She looked over her shoulder. "Not him."

"How can you tell?"

"Your face—it's fuller. You've gained back some of the weight you lost."

Rima picked up a scalpel, sliced off a piece of Bachman's heart, and placed it onto a microscope slide. She carefully put the sample aside and then put the rest of the heart into the black trash bag between Bachman's legs. "Things are back to normal?"

"Mostly."

"That's good, right?"

Rima returned to Bachman's chest and stopped talking. In a couple of moments, she lifted a set of lungs and placed them on the scale. She announced a weight.

"Got anything planned for the summer?"

I shook my head, but she couldn't see me. Rima was in the act of slicing off a bit of lung to place onto another microscope slide. She set the sample to the side and lifted the lungs into the trash bag. They slid from her hands the way a fish might slide off a wet rock into a dark abyss.

Rima looked at me. "Summer?"

"No plans," I said. "You?"

"We're taking a trip to St. John's, Newfoundland." Her hands dropped back into Bachman's chest cavity. "You know where that is?"

I shook my head.

"It's the furthest east portion of Canada." She lifted out the stomach. "You want us to analyze the contents?"

"Please."

"We're going to escape the heat." Rima walked to the counter and set Bachman's stomach into a stainless-steel bowl. I couldn't see what she was doing, but I knew because she once told me. She was slicing the stomach and emptying it. The contents would be packaged, refrigerated, and analyzed later by the lab. "I'm not a big fan of the summer."

She sliced a sample of the stomach and put it on a microscope slide. Then she dropped the stomach into the trash bag.

I shifted my stance. "You're thinking the cause of death is still bleeding out, correct?"

"That would be my opinion, but I'm not done. I don't see evidence of anything else. No, head trauma other than minor bruising from a fall."

I understood why she hedged. Everyone needed wiggle room in a litigious society.

Rima continued. "Three stab wounds would hurt badly. Perhaps Mr. Bachman fell to the floor and waited to die."

"It would seem he would have enough strength to get to a phone or go out his front door for help."

She eyed me. "Maybe he had the strength but not the will."

I thought about Bachman's estranged relationship with his daughter, the loss of his business reputation, how his boss at the car lot described him, and how his bar friends considered him hopeless. "Maybe you're right."

Rima picked up the scalpel and moved to the top of the gurney. Now, she would cut open Bachman's head and remove his brain. She'd have to peel back his skin before she could use a saw, though.

I let my thoughts drift elsewhere.

***

My phone buzzed while I was stopped at the intersection of Division Street and Wellesley Avenue. I pulled it from my pocket when it buzzed again.

"Nash," I said.

"Hey, Dallas, it's Kurt Botzon. We're out at Nora and Elm with Roman McCurdy. Hackworth said to call you when we found him."

The light changed, and I accelerated. "I'm on my way."

I hung up and immediately called Glenn. He answered after the first ring.

"What're you doing?" I asked.

"Updating my Tinder profile." When I didn't respond, he added, "It's a dating app. I'm joking."

"SIU stopped our person of interest in the Bachman murder. Want to meet me there?"

"And hang out with the world's most boring detective? You know it. What's the address?"

I told him and added, "Bring the photos from The Playground's security camera."

13

Roman McCurdy leaned against the front bumper of a flat black GMC Denali. He crossed his arms and scowled. His eyes narrowed as he stared defiantly ahead.

Two officers from the Special Investigation Unit stood in a nearby front yard with McCurdy's cousin. Corporal Kurt Botzon remained by the SUV and observed our interaction. I wondered if his proximity was due to safety concerns or so he could eavesdrop and report back to Sergeant Hackworth.

The SIU team had stopped McCurdy's burgundy Chrysler 300 in a residential neighborhood off the corner of West Nora Avenue and North Elm Street.

Across the street, several young boys draped themselves over the handlebars of their BMX bikes as they watched the scene. They all appeared to be roughly ten years old.

"This stop is bullshit." McCurdy's face reddened as he waved his hands about. "You motherfuckers violated my civil rights. I got witnesses." He jerked his head toward the kids.

McCurdy wore a sleeveless shirt bearing the image of the long-dead rapper Biggie Smalls. Full-sleeved tattoos covered the pale skin of his arms. I couldn't imagine how much money the guy had spent to achieve that look, but it had to be thousands of dollars. Colorful dragons and tigers were intermixed with witches and warlocks on both arms. He reminded me of a Ray Bradbury book I'd read during high school.

"Roman," I said, "I'm Detective Nash." I pointed at my partner with the folder I held. "That's Detective Higgins."

Glenn stood off to my right and watched the man with interest. He would observe McCurdy for ticks or odd behaviors during my questioning.

"You all are doing this bullshit because of that prick, Hackworth." He looked over his shoulder at Kurt Botzon. "Tell that bastard I ain't even seeing his ho daughter no more. Bitch wasn't worth the brain damage he's giving me."

I said, "We'd like to ask you a couple of questions."

McCurdy's gaze returned to me. "Didn't you hear me? Bullshit. Tell me this isn't because of Hackworth."

"Where were you last Thursday night?"

"The fuck if I know." His head bobbed with each word as if to emphasize his outrage. "That's a week ago. How'm I supposed to remember that shit with these Nazi motherfuckers following me around?" He jerked a thumb toward Corporal Botzon, then returned his hand to its position in the crook of the opposite arm. "Them sons of bitches pulled me over for an obscured license. Have you ever heard of such a thing? Check it out, man." He lifted his chin toward the burgundy car. "Does that look obscured to you?"

A plastic cover protected the Chrysler's license plate. Due to age, the transparent cover had yellowed and fogged. The numbers on the plate could still be read.

I glanced over McCurdy's shoulder to Botzon. He shook his head in response to my unspoken question. They had some other reason for the traffic stop.

My attention returned to McCurdy. "Were you at The Playground last Thursday?"

"I already said I don't remember." His eyes narrowed. "Am I free to go or what?"

"Right now, you're being detained as part of an investigation."

"For what?"

"A homicide."

"Serious?" McCurdy uncrossed his arms and slapped his chest. "You think I murdered someone?" He turned to his cousin. "Hey, Leon! They think I killed a motherfucker."

The white man standing with the two other SIU officers hollered back. "Who?"

"They ain't saying. Ain't that some bullshit?"

"What'd you expect, yo?" His cousin threw his hands into the air. "That's how the po-po do."

"Pay attention to me," I said, "and maybe we can get you out of here and on your way."

McCurdy smirked and took a half-step back. His expression reminded me of his DOL picture. "You ever listen to yourself, man? Everything you say sounds like some dumb-ass bullshit. I'm gonna sue this department." He motioned at all of us. "I'm gonna sue all you bitches."

"Were you at The Playground last Thursday?" I repeated.

"You know John Robinson?" McCurdy asked. "He sued this city and got hisself a fat-ass paycheck." He sneered. "What do you think I'm gonna get out of this? Your job is what I'm gonna get. Believe that."

McCurdy was only half right. John Xavier Robinson did sue the city for violating his civil rights, but the case never went to trial. An officer correctly arrested Robinson for a Failure-to-Appear warrant. However, Robinson showed up in court the day before with his lawyer; therefore, the warrant should have been expunged from the system. In a search incident to Robinson's arrest, the officer seized all property the man held. This included a diamond ring that supposedly belonged to Robinson's deceased father. The jewelry was damaged either when the officer had it or when it was secured in the property room. The city settled out of court for a reported $46,000, about twenty times the original value of the ring but much less than Robinson sought in his court filing.

"Nothing to say?" McCurdy said. "That's because you know I'm right."

I opened the folder and showed McCurdy a photograph of him and the unidentified woman inside The Playground. "Recognize this place?"

He glanced at the picture. "That ain't me."

"That was last Thursday, and it is you."

"Whatever you say."

"Who were you there with?"

"Your wife." McCurdy grabbed his crotch. "You know what she's down for."

"Who's the woman?"

"Never seen her before."

"It looked like you two were friendly."

McCurdy shrugged a single shoulder. "What can I say? She liked my charm, but we didn't exchange names." He glanced back at Corporal Botzon. "You should show this picture to Hackworth. Tell him I ain't messin' with his daughter no more so we can stop all this nonsense. Tell him to go find some other sucker to harass."

I tucked the photograph back into the folder and removed a picture of O.J. and Spritzer, the two I believed stole his cell phone. It was of them sitting at their table right before the theft. "Ever see these two?"

McCurdy's eyes flicked toward the picture. He studied it closely. "Who are they?"

"You've never seen them?"

"Was I supposed to? That looks like The Playground."

At least, he admitted to knowing what the bar looked like. I swapped photographs and showed him one of Victor Bachman.

"What about this guy?"

"Nope." He turned toward his cousin. "Hey, Leon! They busting your balls, too?"

Leon turned our way. "Nah, man. It's all good."

"Look at the picture," I said.

But McCurdy didn't. "I already said I don't know him. Can we go?"

I put the photo away and closed the file. "Got a cell phone?"

"What?" McCurdy faced me, and his brow furrowed. "The fuck you need to know that for?"

"Where's it at?"

"I'm not telling you shit."

"I heard you like knives."

Roman looked at me. "Who said that? It was Hackworth. What's he trying to jam me up for?"

"You don't go by Gladiator?"

"You see me with a knife?" He lifted his arms and turned around. "You got some bad information, Detective."

Talking with McCurdy was going nowhere. I faced Glenn. "Mind watching him for a moment?"

"My pleasure."

"You can't go inside my car," McCurdy said. "I got my rights." He turned to the kids. "They're holding me against my will! Call the news! Call the NAACP! Film this!"

The boys on the bikes didn't move, though. They seemed enthralled by the drama playing out in their neighborhood.

I waved for Botzon to walk with me toward the back of my car. We were out of earshot of the other officers and the two suspects.

Botzon tugged downward on the ballistic vest he wore over an equally black golf shirt. His khaki cargo pants bulged at the thigh pockets, and his combat boots were shined. His hair was longer than most cops—a likely product of the SIU assignment, which might occasionally require him to go undercover.

"Why'd you guys stop him?" I asked.

"You want the smorgasbord?"

I nodded.

Botzon ticked them off on his fingers. "Illegal lane change—he signaled less than one hundred feet before movement. Failure to properly signal a right turn—again, less than one hundred feet. Failure to slow at an uncontrolled intersection. And finally, the obscured license plate."

They were all legal reasons to stop a vehicle, but they were chippy. "Decided not to cite him for a missing trash bag, too?"

Vehicles in the state of Washington were required to have a litter bag in them.

Botzon sniffed dismissively. "The SOB had a bag in there, so someone probably dinged him for it in the past.

His driving status is clear, so we couldn't get inside the vehicle. He wouldn't let us when we asked. You can probably guess why."

"Hackworth."

"That's only part of it. He's a real piece. If you're looking for a way to search the vehicle, you're going to have to get creative."

"How's Leon?"

Botzon clicked his tongue against the back of his teeth. "He's a stat-five maggot like his cousin. He's got nothing outstanding right now, either."

"You patted them both down?"

"Not our first dance, Dallas. Of course, we did."

"Any knives on McCurdy?"

Botzon shook his head. "And that surprised me."

"What about a cell phone."

"Nope."

"We need to know if McCurdy's got a cell in his car."

"Why?"

"Because we believe that's what will tie him to the murder scene."

"Ask Leon," Botzon said. "He's usually easier to talk with. Better than Roman, that's for sure."

I held up a finger to Glenn to indicate it would be a couple of minutes longer. He nodded. It appeared he was getting an earful from McCurdy. Glenn moved slightly, and McCurdy turned with him, which cost the man his line of sight on his cousin.

Botzon and I walked over to the other SIU officers. They didn't bother nodding as we approached.

"Leon," Botzon said, "this is Detective Nash. He's got a couple of questions for you."

Leon Harding was a thin man with an acne-scarred face. His black baseball cap was turned backward, and blond hair spilled down his forehead. He wore a Minnesota Timberwolves tank top, baggy black shorts, and dirty Air Jordans. A gold chain dangled around his neck. His pale arms were free of tattoos—a stark contrast to his cousin.

"What'd I do?" Leon asked. He pulled his sunburned shoulders back and lifted his chin. "I didn't do nothing, yo."

"Work with the man," Botzon said, "and he'll get you out of here and on your way."

Botzon patted my shoulder and walked back to where Glenn and McCurdy stood.

"Word is you and Roman are in the Titans. That true?"

His jaw flexed, and he remained quiet. I took that as an affirmation to my question.

"And you're cousins."

"We came up together, yeah."

"So not blood?"

Leon's shoulders bobbed. "We been together since we were little. Our parents called us cousins, so that's what we are. What of it?"

"But not really cousins."

"We're cousins, motherfucker."

The two SIU officers exchanged glances.

I said, "I'm trying to understand your loyalty to Roman."

"Loyalty?" Leon's brow furrowed. "We're boys. He's got my back, and I got his till the day we die." He flashed a West-side gang sign made by crossing the two middle fingers over themselves and tucking the thumb into the palm of the hand.

I didn't understand the significance of the display except it showed up in music videos and movies. Spokane was on the east side of the state, and the Titans were a north-side gang. It made Leon look more of a fool than he already was.

"Where do you work?" I asked.

"I'm between jobs."

"What did you do previously?"

Leon stared at me. "Why are you asking about my resume, yo? You own a business or something? Need an employee? I don't work for minimum wage."

"Why's that?"

"I got skills, yo."

"What skills are those?"

"Skills." He cocked his head in a challenging manner and crossed his arms like he was posing for a rap album cover.

The two SIU officers rolled their eyes.

"Tell me something," I said. "Where were you last Thursday night?"

Leon's expression tightened. "Why's it matter where I was?"

"We're investigating a homicide."

He shifted his stance. "That's got nothing to do with me."

"Who's it got to do with?"

"No one." His gaze hardened further. "I'm just saying it got nothing to do with me."

"Tell me where you were on Thursday night."

Leon looked toward McCurdy, who still had his back toward us. "I was with my girl."

"Why'd you look toward Roman?"

"I didn't."

"You did."

Leon shook his head. "It was an accident if I did."

"Does Roman go by the name Gladiator?"

"Why do you ask?"

"How'd he get that name?"

Leon shrugged. "I don't know."

"Is it because he carries a knife?"

"I guess."

"What's it look like?"

Leon's brow furrowed. "The knife? I don't know. Maybe I'm wrong. Maybe he doesn't carry one."

"Uh-huh. Were you with him on Thursday?"

"I told you—I was with my girl."

"Can she confirm that?"

"Hell, yeah, she can." He grinned maliciously. "I tore her ass up that night."

I studied him.

A moment later, Leon cleared his throat. "Yeah, so we grabbed some Jack in the Box, watched our show, and just chilled in the crib."

"What's her name?"

"You need that?"

"I do."

Leon gnawed on his lower lip. "Jennifer Desouza."

I wrote down her name. "Where's she live?"

"Yo, she lives with her moms. If you go there, you gotta be cool. Understand? She already doesn't like me." He gave me the address. "If a cop shows up, I'm really gonna be in the doghouse. I'm kissing ass all the time she's around, and it don't do nothing. She fucking hates me."

"What's her number?"

"The mom's?"

"Jennifer's."

Leon's shoulders slumped. "Dude, I don't know that."

"Check your phone." I pointed at the rectangular bulge in the right pocket of his shorts.

He removed his cell phone and flicked through the device until he found an entry as *Boo*. Leon caught me looking at the screen and sheepishly said, "That's what I call her."

"Sweet," I said without conviction.

He frowned and recited her phone number.

I jotted it down. "Now, give me Roman's."

Leon looked up from his phone and glanced toward his friend. McCurdy waved his hands exaggeratedly as he spoke to Glenn.

"You guys want to get out of here, right?" I asked.

"Yeah."

"Then tell me his number."

Leon's eyes hardened. "I don't have it."

"You don't have your cousin's number."

"No."

"How do you two contact each other?" I waggled my fingers. "Let me see it."

Leon dropped the phone into his pocket. "Can we go now?"

"Is Roman's phone in the car?"

Leon glanced at the SIU officers and then back to me. "You said we could go."

"I asked if you wanted to get out of here. Big difference. Is his phone in the rig?"

He lowered his head. "I don't know."

"Of course not. Where was he on Thursday?"

"How would I know?"

"You're cousins. You said you were boys."

Leon swallowed. "I don't always know what he's doing."

"If something significant happened in his life, you'd know. Wouldn't you? That's what it means to be family, right?"

He looked down at his shoes.

"Did he say anything about a murder?"

"I don't know shit about shit. Can we go?"

"Not yet." I showed him the picture of Roman McCurdy and the unidentified woman at The Playground. "Who's the woman?"

"This is bullshit." Leon might have thought it was nonsense, but he kept his voice low. He didn't want to call attention to himself. "Put that away."

I tucked the picture back into the folder. "Who is she?"

"You gotta stop talking to me, or he's gonna think I gave you something."

"You haven't given me anything."

"Doesn't matter. He'll think I did." Leon glanced in McCurdy's direction. "And you can get his number all on your own. You bastards have got them computers that find all sorts of shit. I know. My girl and I watch the shows." He lowered his head again. "You gotta keep my name out of this."

"What's his girlfriend's name?"

"Hey!" McCurdy yelled.

Leon's head popped up, and both of us turned in McCurdy's direction.

"The fuck you telling them?" he hollered.

"Nothing," Leon said. "I didn't say nothing." He raised his hands to his waist. It looked like a modified surrender. "I swear to Christ."

"Roman," Glenn loudly said, "Look at me." He grabbed McCurdy's arm and tried to turn him away from us, but the man wouldn't comply. Instead, McCurdy craned his neck to get a better look at his cousin.

"You look guilty," McCurdy said. "What'd you say?"

"Nothing." Leon thumbed in my direction. "This sumbitch keeps asking questions about you."

McCurdy smirked "Whatever he's saying I did, he's lying."

"That's what I figured, yo. I keep telling him you wouldn't be involved in nothing hinky."

"Well, good." McCurdy turned back to Glenn. He hollered over his shoulder. "And hurry it the fuck up. We got shit to do."

"Who is the woman with Roman?"

"If I tell you," he whispered, "can we go?"

"Yeah."

Leon swallowed, and his lips twisted. "Olivia Rizzuto. She's his girl. And before you ask, I don't know her number or where she lives. I swear on my life." He glanced at McCurdy who once again waved his arms while he spoke with Glenn.

I walked over to the Chrysler 300. The windows were tinted, so I couldn't see inside. And even if I could see a phone, what would that prove? I legally couldn't get to it.

But what if I had the right phone number? Maybe I could call it and see the screen light up. That still wouldn't get me legally inside the car. Did I even have enough to go to a judge with a warrant for a call history?

Probably not yet.

A lot of things could have happened to that phone. Perhaps Victor Bachman found it and threw it away. Or maybe Roman McCurdy's girlfriend called the phone, and Bachman answered. They set up a meeting, and he peaceably returned the telephone.

I could have asked McCurdy those questions directly, but I already exposed too much by asking if he had a phone.

More information was needed for a warrant to get McCurdy's phone. Maybe the phone was a wild goose chase, but it seemed important. What if McCurdy already got rid of it?

I had to work on the assumption he didn't. I had plenty of helpful information to push the investigation forward.

I made eye contact with Kurt Botzon and motioned a hand across my throat. "Cut them loose."

***

I dropped into my chair and started my computer.

Glenn wouldn't be back for a bit. He was going to search for Sabina Wrencher at the various shelters. We needed to bring her in and tighten up her story.

My first stop on the computer was the Washington Department of Licensing database. I needed to check three names.

The first was Leon Forrest Harding. It confirmed the address he gave at the traffic stop. His driving status was active, with a long history of traffic infractions. Most of them were similar to the types Roman McCurdy had—chippy stops gave officers reasons for contact. I sent the information to the printer the Major Crimes team shared.

Next, I ran Leon's girlfriend's name—Jennifer Desouza. The system returned with three possibilities. Two lived on the west side of the state, and both were above forty years old. Jennifer Marie Desouza was nineteen and lived in Otis Orchards, a small community in the valley. Her driving status was active, with the only negative mark being a recent traffic infraction for speeding in a school zone. I sent her DOL information to the central printer.

The last name I ran through the Department of Licensing was Olivia Rizzuto. She proved easier to find. There were only two women listed with that name. One lived in the central Washington town of Sunnyside and was sixty-seven years old. Olivia Kay Rizzuto, on the other hand, was twenty-five years old with a listed address in north Spokane. Her driving status was suspended due to several Driving While Intoxicated convictions. I printed her information.

I exited the DOL system and jumped into the NCIC database.

Again, my first check was Leon Harding. It wasn't a surprise to learn the man was a frequent contact of law enforcement. His criminal career started when he was fourteen. It was misdemeanor stuff like malicious mischief and third-degree theft. He graduated to bigger crimes like burglary around his seventeenth birthday. A few felony assault charges popped up by the time he was nineteen. I wondered if that's when he started running with Roman McCurdy. He had had contact with law enforcement since then but not a lot of convictions. Either he was fortunate, or he had a good lawyer—maybe it was a little of both.

It took less than a second for Jennifer Marie Desouza's history to return. She had no criminal history. Unfortunately, that's how many young women get into the life. They get attracted to the bad boy mystique, find themselves quickly in over their heads, and are soon busted for a felony. I wondered how long it would be before Jennifer Desouza stood before a jail in-take camera.

Olivia Kay Rizzuto's background check returned as quickly as Jennifer's, but it was filled with a litany of convictions for misdemeanor crimes. Third-degree theft while a teenager usually meant shoplifting. Minor in possession of alcohol. The DUI convictions I noticed on her driving record showed up again.

There were also four convictions for unlawful issuance of a bad check. The felony limit was $750, so either she limited the amount she wrote checks for, or she pleaded to a lower amount. The charges surprised me as they didn't show up very much anymore. With the advent of the debit card, younger people avoided paper checks. Perhaps someone had helped her open an account, and she didn't understand the ramifications of passing fraudulent paper. However, it was written, the theme of Olivia Rizzuto's life was simple—she was a thief with a drinking problem.

I pulled up the two most recent reports that listed Rizzuto and searched for a specific piece of information. The phone number was the same on both reports, so I dialed it.

"The number you have dialed is no longer in service."

I hung up.

My next stop was Google.

Leon Harding's name produced hits related to several *Spokesman-Review* stories. They listed him as a suspected participant in several crimes. While they were mildly interesting, the articles provided nothing that would help in this investigation.

Like McCurdy, Harding had no social media presence. It would have been a mild surprise had I found one for the man.

I next entered "Jennifer Marie Desouza Spokane" into the search engine and was rewarded with several hits. There were Facebook entries from her high school cheerleading squad, similar posts from her volleyball team, and a post from the Law Offices of Craven, Rivard, and Brennan welcoming her to their office as the receptionist. The job entry was dated seven months ago.

While on Facebook, I searched for Jennifer herself but didn't find an associated account. She probably thought that platform was too old for her.

I returned to Google and conducted the name search again. There was a suggestion to check Jennifer out on Instagram. I followed the link but got nowhere, as the account was marked private, and I would need to be accepted as a friend to view her photographs.

Google suggested I find Olivia Rizzuto on Facebook. I followed the link and discovered she had a public account. The photographs she shared presented a different image than the one her NCIC account told. She posed and smiled brightly in each picture. All were taken outside somewhere—a forest, a trail, or a beach. Most photographs had an animal with her—a horse in one, a cat in another, and frequently there were dogs. And each had some sort of inane thought added.

"Love like you've never been hurt."

"Life is a gift."
"It's not the destination, it's the journey."
"No regrets."

There was some dissonance with the images, the posted thoughts, and her tattoos. Olivia Rizzuto seemed like a young woman trying to present an image she genuinely didn't believe.

I backed out of Facebook and returned to Google's suggestions on Olivia. There were several suggestions for an Olivia Kay Rizzuto in Florida, but I ignored those. I did follow the link to Olivia Kay's Instagram page.

Her screen name was @oliviathethrilla, and the pictures she shared there were radically different than the sweet-natured photographs on Facebook. A quick scroll through her profile showed that almost all occurred inside bars. There were photographs of her drinking, dancing, and laughing with friends. Lots of pictures had neon lights in the background.

Roman McCurdy was in some of them. I scrolled back to the top of her profile and found two selfies taken at The Playground. One photo had her and Roman sitting together and smiling. In the background was the entrance to the bar. The second photo was only of her. She was smiling with a drink held next to her face.

In the background, Victor Bachman stood near the dartboard. He was smiling and talking to someone behind him.

I tapped the print screen button and saved the photo to my computer.

14

When I walked into the Law Offices of Craven, Rivard, and Brennan, Jennifer Desouza smiled. I knew it was her from the brief internet search I'd conducted.

"Good morning," Jennifer said. She lifted her chin and raised her eyebrows as if waiting for me to tell her who I wanted to see.

The twelfth-floor lobby felt antiseptic like it should have been a doctor's office. Marble tile covered the floors. Uninspiring art pieces hung on the walls. The coffee and end tables were glass. No one waited in the uncomfortable-looking leather chairs.

When I didn't provide an immediate response to Jennifer's open expression, she asked, "Who are you here to see?"

She wore a red blazer with a black silk shirt underneath. The clothes seemed more suited for a woman in her forties than a nineteen-year-old. I wondered if it was from her mother's wardrobe. Her long brown hair had fading blond highlights. Her fake eyelashes were a little too long for a law office, the only hint of immaturity.

"I'm here for you."

"Me?" Her smile didn't falter, but she cocked her head. Her gaze dropped to the folder in my left hand.

I pulled my suit coat to the side to reveal the badge and gun on my hip.

She lifted herself out of her chair to get a better look. When recognition set in, her eyes widened, and she whispered, "What'd I do?"

"I'd like to talk with you about the company you keep."

"Did my mother ask you to stop by?"

It was my turn to smile. "Why would she do that?"

"I don't understand."

"Do you know Leon Harding?"

Jennifer glanced down the hall before dropping back into her chair. She lowered her voice even further. "He's my boyfriend."

"Where were you on Thursday night?"

The phone rang.

I waited for her to answer, but she watched me with a strange sense of awe. Or perhaps it was fear.

The phone rang a second time.

"Would you like to get that?" I asked.

She snatched the phone's receiver. "Craven, Rivard, and Brennan. How may I help you? Uh-huh. Okay, hold, please." Jennifer tapped two buttons on the phone and hung up. Her attention returned to me. She whispered, "Why are you asking about Leon?"

"Do you know where he was last Thursday?"

Jennifer stood and looked down the hallway. No one was visible, but it was obvious she was worried about being overheard. "Can we do this later?"

"We need to do it now."

Her face reddened, and she swallowed with some difficulty. "What about someplace else? Downstairs?"

"Sure."

She walked around the desk. "Wait a minute."

Jennifer hurried down the hall with a worried skip to her gait. She leaned into an office and said a few words. A moment later, she reappeared and hurried back toward me. She motioned for me to leave the office.

I entered the elevator lobby, and she followed.

"I've got ten minutes," she said. She pushed the call button for the elevator. "What's this all about?"

"Leon. Last Thursday."

"We were at his house," she whispered. "You sure this isn't about my mom?"

"Why do you keep asking?"

The elevator doors opened, and we entered.

"Because she hates Leon. If she saw me talking to you about him, I don't know what she would do." Jennifer leaned her head against the wall and looked up to the ceiling as the elevator started down.

"Your mom is an attorney?"

"You didn't know?" She didn't move her head, but her eyes shifted so she could look down the length of her nose. "You think maybe I should have her in on this conversation?"

"Your choice."

"Fuck that." Jennifer's gaze returned to the ceiling. "That's the last thing I want."

The elevator stopped, and the doors opened. We exited into the first-floor lobby.

"You mind walking?" Jennifer asked. "I don't want anyone from the office to see us."

We stepped out of the US Bank Building onto Stevens Street and turned right. I half-expected her to run, but she said, "You wanted to know about Thursday night?"

"That's right."

"We hung out at his place and watched movies."

The light up ahead at Main Avenue changed and a cluster of cars headed our way.

"That's it?" I asked.

"You want to know specifically what happened? Fine. I went over after I got off work. We went to Jack in the

Box. He got two Jumbo Jacks, and I got a cheeseburger. We split some fries. He had a Coke or something, and I got a chocolate shake. I like to dip my fries in them."

The last part was hard to hear because a dump truck rattled by. When it faded into the distance, Jennifer continued.

"We watched some Netflix and chilled." She eyed me with contempt. "You know what I mean?"

"I got the gist."

"Well, don't tell my mom." She shook her head. "Not yet at least. I still live there."

We turned right at the corner of Stevens and Main.

"How long were you with Leon?"

"Until after midnight." She stopped walking and looked at me. "You think he did something wrong that night? Is that why you're asking? Well, he didn't. He was with me."

"Until midnight."

Jennifer's face soured. "Whatever you think he did, he didn't. Leon's a good person. I know it."

I didn't feel like arguing the merits of her boyfriend, the gang member.

"Well?" she asked.

"What?"

"What do you think Leon did?"

"Did he talk with Roman McCurdy that night?"

Jennifer threw a hand in the air. "That's what this is about—*Roman*?" She took two steps and stopped again. "I should have known."

Up ahead was Madeleine's Cafe. It made me briefly think of Marlene, but I pushed those thoughts away. Now wasn't the time.

Jennifer pointed ahead at nothing as she spoke. "That guy's a real piece of shit. Whatever you think he did, he did. I know it." She started walking again. "He's always pulling Leon into some trouble. So, what did Roman do?"

"The two of them didn't meet up that night?"

"No. I told you."

We were almost to Washington Street. The Mango Tree restaurant was on our right, and Auntie's Bookstore was across the street to the north. We turned southbound, and the sun warmed our faces.

Jennifer lifted a hand to shield her eyes. "I should have brought my sunglasses."

"What can you tell me about Roman?"

"Besides I hate the guy? Nothing. I don't want nothing to do with him. I wish he'd go away somewhere and die."

"If he did something bad that could send him to prison for a time, you'd tell me?"

Jennifer stopped walking. "Oh, hell yeah. If it got him away from Leon, I'd be a super rat."

"I'm investigating a homicide."

"You mean a murder?"

"That's exactly what I mean."

"And you think Roman did it?"

"I don't know. That's what I'm trying to find out. I'm trying to determine his whereabouts on Thursday. I know he was at The Playground for a bit, but after that, I don't know what happened."

Jennifer's eyes narrowed. "He got his phone stolen."

"How do you know?"

"He called Leon from his girlfriend's phone." The look on her face showed her displeasure with that turn of events.

"I take it you don't like Olivia, either."

"She's a whore." Jennifer Desouza wasn't the type of girl who dropped her Rs. The word came through crisp and full of venom. "And you're right. I didn't like that Roman called him on her phone, and I like it even less that she now has my boyfriend's number."

"Did you hear what they talked about?"

"I made him not answer. Then Roman texted that he had his phone stolen."

"They texted?"

Jennifer nodded. "Roman said he knew where it was, and he was going after it. He wanted Leon to come along and help him get it back. I convinced him not to go."

"How'd you do that?"

She cocked her head and raised her eyebrows in a challenging manner. I understood what she was intimating.

"And they texted this back and forth from Olivia's phone?" I asked.

"That's what Leon said."

"Did he mention anything about the incident again?"

Jennifer waved a hand. "I asked him the next day if Roman ever got his phone back. Leon said he was glad he didn't help because the whole thing ended up being about some nonsense. Roman got his phone back but then wanted a new one. How stupid is that?"

"Roman got a new phone?"

"I guess so. That was what Leon said."

"You wouldn't happen to know Roman's old phone number, would you?"

She shook her head. "I never had a reason to contact the guy."

I looked up Washington Street as a patrol car drove by.

"But I know *her* number." Jennifer twisted her lips. "I got it off Leon's phone when he went to the bathroom. He doesn't think I know his code, but I do." She pulled her phone from her pocket and swiped her finger across the screen.

"Why'd you copy her number?"

"Why do you think?" she said without looking. "She better not try and move on my man. I'll mess a bitch up. You want her number or not?"

I pulled out my notebook and jotted Olivia Rizzuto's phone number down.

"Do you know where she works?" I asked.

"At that veterinarian place on Argonne. You know the one? They have the statue of a horse and dog out front. I wouldn't let any place that hired her work on any dog I love."

I didn't know the business, but how hard would it be to find with the description she provided?

"I hope you get that whore for something." Jennifer slipped the phone back into her pocket. "Maybe she was the one who did it. Listen, I've got to get back to the office."

We entered the alley and cut through the bank's parking lot.

"I swear," Jennifer said. "Leon didn't have anything to do with a murder. I love him. I would know if he did anything bad. He couldn't hide something like that from me." Her expression darkened. "If you need me to go to court on Roman or that bitch, just tell me. I will. I'd love to see those two go down."

Jennifer waved a small goodbye before entering the building.

***

I sat in my car seat and was about to start the engine when I realized the time. It was getting late for lunch, and my thoughts went to Marlene. My fingers released the key, and I dug out my cell phone.

Marlene mentioned something about getting lunch today when we talked yesterday. With our recent misunderstanding, she had remained on my mind. I didn't want to forget to call and upset her again. She didn't answer, and her voicemail started. I leaned back against the headrest as the message played. When it was my turn to speak, I said, "Hey, it's Dallas—"

The phone beeped for an incoming call. It was her, so I switched over.

"Sorry about that," she said with a chuckle. "I walked out of my office for like a minute, and when I came back, I had missed your call. Isn't that how it always goes?"

"No problem."

I imagined her sitting in her office with her hair drooping over her shoulder. Her absently tugging at it with her free hand. She sounded as if she were smiling.

"How's your day?"

"Busy. Yours?"

"As it always is. The world is a mean place, and we try to help women walk through it. Some respond well to assistance. Others, not so much. But we do what we can."

A mother pushed a baby stroller in front of my car. She noticed me sitting there and politely waved. I returned the gesture.

"Did you already have lunch?" I asked.

"I ate an energy bar thirty minutes ago. If you want to get something, I'll go with. Maybe I'll get an iced tea."

I waved my free hand even though she couldn't see me. "Don't worry about it."

"What are you doing tonight? You could come for dinner."

"I'm working that homicide case."

"Oh." She sounded disappointed. "What are you doing now?"

"Trying to locate a person of interest in the same case."

Silence invaded our conversation, and I listened to her breathe for a moment. It was a nice sound.

"Dal?"

"Hmm?"

"Did you call to check in on me?"

"What do you mean?"

"I promise everything is okay. We're good."

"No. That's not it."

"I'm a big girl." She rustled some papers. "Feelings don't work the same for everyone. It's okay."

"What are you doing tomorrow night?" I hadn't expected to ask the question. It just came out.

The paper rustling stopped. "Saturday? I'm not doing anything. Why?"

"A guy I work with invited me over to dinner—"

"So, a friend?"

"I guess."

"He's not a friend?"

"I don't know. Maybe. But he and his wife invited me to dinner. They said I could bring someone."

The silence returned for several seconds. "What's that mean?"

"That we'd have dinner together."

"As friends?"

"I'm sorry." I reached forward and started the car. "Listen, it was probably stupid I asked."

"It's not stupid. It's just— Let me think about it, okay? Even if I wanted to do it, I need to find a sitter for Sadie, and it's short notice."

"Forget it." I dropped the car into gear. "I'm sorry—"

"Dallas." Her tone was sharp.

"Huh?"

"Let me think about it. I'll get back to you."

***

A horse lowered its nose toward a small dog that looked like a border collie. It was a sweet image and one forever frozen in bronze. The statue stood at the entry of the Valley Friends Veterinary Services.

I pulled into the lot and parked. Before exiting the car, I called Glenn. He answered after the first ring.

"Where you at?" I asked.

"Back at my desk. I struck out finding Sabina Wrencher. Homeless people are like ghosts. We should give them ankle trackers or something."

"The ACLU would scream bloody murder."

"Those liberals would scream bloody murder if we saved their mothers."

"Got anything happening now?"

His chair squeaked. "More grinding. Why? What do you need?"

"Mind drafting a warrant for Olivia Rizzuto's cell phone records?"

"You're getting in deep with the favors, my friend. Do you know the provider?"

"I don't."

"No ground balls for this guy. Make it harder, why don't you? Gimme the phone number."

I did, and he read it back. Then I relayed what I'd learned from Jennifer Desouza so he'd have adequate probable cause for the warrant.

"Got it," Glenn said. "Anything else?"

"When you locate the provider, ask if they can give the locations of the towers she pinged for Thursday night. Roughly, nine o'clock and after."

"What about Friday?"

"That, too—if they'll give it. It'd be nice to know where she went."

"I'll make the warrant for forty-eight hours after they left the bar. Did Sepulveda give a time of death during the autopsy?"

"No, but it should be in her report. Maybe it'll arrive today."

"If not today, it'll be Monday." Glenn's chair squeaked again. "Doesn't matter. I can write the warrant without it."

I looked over my shoulder to the veterinary building. "I'm gonna attempt to interview Olivia Rizzuto now. If I can get Roman McCurdy's number, I'll call you with that info as well."

"More work. I love it. Keep talking dirty, and I'm gonna ask for a new partner."

"If she doesn't cough it up, we'll work backward from her records and get McCurdy's number."

"I'll let you write that one. I'm getting the impression you're trying to get out of paperwork."

I shifted in my car seat. "Would you do me one more favor?"

"Let me guess. You want it signed, too?"

"If you don't mind."

"C'mon, man, you're overthinking what the judge said."

"Listen, I gotta go. I'll head back in when I'm done."

I hung up before he could protest further. I grabbed my folder and left the car.

Olivia Rizzuto looked in my direction when I entered the veterinary clinic. I recognized her from the DOL photo I'd seen earlier. She stood near the back wall with a clipboard in her hand. Olivia had short dark hair, full lashes, and dark red lipstick. She wore faded blue jeans and a blue scrub shirt—the type hospital staff donned. Colorful tattoos cascaded down her arms.

Another young woman sat at the front desk and intently studied the computer screen in front of her. She also wore a scrub shirt, although hers was pink.

Olivia and I made eye contact, and she cocked her head. It seemed she instinctively knew I was there for her. I nodded and reached for my coat to show my badge.

"Callie," Olivia said, "I need to step outside."

The woman at the computer looked up. She was about to acknowledge me, but Olivia said, "He's with me."

Callie glanced over her shoulder. "No problem."

Olivia tossed her clipboard onto the back counter and picked up a cell phone. It had a salmon-colored case and a pop-up grip on its back. She shoved the phone into her back pocket as she walked around the counter.

Olivia didn't bother looking at me when she passed. I followed her outside.

Once we were in the parking lot, Olivia turned. "What's this about?"

"I'm Detective Nash with the—"

"Yeah, yeah." Olivia flicked her hand. "You're a cop. What do you want? You come to my job and embarrass me, so this better be good."

"Where were you last Thursday?"

She furrowed her brow. "None of your business."

I opened the folder and showed the picture of her and Roman at The Playground.

Olivia smirked. "If you knew where I was, why'd you ask?"

"I like to know if you'll answer truthfully."

She sucked her cheeks in. "Playing the game like a buster."

"Where'd you and Roman go after the bar?"

"If you know that, too, why don't you tell me?"

I remained silent.

"*That* you don't know."

"Not yet, but I will soon enough."

Olivia crossed her arms.

"Here's what I do know," I said. "Someone stole Roman's phone and threw it into the backseat of this guy's car." I pulled out Vic Bachman's photo.

She glanced at the photo. "I don't know nothing about that."

"Look at the picture."

"I did."

"A longer look."

Olivia stared into my eyes. "I said, I don't know nothing about nothing. What more can I tell you than that?"

"You want to know what I think?" I asked.

"Not really."

"I think you helped Roman find his phone."

She blinked several times. Her lips remained closed, but her mouth moved about. Olivia must have realized I was waiting for a verbal response because she finally shrugged and said, "I don't know what you're talking about."

"I believe you found Roman's phone in this guy's car." I shook the picture I held but she still wouldn't look at it. "How'd you do it? Did you use a tracking app on your phone?"

Olivia's face hardened. "No."

"Roman doesn't strike me as the type of guy who would want any woman knowing his whereabouts."

"The fuck is that supposed to mean?"

"Did he use your phone and log into his tracking app?"

"You think he's got another woman or something?" Her head bobbled. "Because he don't. He dumped that bitch to get with me." She pointed at my face. "And ain't no other hoochies getting near him while I'm around."

"That's how the whole thing went down, isn't it? You tracked Roman's phone to Victor Bachman's house." I lifted the picture higher, but she turned away. "What happened when you got there?"

"I don't know what you're talking about."

"You keep saying that, but I don't believe you." I slipped the photograph back into the file.

"You think I'm lying?" She folded her arms. "Nobody calls me a liar."

"Tell me where you were last Thursday night." I pulled my notebook from my pocket.

"I don't remember." Her gaze dropped to the folder tucked under my arm, then she rolled her eyes. "The bar, I guess."

"Where'd you go after?"

"I don't remember."

I removed my cell phone from my pocket. "You've got to do better."

"And why's that?"

"Because the guy whose picture I showed you—" I tapped the folder with the edge of my cell phone. "He's dead. Murdered. But you probably know that."

"I don't know nothing."

An older woman shuffled toward the veterinary clinic. She carried a shaking Chihuahua.

"You need help, Mrs. Smith?" Olivia asked.

"I'm fine." The older woman spoke to the dog. "Isn't that right, Cricket? Everything is gonna be fine." They walked away.

I flipped open my notebook and located the phone number I wanted. It was a bit clumsy with the folder in my armpit, the notebook in my left hand, and my cell phone in the right.

"I'll be inside in a minute," Olivia said to the departing woman. Her gaze slid to me. "Is this gonna be much longer?"

"Where'd you go after The Playground?"

"This again."

I dialed the number. "You haven't told me where you went."

Olivia lifted her hands in frustration. "Shit. I don't know. We went home."

"Whose home?"

"Roman's. You want to know what we did there?" Her gaze challenged me. "Like the positions and stuff? Does that get you off?"

I pressed the call button. "You went to his house?"

"That's right." Olivia reached into her back pocket. "We stayed there the entire night." She brought her phone around and stared at the screen. Her brow furrowed as she considered the call.

"Go ahead and answer it."

Her eyes flicked to my cell phone, and her thumb swiped over her phone's screen to cancel the incoming call. "The hell does that prove?"

"I verified your number."

"Who gave it to you?"

"Does it matter? I could have gotten it from your employer."

She shoved the phone back into her pocket. "This is harassment."

"Here's the thing. I believe you used your phone to track Roman's to my homicide victim's house, but maybe I'm wrong."

"You're wrong," Olivia said. "Totally."

A car pulled into the parking lot.

"But a warrant is already being written for your cell phone records."

"What?" Olivia took a half-step back. "You can't do that."

"We can, and we are. We're going to use your phone to do two things." I held up as many fingers.

A man walked past us carrying a pet carrier with a yowling cat inside. He didn't make eye contact with either of us.

"First," I said, "I'm going to find Roman's phone number. Then I'm going to pull his records, too."

Olivia shifted her feet. She wore black tennis shoes. They weren't fashionable but were probably required for the job. They didn't look as if they would be comfortable to run in.

"Second," I continued, "I'm going to prove you didn't go to Roman's house like you said you did but instead went to Victor Bachman's home."

She stopped looking around and studied me. "You can't do that."

"The cell phone company will have your location history in their database." That wasn't exactly true. The service provider kept history data related to which towers the phone accessed. Only Olivia's actual phone would tell me where it was courtesy of its GPS data.

Her eyes took me in then, from top to bottom. I'd seen that look before while working patrol. She was sizing me up to see if I could catch her. Was I too old now? She was twenty years my junior and probably fifty pounds lighter—I still hadn't recovered all the weight I'd lost following Bobbie's death. My height and leg length pushed some advantage back into my corner that youth and adrenaline would undoubtedly give her.

"You can't outrun me," I said.

Olivia's lower jaw moved about before she answered. "I'm not running anywhere."

"You're thinking about it."

"No, I'm not." She sounded like a petulant child.

"I'll tell you this much. I don't care if you run. I won't even chase you."

She started to protest but stopped herself.

"I'm gonna go back to the department now," I said. "I might even take my time getting there. Maybe I'll stop for a coffee and have one of those fancy ones. I might get myself a pastry, too. You know why?"

She slowly shook her head.

"Because I feel like celebrating." I didn't feel like doing that, but it felt good to say it.

"I didn't do anything. How many times do I—"

"Where did you go Thursday after the bar?"

Olivia's tongue darted between her lips like a lizard tasting the air. She blinked rapidly. "I already said."

"Yeah." I smiled. "You already said." I reached into my jacket. "The problem, Olivia, is you still haven't thought this whole thing through. There's going to come a point when push comes to shove, and Roman will throw you under the bus."

Her mouth slowly opened. "He loves me."

"They always say that. I bet he has you carry his drugs, guns, or anything he doesn't want to get caught with. You've already got one big strike against you."

"What's that?"

"You got a suspended license."

"He's got a license."

I nodded. "But you're a liability. How long will he put up with you?"

Her eyes narrowed. "You don't know shit."

"Of course, I don't." I handed her my business card. "In case things change."

I headed toward my car. As I left the parking lot, I checked the rearview mirror. Olivia Rizzuto remained standing where I had left her. She watched me drive away.

15

Glenn walked up to my cubicle and tossed the warrant onto my desk. "You're welcome."

I picked up the order for Olivia's cell phone records. "Thank you." I flipped through the pages and gave them a cursory glance. "Anything from the judge?"

"About you? No. I didn't feel like stirring the pot any more than it was."

I set down the warrant and retrieved a list of numbers someone had compiled years ago. It provided the contact numbers for the major and minor cell phone companies. This wasn't as hard as it used to be, but it was still a slog. I needed to work through the list until I found Olivia's cell provider.

"When you're done," Glenn asked, "want to give me a hand looking for Sabina Wrencher?"

"What do you need?"

"More of your shoe leather. I need to go back out and hit the haunts again. See if anyone has seen her."

I grabbed my desk phone and pulled it closer. "Gimme a few."

My finger landed on the first name on the list. I snatched the receiver and dialed.

It took ten minutes and four phone calls.

Olivia Rizzuto's cell phone provider was Metro-PCS, the pre-paid carrier owned by T-Mobile. I finished the call, underlined the email I was to send the warrant to and headed to the copier.

Detective Quinn Delaney stood there as the machine loudly whirred. Papers dropped onto a rack below.

"Makin' copies," Quinn said.

I frowned. "I see that."

"Dallas Nash, the big dog. Makin' copies."

I cocked my head.

"*Saturday Night Live*?"

"Must have missed it."

He shrugged. "It's all right. I've had too much coffee. Standing here watching this machine is frying my brain."

"What are you doing?"

"Final report to send over to the prosecutor. It's that real estate case."

"The double murder?"

"That's the one. Paperwork heavy."

"Too bad you couldn't send that via email."

"Somebody's got to print it. DA wants it on our dime."

"How much you got left?"

"More than I care to think about. You need to step in?"

"If you don't mind."

The machine continued to whir, and the stack on the feeder tray decreased.

"I still have more to go," Quinn said, "but I'll let you jump in after this bit. You okay?"

"Why do you ask?"

He shrugged. "I don't know. You seem off."

"I'm fine."

Quinn raised an eyebrow.

A couple of years ago, a rumor floated around about Quinn having financial troubles. Those seemed to have gone by the wayside. He acted differently now than I remembered him behaving when he was married—

brown-bagging his lunches, no talks about expensive trips, he'd even sold his truck and bought a sensible sedan.

There were also persistent rumors Quinn was involved with his partner, Marci Burkett. I didn't believe that gossip, but cops talked when a man and woman worked together. It was unfair and unprofessional. If anyone could understand department gossip, it was Quinn Delaney.

I lowered my voice. "There's some talk."

He sighed. "This again? I'm not sleeping with Marci."

No," I said. "About me."

The copy machine finished its job and quieted. Quinn pulled his originals and copies and waited.

I set the warrant into the feeder tray and entered my code into the pad. Next, I selected scan and identified myself as the recipient before hitting start. The machine whirred to life.

"Judge Whitaker told Glenn he's heard rumors about—" I considered saying my mental stability but figured that was better left unsaid. "I'm seeing a therapist."

Quinn waited for me to continue. Whether he knew about my counselor, he kept it behind a poker face.

"If the judge knows," I said, "that means the attorneys are talking. And if they're talking…" I let the thought hang in the air.

The machine stopped, and our area quieted.

"Fuck 'em," Quinn said. He wasn't a man prone to swearing, so the expletive caught me off guard.

"It's just I'm worried about my reputation when I get up on the stand."

"You think one of them is going to bring it up?"

"I don't know."

"They're not, so stop worrying. Everyone's human. Plenty of guys in this department have got themselves involved with weird stuff. I'm sure you've heard about their compromising situations. Guess what? They come to work every day and do their jobs. They don't worry about defense attorneys bringing it up, so why should you?"

"It's what I do."

Quinn smiled. "If it helps you get through the day, then so be it. But it's not going to change anything. This place—" Quinn lifted his chin and motioned around the Major Crimes office. "—is like a junior high school, and I'm talking the whole department here. Hell, throw in city hall, too. It's like a bunch of immature kids gossiping in the lunchroom. Who knows why we do it? Because we sure as hell have more important things to do." He thought about it for a second, then shrugged. "Maybe that's why. Because those important things are life-altering, the occasional chatter about someone else's weaknesses takes our minds off of what is so ugly about this job."

"It makes the job uglier, though."

"I'm not going to argue."

I grabbed the warrant from the copier. "You're probably right."

"I'll tell you one thing."

"What's that?"

Quinn glanced around before whispering, "Don't go around telling people you see a therapist."

"I don't."

"Then why'd you tell me?"

Was he not aware of the rumors surrounding him? Were we all unaware of how others saw us? Should I tell him? I decided to keep it to myself.

"I figured I could trust you," I said.

"Your secret is safe with me, Dallas, but you shouldn't be so cavalier with it." He headed toward his desk.

Intellectually, I knew seeing a therapist shouldn't be something worthy of ridicule, but I thought the same thing when the department ordered me to see one. I didn't want to go because of how it might be perceived. At first, I avoided it by visiting the chaplain. When that didn't work, the administration forced me to see Stephen Yoder. I'm glad I went, as talking with the man had helped.

Quinn was right—the department was like a junior high school. Signs of frailty or displays of oddity were opportunities for scorn by others. I had participated in some mockery over the years and felt ashamed to admit it now. All officers formed alliances or cliques—it was impossible not to do such a thing. But those associations were fluid—some patrol friendships broke easily with the annual shift changes.

Could we, as an organization, be better? I should ask the same question of myself.

When I returned to my desk, I dropped into my chair.

"Ready to go?" Glenn asked.

"In a minute."

I found the email with the scanned warrant. I forwarded it to the appropriate contact at the cell phone company and offered a quick salutation. When the email whooshed away, I pushed back from my desk.

"Meet you outside." I couldn't wait to leave the office and headed for the door.

"Wait up," Glenn called.

But I didn't.

***

Peter Decker dressed sharply for a man who helped those down on their luck. He wore a short-sleeved black shirt which hugged his sculpted chest and thick arms. The green slacks were tailored to the perfect length and broke above his black leather shoes. His short dark hair was trimmed to perfection.

He might have been a model if it weren't for the tattoos covering his arms and appearing on his neck above the shirt collar.

Glenn and I pulled to the side of the road immediately after turning onto Madison Street from Second Avenue. When Glenn noticed Decker talking with two men near the mouth of an alley, he said, "It can't be."

"What?"

He shut off the car, hopped out, and hurried across the street. The two men with Decker slunk away. Two cops have that effect on those living on society's fringes.

"Detective Higgins," Decker said with a slight smile. His thumb and forefinger rubbed a small, silver cross hanging around his neck. "Been some time."

"You're looking good, Pete." Glenn nodded appreciatively. "I mean it."

"Being right with the Lord has a way of doing that to a man. You should try it."

A church and two outreach organizations catering to the disadvantaged were nearby. A smattering of homeless men and women lingered about. They seemed very interested in our interaction with Pete Decker.

Glenn glanced at me, then turned his attention to the other man. "This is Detective Nash, my partner."

Decker offered his hand, and I shook it. "Nice to meet you, Detective."

"Pete and I go way back," Glenn said. "How long's it been?"

"Too long." It wasn't a flippant response but instead said with some appreciation. "Meeting you was the best thing that ever happened to me." He tapped the silver cross. "Second best, I should say."

Glenn nodded. "Totally understand." He leaned toward me but kept his attention on Pete. "We met back when I was working in the general dick's office. Pete was walking the wrong path."

"Drugging and stealing," Decker said.

"I seem to remember some assaulting in there, too."

Decker ruefully shook his head. "I also did things that weren't crimes against man but broke the Lord's commandments. That behavior ended when Detective Higgins caught me possessing some property which didn't belong to me."

Glenn laughed. "You make it sound easier than it was. Pete here decided to fight."

"Not my finest moment."

"The fighting or the losing?" Glenn asked.

Decker stopped rubbing the cross. "Pride goes before destruction, and a haughty spirit before a fall—Proverbs 16:18. You're trying to get me to embrace my ego, Detective Higgins."

I considered his clothing and physique again. Totally abandoning his ego didn't seem like something Peter Decker chose willingly to do.

He continued. "The Lord brought us together for one reason—my salvation."

Glenn shook Decker's shoulder. "I can't believe it, man. You look great. Really. I'm happy for you."

"Thank you, but two detectives don't come down here to praise me for my continued good behavior. What brings you among the commoners?"

"We're looking for Sabina Wrencher," Glenn said. "Know her?"

"Gypsy? Everyone knows her. She's quite the character."

"How so?"

Decker shrugged. He spoke as his attention shifted to the group of folks watching us from the south. He lifted a hand as a subtle wave. "I've never heard of any official diagnosis, but I'd guess Gypsy to be bipolar. Not that I'm a medical doctor. One moment she's nice, and the next, she's out on Pluto. Real *Looney Tunes* stuff. Understand?"

Both Glenn and I nodded.

"But that's not abnormal down here. Quite the opposite. It's either mental or medicinal." His grin was wry. "Medicinal being code for, well, you know. Recently, Gypsy got into it with another woman because she—the other gal—showed some affection for a guy named Ranger." He snapped his fingers. "You being down here has something to do with that, doesn't it?"

"Yeah," Glenn said. "We're investigating his death. About this other woman, what's her name?"

"Poppy. From what I heard, Gypsy thought Poppy was making a move on Ranger, so she threatened her. Only thing was Ranger wasn't Gypsy's man."

"What about Mango?"

Decker smirked. "Mister Magnificent himself. There was talk about something between him and Gypsy, but she wasn't having any of it."

"Just to confirm," Glenn said, "Poppy made a move on Ranger which got Gypsy jealous, so she made some sort of threat."

"That's the word, but don't ask me. Talk with Poppy." He looked back toward the crowd. "She's right over there."

Decker pointed at a blond woman in a dirty Army jacket, a Cincinnati Bengals T-shirt, blue jeans, and untied combat boots. She stood among several men. When the men noticed us eying Poppy, they turned and watched her with suspicion.

I waved Poppy over, but she stepped back.

"Poppy," I called.

She took another step backward.

"It's all right," I hollered.

Members of the crowd murmured things to her as she continued to shuffle in reverse.

"Wait!" I shouted.

Poppy spun and ran.

"Good luck," Decker said.

I sprinted after her.

The crowd standing with Poppy didn't get out of the way. They remained rooted to the ground like willfully defiant trees.

"Move!" I shouted and waved.

I sprinted through the middle of the group of men. Someone banged into my right shoulder. I lost balance and collided with someone on my left. They shoved me into another on the right. I bounced off him into the clearing. It took a few awkward steps with my arms windmilling and my body hunched over before I regained my balance and turned the corner.

Up ahead, Poppy ran west on Second Avenue. Her combat boots slapped loudly on the sidewalk. Traffic whizzed by on the arterial, and a car honked loudly— one long sustained blast.

At the next street, she cut right, around the building, and out of sight. I leaned forward and accelerated the best I could.

The pursuit instinct was wrong, but it felt good. Adrenaline pulsed through my veins, and blood pounded in my ears. I sucked air deeply through my mouth as I sprinted ahead.

I felt alive.

Poppy waited for me around the corner. She'd picked up a red brick from somewhere. She swung it like an actress in a bad movie—in a wide arc and with a God-awful grunt. The brick missed hitting the tip of my nose by an inch—perhaps less so.

"Get away," she rasped. "Get away!"

She pirouetted and swung the block of clay again. This time the distance from my nose was more than a foot.

Her element of surprise was gone, and I was no longer worried.

"I'm not saying nothing." She wheezed as she spoke.

Even from this distance, Poppy smelled of alcohol. She hunched, not like a predator about to attack, but like a woman who had just run a marathon only two blocks long. Poppy sucked for breath.

"Leave me… alone." The words came with great effort.

A siren wailed from down Second Avenue. I imagined it was Glenn. He'd be here in less than thirty seconds.

"Put it down," I said.

Poppy shook her head. "You're helping her." She pointed at me. "She's gonna kill me."

I pulled my jacket to the side. "I'm not going to hurt you."

Her eyes flicked to the gun and badge on my waist.

Glenn started past our position in the alley and then slammed the car's brakes. The tires skidded across the pavement. I didn't have to look to understand what had happened. My concentration remained on Poppy.

"You're with her," Poppy said. She straightened and lifted the brick above her shoulder. She looked like a pitcher winding up for a throw.

"Put it down."

The car turned into the alley and jerked to a stop. Glenn jumped out. "Drop the brick!"

I glanced back. Glenn stood behind the driver's door with his gun aimed at Poppy.

"I got this," I said.

Poppy shouted, "You're working with Gypsy!"

"No one is working with her."

"You are!"

Poppy threw the brick at Glenn. It was a weak toss, and it bounced off the hood of the car before careening near the driver's door.

While her attention was on my partner, I tackled Poppy.

It was the type of hit seen on Sunday afternoons in the NFL. It was clean and by the book and unlikely to earn a penalty flag for unnecessary roughness. We hit the ground with a thump. Our heads collided together on the way down. Hers might have hit concrete when we landed. I flipped Poppy to her stomach, and she fought and wriggled to get free. My weight and training outmatched her desire to escape.

Glenn ran over to help put her into handcuffs, but it wasn't needed. I ratcheted a cuff around her first wrist.

"Rape!" she screamed.

"Stop resisting," I said.

She tried to yank her second hand free, but it was a futile effort. The second cuff snapped into place.

We sat Poppy up and leaned her against the side of a nearby building. She glared at us.

"Let's try this again," I said. "I'm Detective Nash. This is Detective Higgins. We'd like to ask you some questions about Gypsy."

Poppy turned her head and spat. "I'm not telling you nothing."

"You said she was going to try and kill you."

"No, I didn't."

I cocked my head. "Why'd you run?"

"I didn't run."

"I chased you." I motioned toward Glenn. "He followed us."

Poppy shook her head emphatically. "I didn't run. You're making that shit up." She spat to the side again. "False news."

"If you tell us about what happened with Gypsy, we'll let you go."

From my peripheral vision, I noticed Glenn adjusting his stance. He wouldn't like me offering to let a woman go who threw a brick at him. Especially if he had to explain a scratch and dent on his car.

"For real?" she asked. "You'll let me go?"

I faced Glenn.

His shoulders sagged, and he rolled his eyes before puffing his cheeks. He was getting there, but I didn't look away. I needed to keep the pressure on.

Finally, he said, "Whatever, but it better be worth it."

I turned to Poppy. "Make it good."

She rested the back of her head against the building. "What do you want to know?"

"We heard Gypsy was upset when you made a move on Ranger. That true?"

Poppy looked into the sky. "Of course, she was. The woman is crazy."

"Then why move on her man?"

"I didn't make no move." Her eyes met mine. "Nobody dared do anything like that with her. She once cut my tent to shreds because she thought I stole some money from her. I can't prove it was her, but I know it was. And I didn't take the money! Think of what she'd do if I went after her man."

"Why'd she think you went after Ranger?"

"Because she's crazy! Aren't you listening? She's like a yo-yo. She'll help you get some medicine, and then she'll steal it from you. Right after that, she'll tell you she loves you." Poppy shook her head. "The woman doesn't make any sense."

"Did she make any statements about wanting to hurt Ranger?"

"Besides saying she was going to kill him for what she thought we did?"

"She said that?"

Poppy nodded. "And we didn't do nothing! She was going to kill me until I got away from her. I went to detox to escape her. Worst forty-eight hours of my life. Then I got out and heard about Ranger. She actually went and did it!"

I removed my notebook and spent several minutes getting her real name, where she received mail, and other ways to contact her.

Glenn called dispatch and ran her name through the system. He waved me over.

"She's as clean as could be expected. No open warrants but a long history related to the life—drug possession, theft, misdemeanor assaults, and a slew of malicious mischief charges. You really going to release her?"

"She was scared of Gypsy. She thought we were working for her."

He pointed at the hood of his car. "Look what she did."

"Arresting her isn't going to fix anything, and it's not like she's going to pay any restitution."

Glenn flicked his hand. "Whatever. Do it so we can go." He walked back to his car and dropped sullenly into the driver's seat.

Poppy rolled to her knees. She stood with some difficulty because her hands were still behind her back. "You really letting me go?"

"I'm keeping my word."

She turned so I could unlock the cuffs. When they slipped off her wrists, Poppy faced me. "What should I do if I see Gypsy?"

"Don't go looking for trouble."

"I'm not, but you want to find her, right? What should I do if I see her?"

I pulled out a business card and handed it to her. "Call 911 and tell them Detective Nash is looking for her."

Poppy held the card with both hands. Her head bobbed enthusiastically. "Detective Nash," she said. "Will do." She backpedaled. "I'm going to find her and call you."

"Don't go looking for trouble," I repeated.

But my second warning was unheeded. Poppy ran northbound.

I settled into the passenger seat of Glenn's car.

"Where's she going in such a hurry?" he asked.

"To find Gypsy."

"Oh, that's going to end well." Glenn rubbed his chin. "Just so we're on the same page. Gypsy convinced Mango to beat-up Ranger because she thought he was moving on with Poppy. And the beating went too far, and Ranger eventually died as a result."

"That's how I'm reading it."

Glenn slipped the car into gear and backed out of the alley. In a minute, he turned eastbound onto First Avenue. "You staying late tonight?"

I thought he might want to talk about the deal with Poppy, but he let it drop. At worst, he would let it rest, and we'd address it on Monday. There were many good things about working with Glenn, and this was a reminder of them. He didn't stay mad for long.

"I might go up to The Playground later," I said. "Take a look for those two who stole Roman McCurdy's cell phone."

"Want me to tag along?" It wasn't an enthusiastic question.

"Not necessary. I've got it." I scanned for Poppy, but she was nowhere among the citizens shuffling along the sidewalk.

Glenn turned northbound on Walnut Street.

"What have you got going on tonight?" I asked. "Another date with the librarian?"

He chuckled as his thumbs tapped a happy rhythm on the steering wheel. "It's Friday, Dal."

"So?"

"This night is reserved for the pilot." Glenn's eyes remained on the road, but a lascivious smile grew on his lips. "After a week flying fighter planes, she's so pent up with aggression—" He never finished the statement. He couldn't.

Glenn braked hard to avoid a collision with the car stopped at the traffic light ahead of us.

***

I stood in my kitchen and considered options for dinner. A quick inspection of the refrigerator showed limited options. Maybe I should run out to a fast-food restaurant, but that would require personal interaction with employees who insisted on telling me to have a nice day. That never occurred when I stopped in for a gas station burrito. The moment it did, I would move on. Maybe I'd get something from a grocery store deli.

The plan was to visit The Playground and look for O.J. and Spritzer after eating. No one responded to the Crime Analysis email about the people in the picture yet. If I didn't find them soon, we could run the photograph through the local media and hope to identify them that way.

That was easier than what I was doing now, but I didn't want the woman to hide. She had stolen Roman McCurdy's cell phone, but that crime was the least of my worries. I wanted to discover Victor Bachman's murderer.

Could O.J. and Spritzer have had a hand in his death? She did throw the phone into the back of his Mustang, so there was a link between the two. However, it could have been a purely coincidental link. I hated coincidence.

What if throwing the phone into the car was not a coincidence? What if they did it on purpose? Why would they do such a thing?

Those were the questions I wanted to ask when I found the two. Perhaps they changed their drinking establishment. That could have happened, yet it was just as likely they remained creatures of habit.

I closed the refrigerator door. Eating could wait. I changed into jeans and tennis shoes, then sat on the edge of the couch and stared out the front window. Was it worth my time to sit at the bar and hope O.J. and Spritzer showed? It might be a wild goose chase as it had been before. Besides, the bartender and the owner had my number.

What else could I be doing?

Cleaning my house, I guess.

I glanced around. It was fine.

I could always call Marlene and see what she and Sadie were up to. I shook my head. That would only confuse things further. I was still waiting for her to get back to me about going to Parker's tomorrow night. It was probably a bad idea to ask her to go.

There was always my brother. I could call Dean and see the pictures of his Italy trip. I didn't want to do that, though. It's not that I didn't love my brother and his wife but seeing the pictures of someone else's trip is like watching someone eat a meal you've always wanted to try. It doesn't make you feel full.

I fell backward into my couch and stared at the ceiling. Maybe I could read a book, although it was probably too ambitious a goal for this night. I hadn't read a book in ages. Not since Bobbie died. I couldn't keep my thoughts quiet long enough.

It was too early to go to bed since it was barely six. If it was eight, I could pretend I was tired and lay down on the couch. Although, who was stopping me from doing it now?

I stretched out and shut my eyes.

***

My phone buzzed, and my eyes fluttered open. The caller ID screen displayed the 509 area code, but I didn't know the number. The clock showed it was 6:37 p.m. I'd fallen asleep for half an hour.

The phone buzzed again.

I answered it. "Nash." My voice sounded groggy.

"Hi, Detective, this is Adam." He paused. "Did I wake you?"

"Who is this?"

"Adam. You know, from The Playground? You told me to call if O.J. and Spritzer came back."

I sat upright. "Are they there now?"

"They just ordered their first drink."

"I'm on my way."

***

Two patrol units waited several blocks from The Playground. I had checked into service while driving to the Public Safety Building to pick up my file of photographs. It was a short detour and only took a couple of minutes to run inside. Then I sped toward the Hillyard business district. Dispatchers coordinated this meeting with the on-duty officers. I pulled in behind the patrol cars and got out.

The officers worked the power shift, a block of time overlapping swing shift and graveyard. It attracted younger, more aggressive cops. I knew these two more as names on reports than as anything else. They were too new to the department to have developed a true reputation.

Steve Talkington and David Galloway waited near their patrol cars. They stopped chatting as I approached. They'd lost the hungry look many young cops carry through their first couple of years—that expression which says they're willing to fight anyone. Now they carried a look of bored anticipation. They knew trouble lurked around the corner and they could handle it. Maybe they'd been on the department longer than I remembered.

I showed them the picture of O.J. and Spritzer. "This is who we're looking for."

"What did they do?" Talkington asked.

"The woman stole a cell phone."

Talkington cocked his head. "Aren't you a Major Crimes detective? What're you doing grabbing a pickpocket?"

"Her theft might have led to a murder."

The two patrolmen glanced at each other.

"What do you need us to do?" Galloway asked.

"Be there in case they run. We don't know who they are. We'll first ID them in the bar and then ask them to step outside."

"And if they don't want to comply?" Talkington asked.

"We'll deal with that when we get there."

***

Inside The Playground, the bartender noticed our entry. He jerked his head toward one of the booths.

It was nearly seven now, and the bar was full of men and women already seeking to forget the work week. A classic rock song played over the radio. I did my best to ignore it.

The chatter in the bar quieted quickly. It had nothing to do with me. My gun and badge were hidden under my untucked shirt. It was the presence of Talkington and Galloway. Uniformed officers inside a liquor establishment are the equivalent of a cold shower on a night of fun.

O.J. and Spritzer sat shoulder to shoulder in the booth. His arm was around her, and they leaned into one another as if sharing a secret. They both smiled and were oblivious to the change in the bar's atmosphere.

"Excuse me," I said.

They turned to the three of us. O.J.'s eyes widened, and Spritzer's mouth opened in surprise.

He had dark, thick hair with flecks of silver at the temples. Worry lines ran the length of his forehead, and wrinkles gathered around his gray eyes. I estimated him to be in his mid-fifties.

She had dishwater blond hair that fell beyond her shoulders. Wire-rimmed glasses magnified her watery blue eyes. Freckles and age spots cluttered her face. She also seemed to be in her mid-fifties.

As the bartender had advised upon our first meeting, the man grasped a tumbler with an orange juice mixer. I briefly wondered if rum remained his liquor of choice. The woman held a stemmed glass with sparkling wine.

"We need a word," I said.

"I can give you a word," the man said. "No."

O.J. turned to Spritzer and laughed. Her reaction was delayed. At first, her attention remained on the three of us. After a moment, she joined in O.J.'s frivolity. She giggled nervously.

I tapped O.J.'s arm with the back of my hand. When he turned to look at me, I said, "I'm Detective Nash with the Spokane Police Department." I lifted the front of my shirt to reveal my badge and gun.

"And?" O.J.'s brow furrowed. "We're not doing nothing to no one."

"Let me see some ID."

"Why?"

Talkington and Galloway fanned out slightly. I could tell they were itching to grab hold of O.J. and yank him out of the establishment. Things were done differently on power shift than they were in the detectives' office.

My ability to reason with the man—inebriated as he was—would still be my best weapon.

"Washington State requires you show your ID when inside a bar."

O.J. glanced at Spritzer.

"I think that's true," she said. Her words slurred as she reached for her purse. "Not a big deal."

"It is to me." O.J. patted his chest. "I didn't do nothing. I'm not showing my ID. We'll leave."

"You're already inside," I said. "It's too late."

O.J. smirked. "Well, I ain't showing shit."

"Have it your way."

I stepped back to let Talkington and Galloway step forward. Talkington reached for O.J., but the man lifted his arm in the air.

"Whoa! Hold on. What's this about?"

"Your ID," Talkington said. "Either give it to the detective, or we drag you outta here." He grinned. "Either way, we win."

O.J.'s shoulders slumped. "Ain't that the way?" He looked at Spritzer. "I told you. Didn't I tell you?"

"Just give them your ID." She handed her driver's license to Talkington, and he passed it to me.

I glanced at the name on the license. Ruby Ann Louden, fifty-four, with an address on Hogan Avenue.

O.J. leaned clumsily to the side and pulled his wallet out of a back pocket. "I don't get why you guys gotta harass working people like us."

"Where do you work?" Galloway asked.

O.J. flipped open his wallet. "I'm on disability."

Galloway smirked. "Working people."

"What about them?" O.J.'s thumb slipped off his license as he tried to pull it free from his wallet.

"That's what you said."

"When?" O.J. tugged the license loose and held it up triumphantly.

Galloway snatched it from the man and gave it to me.

Michael Lee Boyd. Fifty-seven. He lived on North Perry.

I handed both licenses to Talkington. "Would you run their names and take Mr. Boyd for a walk?"

Boyd's head popped up. His gaze darted between the three of us. I don't think he knew which of us had just spoken. "Where'm I goin'?"

"With us," Galloway said. He grabbed Boyd's elbow.

"Am I coming back?"

"If you behave."

Boyd turned to kiss Louden goodbye. He puckered his lips, and she did the same. They were about to touch when Galloway tugged on his arm and broke the moment.

"Let's go, Romeo."

Boyd led the way toward the door with Talkington and Galloway close behind.

I slid into the booth across from Ruby Louden and set my file on the table.

The chatter in the bar returned to its previous volume—maybe it was even louder this time. A new song started, but I did my best to ignore it like the others.

Ruby reached for her wine glass, but I pulled it away.

"Hey," she said.

"In a minute. We need to talk."

"About what?"

"A cell phone you stole."

Her lip curled. "I didn't steal no cell phone."

I flipped open the file and found the photograph of her taking Roman McCurdy's cell phone. "This was last Thursday night. Remember this?"

"What's that prove?" She turned away. "You don't know me."

I pulled out the second photograph. It was the one that showed her tossing the phone into the backseat of Vic Bachman's convertible.

"How about this?"

She glanced at the picture. Once she realized what she was seeing, she turned fully to it. Her eyes registered surprise, but Ruby tried to mask it by squinting. When she looked up, her face contorted into what was supposed to resemble remorse. "Okay, so I took it, but I didn't keep it."

"Doesn't matter."

"Sure it does." She tapped the photograph of Bachman's car. "It's not stealing if I don't keep it. I'm not a bad person. If I get rid of it, it's like giving it back."

"It's not even close to giving it back." Her childish argument was so simple it was amazing. It's not the first time I'd run into this type of thing on the street, but it never failed to surprise me. "You tossed the phone into the backseat of a random car."

"You don't know it wasn't the right car." Ruby smirked, seemingly satisfied she'd just won the argument.

"Yeah. I do." I tapped the photograph. "The guy who owned this car was not the owner of the cell phone."

She shrugged. "Big deal. I moved a phone. That's not a crime."

"You stole a phone. That *is* a crime."

"I didn't keep it. I *moved* it." She flicked her hand. "Where's the harm in that?"

I opened the folder and showed her the picture of Vic Bachman lying on his living room floor. "That's the owner of the convertible."

Ruby cringed but pulled the photo closer to look at it. "What happened?"

"He was murdered."

She leaned over the picture to examine it and absently reached for her wine spritzer. I let her have it. "How?"

"Someone stabbed him to death."

Her face pinched tighter, and she turned slightly to sip her drink, but her eyes never left the photo. "That's horrible." She tilted the glass back.

"We think he was murdered because of the missing cell phone."

She swallowed quickly as her gaze found me. "Well, I didn't kill him."

"I never said you did."

Her eyes widened, and she clumsily set the glass down. Sparkling wine splashed onto the table. "You're not thinking Michael did it? He couldn't hurt a fly." She abruptly looked toward the door. Her brow furrowed, and it appeared as if she were fighting back tears. "He didn't do it! I swear!" I lifted a hand to calm her, but she shouted, "He didn't!" Ruby anxiously tapped the photograph. "Why would we do something like this?"

"I don't know. Why did you take the phone?" My hand hovered over the picture of her taking Roman McCurdy's property.

Ruby studied the various photographs. "It was stupid."

Somewhere a woman cheered, followed by a few others joining in. A player broke a rack at the closest pool tables. A new song started—it was one Bobbie loved to sing along with. I ignored it as if my sanity depended on it.

"Why was taking the phone stupid?" I asked.

Ruby looked up. Her eyes were glossy, and she reached for her drink. As it went to her lips, I motioned for her to refrain from taking another sip. The disappointment was clear in her eyes, but she paused. The glass returned to the table. "It was a goof."

"A goof?"

She shrugged. "You know how it is. I was fucking around. I didn't mean no harm."

I couldn't believe what I was hearing. "You had to have taken the phone for a reason."

"No. I swear." She raised her hand as if testifying before a judge. "I was only having some fun."

I stared at her.

She leaned in and looked at me earnestly. "Don't you ever do anything just to do it?" She looked deeper into the bar. A sneer grew, and her attention returned to me. "God, I hate these people."

I tapped the photo of her taking Roman McCurdy's phone. "Did you know the people at this table?"

"No. But I probably hated them, too. I hate everybody, if I'm being honest. You, too."

I wondered how much of her confession was the alcohol speaking and how much of it was her true personality.

"What am I going to do about it?" Ruby asked. "It's not like anyone cares what I think. I'm not exactly scary now, am I?" She bared her teeth and growled like a bear. "See? You weren't even scared a little bit. So I move stuff." She grabbed her glass but didn't sip from it. Ruby waggled it and watched the liquid slosh about inside. "But I never keep nothing I take, not one thing." Her eyes met mine. "And I'm proud of that. I've never stolen one goddamn thing, and I'll swear on a stack of bibles."

She wiped her mouth with the back of her free hand before lifting the glass to her lips with the other. Ruby sipped her spritzer and moaned with satisfaction. "Amen and all that jazz."

Frustration welled in my chest.

If Victor Bachman's murder occurred how I imagined it, the catalyst for it started as a lark—a drunken prank. Ruby Louden stole Roman McCurdy's cell phone because she felt powerless in her life. Whether it was true she had no intention of keeping the cell phone carried no weight. It was theft, plain and simple.

The problem was I needed a victim for the crime of theft, and Roman McCurdy wasn't forthcoming. And why would he? I believed Roman McCurdy and Olivia Rizzuto tracked the missing phone to Victor Bachman's house. Admitting the theft would help prove his guilt.

Ruby Louden wasn't going to answer for a crime that set everything in motion.

Officer Galloway walked up to the table. He set her driver's license in front of me. "Record's clean. No history."

"What about her boyfriend?"

"DUI, but that's it."

Ruby and Michael's information was in the system now. I didn't need to pull out my notebook.

"Where do you work?" I asked.

Ruby blinked slowly. "Why do you need that?"

I held her license up. "Want this back?"

She frowned. "Western Bank. The downtown branch."

"What do you do there?"

"I'm a teller. Part-time."

"Will you be there Monday?"

"Unfortunately."

"We're going to talk again when you're sober."

"But I didn't do nothing," she whined.

I tapped the driver's license against the table. "You're going to give me a written statement of what occurred last Thursday night."

"But why you gotta come downtown? That's my job."

"We can take you down to the station now."

Ruby's eyes settled on what remained of her drink. The lines around the edge of her mouth deepened. "Monday's fine."

I tossed the card into the middle of the table and stood.

"Is Michael coming back?" she asked.

"Yeah," Galloway said. "We'll send him in."

Ruby waved to the bartender with two fingers and then pointed down to their table.

We'd been dismissed.

***

The burritos on the display rack looked freshly cooked. The pizza rolls appeared the same. The top of each item peeked out of its paper wrapping. A heat lamp did its best to keep the food warm.

Next to the rack, a series of hot dogs and sausages glistened on a spinning rack. They also lingered under a cooking lamp, but these seemed more appealing. I had come for a burrito, but the glistening, turning dogs continued to catch my attention. Maybe it was the motion—the hypnotic spinning—that lured me away from my original choice.

I was at the Quik-E Mart at the corner of Bridgeport Avenue and Nevada Street. Over the past couple of years, it had turned into a regular stop.

Some annoyingly bass-filled rap music played from hidden speakers. I didn't know the music and could only understand an occasional word. Above me, a fluorescent light flickered. The store smelled like most convenience stores I'd ever been in—a concoction of cleaning supplies, coffee, and packaged foods.

I glanced at the clerk behind the counter. Marvin was a thin, dark-skinned man with a handsome face and kind eyes. He smiled and lifted his chin toward the food warming in the showcases.

"What're you thinking?" he asked. "Going with the usual?"

I lifted the top of the burrito rack and reached for a bean and cheese blend. My hand hovered over it.

"I don't know. I'm not feeling it tonight." I removed my hand without selecting a burrito and closed the lid.

"Hot dog then?" the clerk asked.

"I can't decide."

"Get one of each. Can't go wrong that way."

I wasn't hungry enough for both. Maybe I could eat half of each and discard the portions I didn't want. That seemed wasteful, so I went with the third option. I lifted the lid and grabbed a pizza roll. It's not what I wanted, but it would do.

I picked up the soda nearby and carried my dinner to the counter.

"Didn't see that coming," Marvin said. "You never get a pizza dog. You feeling all right?"

"Trying something new."

"Good for you, my friend." The cashier tapped several keys on the register. "Haven't seen you in a couple weeks."

Had it really been that long?

"Started to think you might have jumped to that new joint over on Division."

"The fancy one with all the pumps?" I shook my head. "I'm loyal to you guys."

"Because of our burritos?" He announced a total. "I hear they got pretty good snacks over there."

I pulled a few bills from my pocket and handed them to Marvin. "You trying to get rid of me?"

"Not a chance. I like cops coming in. It keeps the trouble down."

"You get a lot of trouble around here?"

He straightened out the dollar bills. "Probably no worse than anyone else."

I didn't have an excuse for why I had stopped coming by the Quik-E Mart. There was no need to justify it to Marvin, but it caught me off-guard that I hadn't been there for a couple of weeks.

Marvin watched me with curiosity, so I asked, "How you been?"

"Business has been off because of the—" The cash register banged open. "It's hard to compete with new pumps and flashy new snacks. Other than that, things are normal." He tucked the dollar bills away. "Thanks for the loyalty."

Outside, the sun was setting, and two cars were at the pumps. Neither of the drivers looked in our direction as they filled their gas tanks.

A textbook sat on the counter near Marvin's elbow.

I lifted the pizza roll. "What are you reading?"

Before he could answer, I bit into my dinner and was immediately disappointed. It wasn't what I wanted, and I should have expected as much. I could have stayed with the burrito or gone with the hot dog. Those would have been satisfying.

Marvin reached for the book and flipped it closed. The cover read *Fundamentals of Financial Management.*

I continued to chew, but the taste was less than mediocre. I should have stopped eating right then and bought what I wanted. What would a few dollars have been compared to my happiness? Nothing. But I swallowed, nonetheless.

"Like it?" I asked and motioned toward the textbook.

"It's all right. Need it for my degree."

"How's that coming?"

He looked toward the ceiling. "Slower than I want. The online process is taking forever."

I bit into the pizza roll again. The taste remained unfulfilling, but I continued to eat it anyway.

"You digging that?" Marvin asked.

"It's fine," I said through a mouthful. "Duke still agreeing to sell you the place?"

He lifted the edge of the textbook. "He is, but I gotta graduate first."

Duke was the owner of the store, along with several other locations around the county. We'd met while I was working a homicide a couple of years ago. According to Marvin, Duke made a deal to sell him the store on an owner-carried contract, but Marvin had to finish his college degree first. The deal was about legacy. Duke had no children but wanted to leave the store to someone who would care for it the way he did. Marvin's college degree was a commitment to furthering the store's success.

I motioned toward him with the pizza roll. "How much longer?"

"At this rate, a couple years. But it's worth it, and Duke is helping me more than my family ever could." He shrugged. "What can I say? I like the old guy."

I bit into the pizza roll for the third time. It wasn't as bad as the first two. It remained unsatisfying but I had become quickly accustomed to the uninspiring taste. The idea of wasting a few dollars on a replacement choice seemed slightly foolish now. I could gut this down and be full in the end.

"Working late tonight?" Marvin asked.

I nodded, then swallowed. "Was hoping to wrap up a case."

"So you can enjoy the weekend, huh? Did you get it done?"

"No." I flashed a closed-lip smile. "Got a little closer, though, so there's that."

"Any plans for the weekend?"

Dinner at Parker's house entered my mind. I still hadn't heard back from Marlene. I absently patted my phone with my left hand in hopes of generating a buzz from a text message. Nothing happened, so I jammed the last bite of pizza dog into my mouth. I wasn't worried about the taste now.

"You're really getting after that." Marvin laughed. "Lots of people like them. They're our biggest seller after the bars close. You got lucky by grabbing one early."

I swallowed the mouthful and decided the pizza roll wasn't as bad as I first thought. "Bestseller, huh?"

"Two to one over the burritos."

That seemed a stretch, but what did I know? I grabbed my soda and offered a slight wave. "I should get going."

"Take care, Detective. Until next week."

16

I awoke and sat up on the couch. A crick in my neck elicited an unwarranted moan. I felt foolish for making the sound. Worse than that, I felt pathetic.

Sunlight peeked into the living room through the opening, where the curtains didn't meet. Streaks of gold splashed across the floor.

Someone in the neighborhood mowed their lawn. Not the jerk across the street because it was early, and the sun was up. The small engine whirred loudly and incessantly.

I leaned forward to rest my elbows on my knees. A dull headache worked its way into my consciousness. It was at the back of my head.

A crick and a headache—I blamed that stupid pizza roll. A burrito never gave me problems in the morning.

I picked up my phone from the floor to check the time. There was a text message from Marlene. It came in at 12:37 a.m.

DINNER WITH YOUR FRIEND SOUNDS CONFUSING. I TRIED NOT TO READ ANYTHING INTO IT, BUT I COULDN'T. IF I'M ONLY YOUR FRIEND, THEN I WILL PASS. HAVE A GOOD TIME—TRULY. IF DINNER IS TO BE SOMETHING MORE, THEN I WILL GO. LET ME KNOW.

I dropped the phone to the floor and fell back onto the couch.

"Shit."

***

Thirty minutes later, I got up and showered while a pot of coffee brewed. Once dressed, I poured myself a cup and left the house. It had been a while since I'd walked through the neighborhood. I don't remember the last time I did such a thing—probably with Bobbie.

A wave of melancholy rolled over me, and I almost spun around to return to the safety of the couch. The thought resulted in a bit of shame joining the sadness.

Two years and still hiding.

I sipped some coffee and eyed a neighbor's rose bushes Bobbie had frequently commented on. The morning sun warmed my face.

Several things played out inside my head then. They came in starts and stops, and I tried to keep them straight.

Dinner with the Parkers was the most pressing issue. I should have said no when first asked. I could still cancel—there was time. If I did it soon, it wouldn't be overly rude, but there would be ramifications for doing such a thing. Parker seemed to look forward to it, so hurt feelings were a real possibility.

Marlene wouldn't be disappointed either way. She didn't want to go with me and make us something more than we were. That made sense, and I appreciated her reasoning. I didn't want to complicate things more than they already were.

I would have liked to have taken Bobbie. Although, I could imagine her playfully chastising me for accepting the invitation without talking to her first. I pushed further thoughts away so as not to do any more harm to myself.

One of my neighbors—a younger man who must have moved into his house over the past couple of years—waved from his garage. A child's bicycle was upside down, and he appeared to be fixing a tire. I waved back.

A little girl burst from inside the house with a plastic toolbox. She wore a yellow hard hat. The child dropped down next to her father. Her attention was locked on the bicycle. The father put his arm around the girl and pointed at the tire.

Parker said he had kids. Bobbie and I never had them. The idea of starting a family came up early when we first married. After a time, that conversation quieted. I didn't think I wanted children. If Bobbie wasn't going to broach the matter, then why would I? Life seemed perfect with just the two of us. Now, she was gone, and there was only me.

Marlene had Sadie, who I adored. Was that because the kid liked me? The only children I had been around never connected with me. And why should they? I saw them once in a blue moon. I saw Sadie only slightly more than that, but she lit up when I walked into a room. The kid was special.

So was her mom. She carried an underlying sadness but remained hopeful, especially in the world where she worked. I understood her for a variety of reasons. What did that mean, if anything?

It certainly wasn't a reason for a relationship—at least, I didn't think so. But what did I know? I'd only been with one woman. Bobbie and I fell in love in high school. I never wanted anyone else.

Marlene's life was radically different than mine. She was at the opposite end of the spectrum. I didn't hold that against her even though I knew others would. Glenn had held it against her when they first met. If anyone on the department remembered her from when she worked the street, they would judge her. It was human nature. Cop nature was even more intolerant.

It was probably better she didn't go to dinner tonight. Parker had met her during the case we worked together. Someone had murdered a couple of pimps, and we each caught a case. Who knows how the evening would turn out if she showed up at Parker's house?

Maybe that's what I secretly wanted to happen by inviting her—to ruin everything.

I sipped the final bit of my coffee.

No, I decided. That wasn't it.

I liked Marlene. How much, I wasn't exactly sure, but I did like her.

And I guess I liked Parker, too. Things around the office were better lately since he and I had found common footing. I didn't want to go back to those days when we were antagonistic toward each other. Maybe I didn't want to have dinner with the man, but I didn't want him to dislike me.

I headed home.

***

After a shower and a change of clothes, I checked my phone.

An email from a representative of MetroPCS was waiting. Along with a polite salutation were two pdf files. One was named Leon Harding, the other Olivia Rizzuto.

The information technology types didn't work typical 9-5 jobs, so I had hoped the info would come in over the weekend.

It was hard to read the files on my phone.

I grabbed my keys and headed into the office.

***

The Major Crimes office was quiet. Hell, the entire Public Safety building was silent, and I felt like a burglar sitting at my desk. After the computer whirred to life, I printed both Leon Harding's and Olivia Rizzuto's cell phone records. I retrieved them from the central printer and sat at my desk.

First, I reviewed Harding's report. The report contained a list of phone calls for a five-day period. There was only one number I knew—his girlfriend's, Jennifer Desouza. Calls to that number were made repeatedly.

There were calls to other numbers made frequently, but only one number stood out as a close second to the girlfriend's. I highlighted that number and wrote it in my notebook. I pushed Harding's report to the side.

Next, I reviewed Olivia Rizzuto's report. I found calls and texts to Leon's number on the Thursday night Victor Bachmann was murdered. Prior to that, there were four unanswered calls. The same number was called and texted multiple times each day before that Thursday night. After those unanswered calls, Olivia Rizzuto's phone never attempted to contact that number again.

A reasonable assumption could be made the phone number previously belonged to Roman McCurdy. Knowing McCurdy's phone number, I reached for our call sheet on cell providers. Both Leon Harding and Olivia

Rizzuto had purchased their cell phones from the same company. I bet McCurdy had done the same.

It took less than three minutes to confirm my suspicions. McCurdy's phone number was also affiliated with the MetroPCS network. That surprised me. I thought for sure it would have been one of the lesser-known networks, the ones associated with burner phones—the type a person might throw away if a cop were approaching. But MetroPCS was that middle tier and provided an option to those customers on a limited budget. They offered the same brands and styles of cell phones as the major networks.

I set to work on three warrants for MetroPCS.

First, I wanted all the records associated with Roman McCurdy's phone for twelve hours after Victor Bachman left The Playground. That meant calls, texts, and the cell-site location information (CSLI) log. The CSLI log showed which towers McCurdy's phone pinged and where those towers were located. This gave me a general idea of the phone's location at that time.

Second, I wanted the texts from Olivia Rizzuto's phone to Leon Harding's. That would truly show me what was said. I also wanted the cell phone tower pings for twenty-four hours after Victor Bachman left the bar. Not only did I believe it would show me Roman McCurdy and Olivia Rizzuto went to Victor Bachman's house, but I wanted to know where they went next.

And finally, I wanted the cell phone tower pings for Leon Harding's phone. This would collaborate his story that he stayed at home with Jennifer Desouza. He could have easily left his phone at her place and gone to wherever Roman was, but she alibied him. A phone wasn't a strong alibi, but it would put another piece of evidence into his corner and allow me to believe his story.

Afterward, I completed three warrants for the actual phones. I wanted to collect them from McCurdy, Rizzuto, and Harding when I saw them next. McCurdy might have disposed of his, but I still wanted to be prepared.

It took about two hours to complete the six warrants. I needed a judge to sign them. The one on call this weekend was the guy I had most hoped to avoid.

***

Judge Whitaker opened the door to his north Spokane home. Located in the Windermere neighborhood, the Upper Spokane River ran behind it. A slew of cars lined the half-moon driveway, and more were parked along the street. Colorful balloons were staked into the manicured lawn.

I rang the doorbell and waited for several moments. When Whitaker opened the door, he seemed surprised to see me.

"Nash, this better be important. We're celebrating my grandson's birthday."

Whitaker was a man in his mid-sixties. He had a shock of white hair and piercing steel-gray eyes.

Behind him, a group of children ran by, screaming and laughing.

"I'm sorry to interrupt, sir. This is important." I handed him a folder containing the various warrants. "They're related to a homicide."

He accepted the file and frowned. "Give me a rundown."

I explained the case as quickly as I could.

Whitaker's brow furrowed. "Didn't I just sign these for Higgins?"

"You signed the initial warrant for Rizzuto and Harding, but all we got were the call logs. Now we want their text messages and tower pings."

The judge cocked his head. "Wouldn't it have been prudent to request that the first time?"

"Our goal at the time was to locate the cell phone belonging to Mr. McCurdy." I tapped Roman's warrant. "We now know that number. From our pursuant investigation, we believe there may have been relevant text exchanges. The tower pings may show the suspects in the proximity of the deceased."

Whitaker read the warrants while I talked.

"And this couldn't have waited until Monday?"

"Perhaps, sir, but it takes the cell service provider time to get this information."

The judge looked up. He studied me for a moment, then slowly nodded. "All right. Got a pen?"

I handed him one, and he turned to the wall. He held each up and signed them. "Haven't seen you in some time," he muttered.

"Been awhile."

Whitaker handed back the folder and the pen. He then motioned inside. "I need to run. Otherwise, I'd stay and chat."

Before I could thank him for signing, he shut the door. I suppose that was better than discussing the rumors about my mental health. I turned and left his house.

***

"Dallas, this is my wife, Brooke." Parker beamed as he motioned toward a dark-haired woman. She was nothing as I expected.

Brooke Parker stood roughly the same height as her husband. She had a round, attractive face with laughing green eyes and full brows. Brooke wasn't the lean, sinewy woman I imagined Parker to spend his time with. Instead, she curved exaggeratedly in all the right places that a men's magazine from the 1950s would have celebrated. She wore a red shirt, black shorts, and black canvas shoes. Unlike her husband's fake gym tan, Brooke's skin was pale.

We stood in the foyer of their South Hill home. Some soft piano music played from the living room.

Brooke grabbed my offered hand with both of hers. She didn't shake it, though. She simply held it. Her smile was genuine, and it exposed bright white teeth. "It's extremely nice to meet you, Dallas. Andrew speaks very highly of you."

I handed her a bottle of wine I stopped to pick up from a grocery store along the way. I'd already forgotten the brand. "For you."

"You didn't have to." Her smile brightened further. She accepted the bottle and then clutched it to her chest. "But thank you."

"And these are the girls," Parker said with evident pride.

Three young children huddled nearby. They giggled as if they shared a secret.

Parker lightly patted each girl on the head as he announced their names, moving from oldest to youngest. "Hailey, Charlotte, and Willow."

I bowed slightly. "It's nice to meet you."

The three girls each said the same thing back.

"All right, everyone," Brooke said, "dinner's ready."

I raised an eyebrow. "Already?"

Brooke smiled. "When you're raising Andrew and three kids, food is no joking matter."

***

Dinner for Brooke, the children, and me was beautiful hamburgers with pineapple rings, sweet potato fries with spicy ketchup, and cut watermelon.

Parker ate a grilled chicken breast with no sauce, a heap of grilled vegetables, and cut watermelon. He ate it hungrily and happily. There wasn't any discussion from the family about the difference in meals. It all seemed natural to them.

The dinner conversation included the children. Brooke carefully ensured each girl got an appropriate amount of stage time. Parker laughed and smiled throughout the entire meal. I caught him several times watching his wife the way I used to watch Bobbie.

I changed my mind about them. I think she would have liked the Parkers.

Brooke reached for my plate. "Did you save room for dessert?"

"There's dessert?"

"She made an apple pie," Parker said. "You're gonna love it."

"Homemade?"

Brooke's brow furrowed. "You question my piemaking skills?"

"Not at all, but I'm surprised Parker's going to eat some."

"Andrew makes an allowance for my baking."

He held his thumb and forefinger about an inch apart. "That's it."

"If he eats more than that," Brooke said, "I'd quit making them."

Parker smiled satisfactorily. "We make a good team."

Brooke set the plates in the sink. "I'll clean up here and then come get you two when dessert is ready."

Parker took me out to his garage. It was filled with a fair amount of stuff most families have—bikes, children's toys, sports equipment, and some tools. The walls had a smattering of movie posters featuring the likes of Arnold Schwarzenegger, Sylvester Stallone, and Mark Wahlberg.

A waist-high refrigerator stood in the corner. Parker opened it. "Beer? I got light and ultra-lights."

"Light," I said.

Parker handed me a can of Coors Light and opened a bottle of Michelob Ultra for himself. He then opened the garage door, so we could look out into his neighborhood. His and Brooke's cars were parked in their driveway. Mine was on the street.

Several boys raced past the house on their BMX bikes. One of them waved at us. Parker motioned back.

He turned on a small clock radio sitting on the workbench. It was tuned to a local classic rock station. A song I used to love in high school came on. The volume was soft, and the speaker sounded tinny. I was glad I could barely hear the music.

"We don't drink around the girls," Parker said. I had wondered why they hadn't popped the bottle of wine I brought for them. "We feel it wouldn't set a good example."

"Is that a church thing?"

"Say what?"

"I didn't know if you guys maybe went to church."

A smirk grew before he laughed. "Fuck, no." He flinched and glanced toward the door to the house. "I don't swear around the girls either."

"Probably a good rule."

He shrugged. "I don't know. It's a mess out there." He pointed toward his neighborhood, but I understood what he meant. "Maybe it's stupid to try and protect them from the occasional bad word or seeing us have a beer when the whole world is on fire, but we want them to hold on to their childhood as long as they can."

I sipped my beer.

"Did you ever want kids?"

The thoughts from earlier in the day returned briefly. I shrugged.

"It's not too late, you know? Guys can have them until they die." Parker scrunched his nose. "Although, it hits a point of being gross. Like old actors getting their young wives pregnant." He stuck out his tongue. "Blech."

We stood silent for a few moments, and I tried to ignore the tinny music coming from the clock radio.

"Hear you caught a couple of cases this week," Parker said. "How they looking?"

When he invited me, he said he didn't want to talk about work, but something in the way he asked this question sounded funny. Like he didn't really want to talk about the cases but was leading into something.

"They're fine," I said.

"That's good." He sipped his beer and nodded. He didn't make eye contact but instead stared out into his neighborhood.

The silence between us returned, and we both nodded like a couple of idiots. A commercial played on the radio for Banner Fuel. It had a catchy jingle. I hoped it wouldn't stick in my head.

"You seeing anyone?" Parker asked.

"Excuse me?"

Parker's eyelids drooped, and he shook his head. "That sounded stupid. Never mind."

I eyed him.

"Brooke made me ask."

"That's why she grabbed you before we came out?"

Parker nodded. "She likes setting people up. I'll tell her I forgot to ask you about it."

"I'm not dating anyone, but I have a friend."

"A friend?" His eyes narrowed. "Like with benefits?"

"Just a friend."

"Oh." He sipped his beer.

A few seconds passed before I said, "You know her."

He cocked his head. "I do?"

"Marlene Anderson."

I don't know why I told Parker her name, especially after such a nice dinner. What good could come from it? None that I could see. There was certainly a lot of bad that might result from sharing it, though.

Parker's gaze drifted downward, and his head soon followed the same trajectory as he struggled to recall her name. When he latched on to it, his attention returned to me. "The prostitute?"

"She's a counselor now."

"Shit. Yeah. Right." He closed his eyes briefly and shook his head once. "I'm sorry, Dallas. *Counselor*. I knew that."

I looked outside and wondered where the kids on the BMX bikes went.

"You see each other?"

"For coffee and lunch." I shrugged. "Dinner occasionally." There was no reason to add the latter. What was I hoping would happen?

"That's cool." Parker studied his beer. "She seemed nice when I talked with her. Real professional." He nodded several times as if his words weren't enough to show he was okay with me seeing Marlene.

The silence returned to our conversation. Parker finished his beer and dropped the bottle into a small trash can. "Another?"

"Still working on this one."

"I'm gonna have one more." He went to the fridge. When he returned, he said, "If you like her, why don't you be with her? To hell with what anyone else thinks."

Even if I didn't want to get involved with Marlene, I didn't want to get into this discussion with Parker. If that were true, why did I mention her name to him?

I stared outside. The kids on the BMX bikes rolled past again. I raised my beer in a toast, but none waved back.

Parker asked, "Do you like what we do?"

His question's bluntness surprised me. "You mean being a cop?"

He shook his head. "Major Crimes."

I tugged the pull top of my beer and snapped it on the can. "Some days, the job feels like the only thing holding me together."

"Because of what happened to your wife?"

I nodded. I could have elaborated more on it, but why? First, Marlene and now Bobbie. Geez. I wondered if this night could get any weirder.

Parker eyed me. "Are you seeing a therapist?"

I turned abruptly to him.

He lifted an apologetic hand. "I'm sorry if I'm prying, but Jessie said he saw you coming out of that building where the department shrink is, and I heard some other guys talking about you. Sorry if you didn't know."

My face warmed, and I did my best to keep myself under control.

He started to say something, but he stopped and lowered his gaze. He sipped once from his beer, nodded twice, and then looked up. "Does it help?"

The earnestness in his eyes was unmistakable.

Parker looked toward the workbench. "If you're going, I mean. Maybe you're not. Maybe it's all a mistake. But if you are, has it helped with whatever you've got going on in your life?"

I studied him. "Why do you ask?"

He waved off my question. "It doesn't matter. Forget it."

A few minutes earlier, Andrew Parker might have been the happiest guy I'd seen in a long time. He laughed with his children. He looked longingly toward his wife. It was clear how much he adored his family.

Out here in the garage was a tortured man who ached to ask about therapy, but something held him back. I quickly replayed our conversation. Where had it gone wrong?

Parker absently picked at the label on his beer.

"Do *you* like what we do?" I asked.

He stopped pulling at the paper and looked at me. His lips rolled into his mouth, and he inhaled deeply through his nose. Parker held his breath for several moments before announcing, "I fucking hate it."

The door to the garage opened, and Brooke stuck her head out. She smiled and said, "Dessert's ready."

Parker's eyes softened, and he smiled at his wife. "I can't wait."

He set his bottle on the workbench, and that's the last we talked about therapy.

17

My phone buzzed, and I sat up from the couch.

I hadn't been sleeping. I'd been lying there, listening to another neighbor mowing their lawn. It was a reminder it was Sunday. I should trim mine, too.

My lawn was previously a lush green, trimmed tight along the curb. No weeds sprouted in barked areas. Now, the grass had yellowed in spots and seemed to grow in neurotic spurts. Dandelions were everywhere.

If I didn't get to the lawn today, there was always tomorrow.

I reached for the phone as it buzzed again. The display showed Glenn was calling. My thumb swiped across the screen to answer.

"You awake?" he asked.

"Just lying here."

"It's after eight."

Glenn didn't normally call on my days off. We were partners, not friends. When I didn't respond, he continued.

"How was your dinner with Parker?"

I rubbed a knuckle into my eye. Is that really why he called? "His family is nice."

"What about his wife? Is she a freak like him? I bet she's a freak."

"Is there a purpose to this call, or did you only want to gossip?"

"Gossip *is* a purpose." He laughed.

Why was he so happy? Whatever it was, I didn't want to deal with it.

"I haven't had my coffee yet," I said. "I'm hanging up."

"Wait."

I heard him even though I lowered the phone to end the call. I switched it to speakerphone, so I didn't have to hold it next to my ear. "Yeah?"

"Patrol found Sabina Wrencher. They're transporting her to the station. I'm heading down there now."

I forced my eyes wider and looked at the ceiling. "I need to shower."

"It'll take them some time to get Gypsy there but make it quick."

"I also need to grab something to eat." I thought about the piece of apple pie in my refrigerator Brooke Parker sent home with me last night.

"Well, get a move on, buddy boy. The day's already half over."

"You said it was eight."

"After eight. It's a great day to be alive, Dallas." He sounded chipper. And what was with his "buddy boy" comment?

"Why are you in such a good mood?"

He chuckled. "Funny you should ask."

I remembered and groaned. "The fighter pilot."

"What can I say?"

"Have you two been together since Friday night?"

"You should be a detective." His voice turned serious. "Seriously, though. Get a move on. I'm already headed that way."

A car door slammed, and the call ended.

***

Sabina Wrencher sat in the small interview room. She wasn't handcuffed to the railing running the length of the short wall. A table sat between her and Glenn. He had a closed manila folder and a yellow notepad in front of him. A can of Coca-Cola and a Snickers bar sat near her.

I stood in the corner, watching the two.

Sabina wore the same tattered clothes from our previous contact. Her hair remained a tangled mess, and dirt smudged her sunburned face. She stank horribly—like a mixture of rancid body odor, feces, and urine. There also seemed to be a hint of gasoline, but that might have been my imagination hoping for something more pleasant.

Glenn's face didn't show any emotion. "We appreciate you coming down to talk with us."

"Yeah, sure." She swiped the can off the table. Her dirty hands held the can to her stomach as she slumped back into her chair. "They made it seem like I didn't have much of a choice."

"You have a choice, Sabina."

"Gypsy," she corrected.

Glenn lifted a deferential hand. "Gypsy," he said. "You have a choice. If you want to end this interview, you can leave right now."

"For real?"

The funk from Sabina was so bad I wanted to open the interview room's door, but doing so might send the wrong signal. I didn't want her to walk out. Telling her she could leave was one thing but showing her the path was something entirely different. I crossed my arms and casually reached up to pinch my nose.

Glenn set his hand on the yellow notepad. "If you leave, that'll mean we have to believe what Mango said."

Sabina's brow furrowed. "What's he saying?"

"Tell me about your relationship with Mango."

She smacked her thumb twice against the top of the soda can before popping open the cap. The soda inside sizzled. Sabina tilted the can back and drank deeply. When her head returned to its normal position, she looked at me. Her face reddened, and her lip curled. "You going to stand there all day?"

"Don't worry about him," Glenn said.

"I don't like the way he's looking at me."

"He's the one that brought you the soda and the candy bar."

She glanced down at the can and furrowed her brow. "He's not trying to poison me, is he?"

"It was sealed," Glenn said.

"They got ways. If the government can plant tracking chips in our heads, they can put poison in our Cokes." She sipped from the can again. "I pay attention to these things. I know all the ways they can get me."

"So, Mango?"

She set the can on the table and reached for the candy bar. "What about him?"

"Tell me about your relationship."

Sabina pushed the candy bar repeatedly through a circle created by the forefinger and thumb of her opposite hand. "He wasn't as good as advertised." She ripped open the candy bar. "Don't tell a girl you're magnificent and fail to deliver the goods." She was about to bite into the candy bar when she stopped and pointed at me with it. "What about this? You poison it?"

"No."

Her eyes narrowed, and she hesitantly bit into the bar. Finding the taste to her pleasure, she nodded a couple of times. Sabina extended the candy to Glenn. "Want some?"

"No, thank you. And you were having a relationship with Richard Ranger, too?"

Her smile revealed chocolate on her teeth. "*Richard*. No one ever called him that, but yeah, we—" She pushed the partially eaten candy bar back through the circle of her forefinger and thumb. "—did it. So what?"

Sabina happily chomped on the chocolate.

Glenn's left hand settled on the manila folder. "We found a pocket watch in Mango's belongings."

"That's Ranger's." She snatched the soda from the table and drank heavily.

I couldn't handle the stink any further and moved toward the door. I cracked it open. Unfortunately, it was the weekend, and the HVAC equipment wasn't moving the air at peak efficiency. The bad smell hung in the small room, it clung to my clothes, and it remained in my nose.

Through it all, Glenn remained poker-faced. "Mango said you gave it to him."

Sabina's chewing slowed, and she faced me. "Stop watching me." She turned back to Glenn. "Can you make him stop?"

"Please answer the question."

She lifted the candy bar and the soda can. "This is bullshit. You think you can buy me with this stuff?" She stood. "I'm outta here."

Glenn pointed at her chair. "You're not going anywhere."

"Huh?"

He flicked a switch in the wall. The light above them glowed red. "We're being recorded now. Both audio and visual. Do you understand? The camera can see and hear us." He removed the Miranda Warning Card from the manila folder. "Sabina Wrencher, I'm advising you of your rights."

She glanced at me. "What'd I do?"

"Listen to him."

"You have the right to remain silent," Glenn said.

Sabina stood dumbly watching my partner as he read the rest of the Miranda Warning. It wasn't the first time she'd heard the rights, so she likely remembered the process.

When Glenn finished reading, she dropped into her chair. "Did I do something to make you mad?"

"Do you understand each of these rights as I have explained to you?"

Sabina lifted her hands slightly. "Yeah."

"Having these rights in mind, do you wish to talk to me now?"

"I don't know. What'd I do?"

"Yes or no," Glenn said. "Do you wish to talk to me?"

"Yeah, fine. What'd I do?"

He didn't bother asking her to sign the Warning Card. Her agreement to the questions was recorded. "You asked Mango to beat up Ranger."

"No." Sabina shook her head. "I wouldn't. You can't prove I did nothing like that."

"Mango said Ranger didn't want anything to do with you."

Sabina bit into the candy bar. She chewed once, then sipped the soda. "That's not true. Ranger loved me. He wanted to marry me."

"You never said anything about that the first time we met."

Sabina glanced at me and then quickly looked back to Glenn. "I musta forgot."

"You forgot Ranger wanted to marry you?"

"It happens."

"Do you know Pete Decker?"

Her face darkened. "Mr. Fancy Pants. What about him?"

"He knew Ranger. Knows you, too."

"So? I once met Ronald McDonald. What's that prove?"

Glenn tapped his forefinger against the table. "Pete also said Ranger didn't want anything to do with you."

Sabina sneered. "That's not true. We fucked."

"So you said."

"That means he wanted something to do with me. That's what that means!"

"Ranger told Decker you wouldn't leave him alone. He started camping alone because he wanted to avoid you."

She kicked a table leg. "That's a damn lie!"

"Mango said the same thing."

"He's a liar, too." Her face reddened, and she looked in my direction. "Stop watching me!"

Sabina's fascination with my observing her was becoming a distraction. I casually moved toward the door. I would watch the interview from the observation room.

"Ranger didn't want your affections," Glenn said, "so you got Mango to assault him."

"No!"

"Mango thought you two were going to get back together. Unfortunately, Mango did too good of a job, and Ranger died."

"Shut up!" Sabina threw the half-empty can of soda at Glenn. He moved, and it hit the back wall. Liquid squirted upward upon impact. Glenn leaned over, picked up the can so it would stop leaking, and set it against the wall.

I froze with my hand on the doorknob. I wasn't leaving the room now.

"You went to check on Ranger, but he was already dead," Glenn continued, unfazed. "Isn't that what really happened?"

"No!" Sabina looked down at the chocolate bar in her hands. "Mango killed him all by himself."

"You didn't mean for any of it to happen, did you, Gypsy? You didn't want Ranger to die, did you? You only wanted Mango to rough him up."

Sabina didn't look up when she set the remaining candy bar on the table.

"Isn't that right?" Glenn asked. "That's why you took the pocket watch. Because Mango went too far with the beating. He was only supposed to knock Ranger around, but Mango took it too far. So you wanted to get back at Mango. That's why you gave him the pocket watch and told us about it. Then you called us about finding Ranger."

Sabina bolted from her chair and lunged toward the door, but I had already blocked the exit. She swung at me, and I wrestled her to the ground. She screamed and twisted as I fought for control.

Her left arm shot backward, and her elbow hit me in the head. I didn't let go. I outweighed her by forty pounds, so my body remained on top of hers.

"Stop resisting," I yelled.

My hands latched onto her right arm, and I yanked it upward behind her back. She howled in pain.

Glenn joined the melee then and grabbed her other arm.

She screeched as we ratcheted a set of handcuffs around her wrists. When we pulled her upright to her feet, Sabina spat. Phlegm hit my shirt. She kicked Glenn in the shin. He jerked her by the elbow and then shoved her into the wall.

He leaned his shoulder into her back. "Stop fighting."

Spittle flew as she shrieked. "You're killing me! You're killing me!"

Glenn said, "Call a supervisor. Let's get someone down here before we book her."

Even though the camera was recording her antics, having an on-duty supervisor witness her behavior was a good idea.

I stepped just outside of the room. While calling dispatch from my cell phone, I kept Glenn and Sabina in sight.

***

I arrived at Marlene's house unannounced.

Sadie opened the door and smiled. "Dallas!"

"Hi, kiddo." I knelt. "How's the arm?"

She held up her cast. "Wanna sign it?"

Before I could answer, Marlene stepped around the corner and put a hand on her daughter's head. "Go inside, honey."

Sadie looked up at her mother. "But it's—"

"I know who it is. Go inside."

"It's okay," I said to Sadie. "I'll see you later."

"Bye, Dallas." The little girl hung her head and tromped to her bedroom.

Marlene stood in the entryway and put her hand on the door, blocking any access to the house. "What are you doing here?"

"I came to apologize."

"You have nothing to apologize for."

"I didn't text you back yesterday."

Her jaw flexed, but she didn't respond.

"I should have called."

"But you didn't. It's becoming a habit with you, Dallas."

A moment passed, and we watched each other.

She broke the impasse. "It's Sunday evening. You waited the whole weekend to respond. That says more than enough."

"I worked today." My head bobbled from side to side. "That's a weak excuse, I know."

"No kidding, that's weak. You could have called at any time. Two minutes is all it would have taken."

"I know."

"A text would have taken less."

"I know," I repeated.

"Christ, Dallas. It's no secret how I feel about you. How I want you to feel about me."

I looked down at my shoes.

"I can't help it," Marlene said, "but if you're going to shit on me because of it, I don't need you in my life. God knows, there are other men who will do the same."

"Listen—"

"If you're going to give me some macho bullshit about my past as an excuse for why you're acting this way, I don't need it."

I met her gaze now. "Who you were is who you were. That's not what this is about."

"Then what is it?"

"I don't know."

She threw her hands in the air.

"Marlene, I'm serious. I think the world of you."

"You're not showing it."

"But I've only loved one woman. My whole life, there was only one."

Her eyes narrowed.

My lips felt dry, and my throat was tight. "I don't know how to move on, to get over her, to love anyone else." I rubbed my face. "No one ever broke my heart the way she did. Do you understand?"

It was a dumb question to ask. Marlene's life was filled with heartbreak. If anyone could understand a broken heart—

She inhaled deeply and slowly let it out. "She died, Dallas. She didn't break your heart."

Tears welled in my eyes. "You're wrong."

We stared at each other for a moment.

Marlene's hand slipped from the doorknob, and she crossed her arms. "I've never been loved the way you loved her, the way you still love her." She shook her head and looked over my shoulder into the neighborhood. "I'm jealous, Dal. I'm fucking jealous of a dead woman." Her gaze returned to me. "I'm sorry if that sounds terrible, but she's had what I haven't and it's something I want."

I checked my shoes again. They hadn't changed since the last time I looked down.

"I would never ask you to stop loving her."

I nodded but didn't lift my gaze.

"But I'm not going to wait if you continue treating me like something on the bottom of your shoe."

"I would never—"

"You are, and you keep doing it."

"I'm sorry." The phrase wasn't enough to express how badly I felt, but I couldn't find the correct words then. I stepped back. "Why don't I call you later?"

"Wait." Marlene pushed the door open. She glanced over her shoulder into the house as if deciding something. When she looked at me again, Marlene forced a smile. It wasn't filled with the kindness usually there, but it was still a smile. "Sadie and I were going for an afternoon picnic at the park. You can come with if you like."

"I don't know."

"No pressure. Just friends."

Little footsteps hurried across the room.

Sadie slipped under her mother's arm. "Please, Dallas! Come with us."

Marlene cocked her head. "I thought I told you to go to your room?"

She looked up at her mother. "You said go inside. That's where I was." Sadie smiled at me. "So you'll come? You can sign my cast!"

***

Later, I stood in the entryway of my house and embraced the silence. Bobbie was there with me. I slowed my breathing, closed my eyes, and searched for her memories.

The refrigerator kicked on, and its motor hummed. Before I could mutter an expletive, my phone buzzed. My eyes remained closed with the futile hope the refrigerator's motor would suddenly fail. The phone buzzed a second time. I pulled it from my pocket and opened my eyes.

"Nash," I said.

"Your brother comes home after being gone for a couple weeks, and that's how he's greeted?" Dean laughed. "Geez, Dallas, I'm starting to think you're on the spectrum."

"Sorry."

"What's your week look like?"

The pictures, I thought. He wanted to get together and talk about his trip.

"You know how it is."

"I know how you are. Thursday. Our house. Bring yourself. No need to bring anything unless you want to bring a lady friend." His voice rose slightly.

I thought of Marlene. She had said she wanted to go to Italy.

"Maybe."

"No maybes about it. Thursday."

I stepped into the house. "Okay, Thursday. I might bring a friend. Her daughter, too, if that's okay."

"Yeah, sure, Dallas. You bet. That'd be great."

"She's just a friend."

"Whatever you say."

18

When my computer came to life, I entered my password and waited for the system to run through its start-up process. I called up my emails and sifted through the usual weekend clutter.

Two emails came in from the city's Human Resources department. The first was filled with nonsensical garbage like heart-healthy recipes, tips to drink more water, and ways to increase my happiness through walking. I deleted it. The other email was a reminder to update my beneficiary file. I hadn't changed it from Bobbie yet, and this was their fourth reminder. I deleted that one, too.

A third email lingered from a MetroPCS address. I opened it and read the brief salutation. Attached was the information requested by the Roman McCurdy warrant. My pulse quickened as I double-clicked on the file. The excitement wasn't lost on me. I felt like a kid at Christmas.

A letter from a company representative was at the beginning of the file. It explained the first part of the file was the call log for the days the warrant requested. The letter also explained the second part of the file included a cell-site location information log.

I scrolled to the top of McCurdy's records. The last activity on his phone was four calls from Olivia Rizzuto's phone number. They came in shortly after Victor Bachman left The Playground. That would coincide with the time McCurdy discovered his phone missing.

No calls ever originated from McCurdy's phone again.

I thought about reviewing The Playground's security footage, but I'd seen it enough times to remember it.

Ruby Louden had stolen Roman McCurdy's cell phone. When McCurdy realized his phone was missing, he asked his girlfriend to call it. Olivia Rizzuto dialed his number but got no answer—the cell phone records now proved as much.

When Glenn and I originally discussed the case, he suggested Roman McCurdy kept his phone's ringer silent. If that were the case, Olivia Rizzuto's four phone calls wouldn't have had any effect since the phone sat in the backseat of Victor Bachman's car.

No calls originated from McCurdy's phone after Rizzuto's attempts—ever. The phone number was canceled the day after Bachman's murder.

I moved to the CSLI log. It wasn't as helpful as a GPS log which would be stored on the cell phone itself. That information could have put me within five feet of McCurdy's location the night of Bachman's murder. Based upon Jennifer Desouza's claim and the fact McCurdy canceled the number, I now believed the missing phone was beyond my reach, even though I had a signed warrant for it.

However, the cell phone company had provided the initial data, which showed McCurdy's phone using a tower around The Playground. We could apply for an additional search warrant and ask the company to pull historical records to triangulate the signal. It would take more time but it would dial in a better location. It still wouldn't be as exact as GPS, but it could get us within an area roughly the size of a city block.

McCurdy's phone records showed he'd been on the same tower for more than two hours before it began moving shortly after Victor Bachman left The Playground. The phone hopped two towers as it moved across town and stopped on a third when it got into an area roughly fifteen blocks from where Victor Bachman lived. This wasn't near enough to prove anything, however. An old adage says close only counts in horseshoes and hand grenades. Fifteen blocks wasn't going to win anything before a jury.

The missing phone pinged off this cell tower until it stopped at 12:17 a.m. on Friday morning.

I leaned back and crossed my arms. I now firmly believed McCurdy tracked his phone to Bachman's house, found it in the back of the Mustang, and killed Bachman. Or perhaps he had Olivia Rizzuto do it. Either way, one of them killed the man. Then McCurdy deactivated the phone. Perhaps he broke the phone or removed the battery. We didn't find any evidence of a smashed phone on Bachman's front lawn, so it must have occurred away from the scene.

A message box popped up in the corner of my screen to announce the arrival of a new email. The salutation inside stated the attached files included the text message records from Leon Harding's and Olivia Rizzuto's text message records.

My pulse quickened again as I opened the file and read the texts sent by Roman from Olivia's phone to Leon's.

***

By the time Glenn walked in, I was putting the finishing touches on a new search warrant for Roman McCurdy's phone records. This one would request triangulated histories for the times corresponding to when McCurdy's phone was stolen until right before it stopped pinging towers.

Glenn dropped heavily into his chair. "You're here early."

"We got him," I said.

"Who?"

"McCurdy. His cell phone records came in." I sent the new warrant to the printer and stood. "We need to locate him, his girlfriend, and his cousin, too."

"How can I help?"

"Grab the warrant from the printer. Get a judge to sign it."

"There are other judges besides Whitaker."

"It's Monday. He's no longer on call."

Glenn frowned. "What I'm saying is, maybe they all haven't heard what he has."

"That's not what I'm worried about." I grabbed the desk phone. "Let's catch a killer."

He grabbed the edge of his desk and pulled himself to his feet. "I didn't even get to tell you about this weekend."

I ignored his complaint and dialed SIU. It was answered on the first ring.

"Hackworth," the voice on the other end of the line said.

Glenn shuffled off, muttering to himself.

"It's Nash. I need your help."

After I explained what I wanted, the sergeant laughed. "Dallas, this is why I like you. We would love to help."

***

Leon Harding leaned against the side of his Nissan Sentra. "This is some bullshit, yo."

Sergeant Hackworth and one of his men stood nearby. They had stopped Harding as he traveled southbound on Crestline Street. After patting him down, they removed his cell phone and put it on the car's hood.

"We could have done this down at the station, Leon."

He disgustedly waved his right hand while his left hand grabbed his crotch. Leon faced me and said, "But I didn't do nothing."

I opened the manila folder. "These text messages look familiar, Leon?"

He leaned in and read the transcript his cell phone provider had sent. His eyes widened. "This is some bullshit, yo."

"But these are your texts, right?"

"You can't do that."

"A judge said differently."

"Do you want to add anything?" Hackworth asked.

Leon looked at the sergeant. "What do you mean?"

"I mean, we're snatching Roman right now. His girl, too. You know the rules—who speaks first, wins."

Leon threw his hands into the air and spun in place. "Yo! This is some bullshit."

He had a one-track mind when it came to protesting his detainment.

"You aren't leaving here until you start talking," Hackworth said.

Leon's face reddened. "What did I do?"

I lifted a hand to calm him down. "Leon, we've got everyone's cell phone records."

His face slackened. "You got mine, too?"

"How do you think I got the text messages?"

Leon blinked repeatedly. "Well, yeah, I guess that makes sense."

Hackworth cocked his head. "You sure?"

"There's nothing in there." Leon pointed at the papers I held. "I didn't say anything bad."

"Roman said he needed your help getting his phone back."

"But I didn't help. I didn't do nothing."

"So be it, but here's where things stand." I wriggled the papers. "Roman and Olivia killed a man—the *wrong* man."

Leon's brow creased. "What?"

"The guy they killed didn't take Roman's phone. Someone else did and threw it into this guy's car as a joke."

"I don't know what you're talking about."

"The woman who took it said she did it as a goof. Can you believe that? For the guy who got killed, the whole thing was a case of bad luck. The question is do you want to protect yourself or do you want to go down with them? All because of bad luck."

"I didn't do nothing, yo."

"You knew what they did, and you didn't notify the cops. That's something."

Leon shook his head. "That's not a crime."

"Sure it is. It's called rendering criminal assistance."

It was a stretch. If he hadn't actively provided help to Roman McCurdy or Olivia Rizzuto, then Leon likely hadn't violated any laws. However, I wanted him to think he had and give me something additional I could use against Roman.

"I didn't render anything," Leon said.

I stared at him.

He tugged at the bottom of his shirt. "Listen, all I know is Roman got a new phone. That's it."

"He didn't tell you he killed anyone?"

Leon looked away and shook his head. "Nope."

"You remember this moment, Leon. It's going to come back to haunt you." I pulled a copy of the warrant for his cell phone from my folder. "I'm taking your cell phone."

"You can't do that!"

"That's a judge's order saying I can."

Hackworth grabbed the phone from the hood of the car and handed it to me.

"Our tech guys are going to process your GPS history. When we're done with it, you can pick it up. If you didn't help Roman as you said, then you got nothing to worry about."

He flicked his hand. "This is some bullshit."

"This is your last chance to come clean," I said.

"I already said everything I have to say."

Sergeant Hackworth stepped forward. "Just so you know, after we put Roman away—and you know that's going to happen—you are going to become my focus, my pet project. You know how much Roman likes my focus, right? I'm sure he talks to you about it."

Leon swallowed with some difficulty but didn't look away from the sergeant.

Hackworth leaned closer into Leon's face. His nose almost touched the man's cheek. "Think about it, Leon. Every moment of every day, my team is gonna crawl up your scrawny white ass. That girl of yours? She's gonna get real tired of all the cops in your life. Maybe one of my boys will even take a real interest in her personal life."

"What does that mean?"

"Maybe we'll start talking to her mother."

Leon leaned away from the sergeant and turned to me. He licked his lips and looked around before announcing, "I want a lawyer."

"And here I thought you were the smart one," Hackworth said. He grabbed Leon by the arm and shoved him toward one of the SIU guys. "Put him in the car."

When Leon was out of earshot, he said, "We've got McCurdy and Rizzuto down at the station. We'll hold this one as long as you want."

"If you got those two, you can let this one go."

Hackworth shrugged. "I might hold on to him for a few minutes—seeing as how he's going to be my new project. Then we'll kick him loose."

I headed toward my car. Hoping to get something from Leon was a long shot. Now, I would have to go into the interviews and hope to turn McCurdy and Rizzuto against each other.

***

Olivia Rizzuto signed the white Miranda Warning card and pushed it across the metal table toward me. "You people. First, your goons take me outta my work, and now I gotta waste time with this. I'm probably gonna lose my job, you know?"

We sat at the small table in the first interview room. A metal railing ran the length of the short wall. Arrestees would normally be handcuffed. Olivia had been detained, so she wasn't hooked to the bar.

Overhead, the fluorescent lights buzzed, and the air-conditioning hummed. The moving air was a nice change from the stuffy interview with Sabina Wrencher over the weekend.

Glenn stood in the corner of the room with his arms crossed. Outside, a group of SIU officers waited. Two brought in Olivia, while three others brought in Roman McCurdy.

Between Olivia and me sat a clear plastic bag. Inside were the items she had carried in her pockets when picked up for questioning—keys, vape pen, ChapStick, a condom, and her cell phone.

I tucked the Miranda card into the manila folder under my left hand. "As a reminder," I said, "we're being recorded." I pointed to the illuminated red light above us.

Olivia looked much the same way she did when I first met her. Her short black hair was tucked behind her ears. The full lashes and dark red lipstick still made her appear as if she were trying for a modeling gig that didn't exist. The blue scrub shirt looked out of place inside an interview room. The tattoos down the length of her arms were in stark contrast to her work garb.

She smirked. "We couldn't have done this over the phone?"

"No."

"Why not? You could have come by my apartment. I gave you the address the last time we talked."

"The last time we talked, you weren't honest."

Olivia eyed Glenn. "You brought some muscle today. Think I'm going to cause a problem?"

The left side of Glenn's face lifted into a cocky smile. I'm sure I would hear about that muscle comment for some time.

Her gaze shifted back to me. "And how was I not honest, huh? I told the truth. What did I say that wasn't?"

Interviewing suspects is an art form. There are times when dancing with them is necessary. Establishing a rapport and letting them believe we have their best interests at heart is important. We lead them to their confessions—much like a trainer directs a horse to water—where they can drink deeply from a pool of honesty. There are other moments with suspects when it's better to confront them head-on. There's no advantage to being nice since they are the type who see kindness as a weakness.

Olivia Rizzuto seemed to be one of the latter.

I opened the manila folder, removed a copy of a search warrant, and slid it to her. "This is for you."

"What is it?"

"We're taking your cell phone." I pulled the clear plastic bag to me.

"The fuck you are." She snatched the bag and tried to pull it back.

"Let go."

"It's my phone!"

"Let go."

"I want a lawyer!"

"Fine, but we're still taking the phone."

Glenn crossed the room and grabbed her wrists. She reluctantly released the bag. Glenn then let go of her.

Olivia smacked the table and glared at me. "That's why you needed the muscle."

I removed the phone from the plastic bag and handed it to Glenn. He dropped it into his pocket and returned to the corner.

"You can't take that," she said. "It's mine."

I slid the folder in front of me. "We'll give you a receipt."

"Fuck a receipt. When do I get it back?"

"When we're done with it."

She dropped back into her chair. "What are you going to do with it?"

"You still want that lawyer?"

Olivia crossed her arms defiantly. "Yes."

Glenn moved toward the door, and I stood.

"Hey," she said. "Where're you going?"

"If you want a lawyer, we're done talking."

Olivia's lips twisted for a moment then she nodded. "Yeah. Lawyer."

She turned and looked at the wall.

Glenn and I stepped outside.

***

"I don't need a lawyer." Roman McCurdy motioned toward the Miranda Warning card. "I'll sign that bitch. Let's go."

I slid the little white card across the table.

"We're being recorded—"

"Yeah, yeah." He scribbled his authorization on the card. "Not my first rodeo. Let's hear what you bitches got." He shoved the card across the table and leaned his chair onto its rear legs. His right hand held onto the metal railing running the length of the short wall. He wasn't handcuffed.

"Let's talk about the night—"

Roman held up his left hand. "No. You tell me what you got. When you're done, I'll tell you what I think. If you start asking me questions, I'm gonna want a lawyer. Them's the rules."

I glanced at Glenn. His face remained impassive.

Laying out a complete scenario to a suspect wasn't advisable. It was like playing a game of poker by exposing your hand while the other guy held his cards close to the vest. However, I thought I was playing with a full house, and there was little Roman could do to beat the hand we held.

Roman wore a Sacramento Kings basketball jersey, baggie sweatpants, and loose-fitting tennis shoes. Several gold chains dangled around his neck. Tattoos covered his upper chest as well as his arms. I wondered if the ink covered most of his torso.

I opened my folder and removed a time-stamped photo of Roman and Olivia Rizzuto. "You were at The Playground two Thursdays ago. So was Victor Bachman."

"Who?"

I set the picture of Bachman at the dartboards on the table. Roman didn't drop his chair on the floor. Instead, he craned his neck outward to see the photo.

"Had you met Bachman before?" I asked.

His gaze lifted upward. "No questions or I call a lawyer."

Glenn shifted his stance in the corner, but I nodded and touched the two photos.

"You and this guy were in the bar at the same time."

"So were a bunch of other people."

"Including these two." I removed a photograph of Michael Lee Boyd and Ruby Louden from the manila folder. In the picture, Ruby was reaching for Roman's cell phone, which sat at the edge of his table. "As you can see, this was the woman who stole your cell phone."

"We've been over this before. Who says my phone was stolen?"

"We know it was. Multiple people have confirmed this. I'm not asking a question here. I'm telling you what we know. Your phone was stolen."

Roman's chair fell forward, and he picked up the picture. His brow corrugated as he studied the picture.

"Do you know those two?" I asked.

He shook his head. "Never seen them before."

"I interviewed them. They said they didn't know you either."

Several moments passed before his face relaxed, and he let the picture slip from his fingers. He pushed his chair back up on its rear legs.

"If you haven't figured it out by these pictures," I said, "The Playground has video cameras. They've had some trouble in the past. Their insurance company insisted they do it. Anyway, we have a video of that whole night. We can watch it together if you like."

He shrugged. "Maybe later." He tried to affect a bored demeanor. "Get on with the story."

I pulled another photo from the folder. "This is outside. The woman threw your phone into the backseat of a Mustang belonging to this guy." I tapped the picture of Vic Bachman at the dartboards.

"Why'd she do that?" Roman asked.

"She called it a goof."

His eyes narrowed as he studied me.

"A laugh. She was messing around."

Roman's head jerked a couple of times as if he had trouble computing what I had just told him. He looked at Glenn, who nodded. Roman's attention returned to me. "A joke? But they didn't know me."

"That's right."

He clenched his jaw and inhaled deeply through his nose.

"You sure you guys didn't have an altercation that night?"

"No." Roman's face reddened. "Get on with it."

"There's a video showing Victor Bachman leaving the parking lot a few minutes after she throws the cell phone into the car. I didn't take any snapshots of it, but you can imagine it, right? That's about the same time you discovered your phone was missing. It all happened—" I snapped my fingers three times. "You looked for your phone. Olivia even called it. Four times, in fact. We have your phone records."

I opened my folder and pointed to the highlighted calls from his girlfriend.

He cocked his head.

"Your records reveal a lot." I flipped a couple of pages. "These are cell phone tower hits. This shows your cell phone being in the Hillyard area until shortly after Victor Bachman left the bar. Then there are a series of tower hits across Spokane." I tapped the table repeatedly with my fingers. "What that means is your cell phone pinged off various towers as Victor drove across town. It's more technical than I can describe, but we could get an expert to come into court and break it down nice and simple for the jury. You understand how that would work."

Roman slowly lowered his chair. He pulled his phone records from my hands and turned them so he could read them.

"Eventually, your phone pinged off a tower supporting Bachman's neighborhood." It supported a much larger area than that, but what I said was essentially true. "Your phone remained there for almost an hour. We've requested additional information from the cell phone company to triangulate the exact location of your phone. It won't be as perfect as GPS, but it should get us within a city block of Bachman's house."

Roman pushed the records away from him. "So far, all I'm hearing is I was a victim of a crime. Sort of feeling like I'm a victim of police harassment, too."

"Want to talk to a lawyer?"

Normally, I wouldn't ask, but Roman had felt confident at the beginning of this interview, and I wanted to show him I felt as confident as he was.

His mouth twisted as he thought. Eventually, he spun his hand in a circle for me to continue.

"We pulled your cousin's phone records," I said, "and saw your text exchange with him."

I thought about showing that communication but decided against it. Maybe I would later, but I wanted Roman to stew on it.

His gaze shifted toward the wall, then dropped downward. I figured he was trying to remember what he wrote. When his eyes returned to mine, he said, "What about it?"

"Do you remember what you said?"

"My phone was stolen. I never texted him."

I smiled. It was a good answer, but I reminded him of the truth. "You were using your girlfriend's phone."

"No, I wasn't." He smirked. "I don't know what you think I did, but I didn't do anything. Maybe *she* did something."

Glenn pushed off the wall. "Excuse me." He left the room.

"Look it," Roman said.

I lifted a finger and stared at the door. Glenn had left in a hurry. I thought I knew why and if he needed a minute to get set up, I would give it to him.

"Hey, man," Roman said, "I—"

"Wait."

"I'm the one getting interviewed."

"Just a second."

"Are you gonna make me call my lawyer?"

I turned to him. "Now, you want to call the lawyer? Before I'm done laying my cards on the table?"

"You aren't listening—" His lips twisted before he continued. "—and I wanna be heard."

"I'm listening."

Roman leaned over the table. "You think I killed this guy? That's what you said when we met on the street. Well, I didn't."

"We have your phone records. It shows it was in Bachman's neighborhood."

"That doesn't prove nothing." He sat upright. "I never got my phone back. It could still be in that neighborhood for all I know."

"We requested the location records from Olivia's carrier. Her phone was pinging the same tower your phone was. The same tower serving Victor Bachman's neighborhood."

"What's that got to do with me? It's her phone, not mine."

"Hey, here's something I want to know. You and Olivia are both with MetroPCS. Leon, too. Why are you all on the same carrier?"

Roman's lip curled, and he flicked his hand. "That's a question."

"Fine," I said. "Them's the rules."

"That's right. Them's the rules."

"Okay, so let's get back to the things you don't know. We just seized Olivia's phone."

He scowled. "So?"

"We're going to analyze the GPS on it. Did you know a phone's GPS gives more accurate detail than a cell tower report? I'll bet you did, and that's why you got rid of yours. What do you want to bet her phone puts her right at Victor Bachman's house?"

Roman's face remained tight, and he stayed silent.

"You should have told your girl to get rid of her phone. Maybe you did, and she didn't do it. I'd love to ask you that, but I'll save it for later."

"She did it." Roman said it so softly I almost missed it.

I stiffened. "Say that again."

"Olivia killed him." He reached out and tapped Bachman's photo. "I had nothing to do with it." Roman looked at me earnestly. "You gotta believe me. I'll take a lie detector test. Whatever you want."

My mind reeled. Was he telling the truth? I wanted to dissect the information, to poke holes in his story, but he was on a roll. I twirled my hand, mimicking the same gesture he had given me only moments prior.

"We found the phone just like you said." Roman nodded. "We used that Find My Phone app. Led us right to old boy's house. What did you say his name was?"

He patted Bachman's photo. "While I searched the car—the top was down—Olivia went up to the house to confront the guy."

I cocked my head. "She contacted Bachman?"

"That's right. I told her to wait, but she got it into her head that she was going to make him pay for what he did."

"Someone stole your phone, you used your girl's phone to track it across town, and when you arrived there, you hunted for it inside the convertible while *she* confronted the guy?"

He nodded. "Just like that. She wanted to impress me."

"You know what that makes you look like?"

"Say what you want." Roman's face twisted with urgency. "She killed that man, not me. I was an innocent bystander."

"You saw her do it, or did she tell you she did it?"

"I saw her do it. Plain as day. She was standing in the doorway when she stabbed the motherfucker." He mimed the action. "One, two, three."

That's how many wounds were found on Victor Bachman.

"Did you see him?" I asked.

Roman shook his head. "He was inside. When I realized what she did, I grabbed my phone and got us out of there."

"Where'd she get the knife?"

"How would I know? You'll have to ask her."

"You carry a knife."

"It wasn't mine. You gotta believe me."

I pulled Leon Harding's phone records from the folder. "Do you remember sending these texts to your cousin?"

Roman leaned forward slightly. "Yeah. Okay, I sent those. So?"

"You said earlier that you didn't send anything from Olivia's phone."

He turned a palm upward. "I made a mistake. Look. I asked Leon for his help to recover the phone, but the guy pussed out." Roman smirked. "It's that bitch he's running with. She's got him by the nuts. He should cut her loose."

"Later on, you texted Leon again." I flipped to the second page of the transcript and put my finger near the part I wanted him to read. "You texted, 'Never mind, I took care of it.'"

Roman studied the message for a moment. His eyes jumped higher on the page, and he reread something there. Then his gaze returned to the words my finger lingered next to.

"I didn't write that," he said.

"You just said you sent those messages."

Roman nodded. "The ones before."

"But you didn't write this part here?"

He shook his head. "Nope. That was Olivia. She'd taken her phone back by then. She wrote it. She took care of it by killing that guy." Roman crossed his arms. "That was her saying that." He looked at the camera in the wall and held up his hand as if swearing in before a judge. "She did it. She killed that man."

"What did you do with your phone?"

His attention returned to me, and he recrossed his arms. "I broke it. Threw it away."

"Why?"

"Why do you think? She killed a man. I know how you guys are. Me just being at the scene was going to jam me up. I'm telling you, Olivia did it while I was next to that car, getting my phone."

"Where'd you throw away the phone?"

"On the street as we were driving. Pieces everywhere."

"Why didn't you tell Olivia to do the same?"

He shrugged. "I guess I was in shock."

"You still had enough sense to get rid of your own phone."

"Self-preservation, I guess. Instinct."

"What did she do with the knife?"

He shrugged again.

"You can still be charged with murder."

Roman batted the air with his hand. "Get out of here with your bullshit. I was upside-down in the backseat of that car. There's no way I could have stopped the crazy bitch. I'll take my chances in court."

"You said you saw her stab the guy. Now you're saying you were upside-down in the backseat when it happened?"

He rolled his eyes. "You're trying to trip me up. I saw her do it. That's my story."

I collected the photographs and stood. "Wait here."

He clicked his tongue against the back of his teeth. "For how long?"

"Just wait."

I stepped out of the interview room and closed the door behind me. SIU Corporal Kurt Botzon leaned against a nearby wall with his arms crossed. "All done?"

"Not yet. Mind watching him for a few?"

"I'd be happy to. Higgins told me to tell you he's with the woman."

"I figured."

Botzon moved into the first interview room.

I walked down the hall and stepped into the observation room. Seated in front of several televisions was Olivia Rizzuto. Glenn sat next to her. Both turned in my direction when I walked in. Mascara streaked down Olivia's face. She'd made it worse by rubbing at her eyes.

Glenn said, "Olivia no longer wants to talk with her lawyer."

19

Olivia Rizutto settled herself into the chair and pulled it closer to the table.

I flicked the wall switch to activate the camera, and the light above us glowed red. "We're recording."

She nodded.

"I'm going to reread your rights," I said.

"I already know them."

"You asked for a lawyer."

"But I don't want one."

"Still." I reached into the manila folder in front of me and pulled out a small white card. "You have the right to remain silent."

Olivia sat dutifully while I read through the remaining rights.

Glenn stood nearby and watched. His hands were in his pockets. Tactically, it was a bad choice—it would slow his reaction time if Olivia became violent. Psychologically, though, it was a great position. He appeared relaxed and friendly. He nodded and politely smiled when she looked his way.

When I finished reciting Olivia's rights, I said, "Do you understand these rights as I have read them?"

"Yeah." She reached for the card and my pen.

"Will you waive these rights and answer my questions?"

"C'mon, let's do this." She ticked the box asserting she would waive her rights and then signed her name. Olivia set the pen on top of the card and slid both back to me.

"I can't believe that piece of shit," she said. "How do you want to do this?"

I wanted to pin Victor Bachman's murder on Roman McCurdy, but there was a process. I needed to build enough of her testimony to do such a thing.

"Let's start at the bar," I said.

"Fine. Someone stole Roman's phone, and he freaked out. I'm not sure why since I'm the one paying for the stupid thing. I paid for the new one, too. I'm an asshole for letting him treat me that way."

"You paid for his phone?"

She nodded. "I could get a discount if I put it on my account, but he made me put it in his name so he could pretend to be a big man. He doesn't want people to know I pay for most of his shit."

"Did you pay for Leon's as well?"

"Why would I pay for his?"

"He also had his through the same provider."

She smirked. "Leon follows Roman. That's all."

"If you're paying for everything, why would Roman freak out if his phone was missing?"

She ruefully shook her head. "Because the dumb son-of-a-bitch had pictures on it. Stuff he and the Titans did. Drugs. Guns. Break-ins. You name it, he took pictures of it."

"Can you provide us with information on those items?"

Olivia's head bobbled. "If that's what you want. That motherfucker is dead to me. You let me know what I can do to hurt him, and I'll stick it right up his ass."

"For right now, let's stay with the night the phone was stolen."

Olivia rolled her eyes. "Whatever."

"You used your phone to track his?"

Her lips twisted. "Yeah, right. Track My Phone. Ever heard of it? Everyone has. I called it up, and we started following his phone. Right to where it was in some guy's Mustang. I called the number I don't know how many times, and no one answered. Roman never had his ringer on. Only had it set to buzz. You think he did that to cheat on me?"

Olivia glanced at Glenn, and he shrugged.

Her attention returned to me. "Well? What about you?"

"I don't know."

My ringer was set to buzz. So was Glenn's. We did it so it wouldn't interrupt interviews or crime scene investigations. I also hated people intruding into my daily life. Explaining any of that to her seemed detrimental to the situation since I wanted her to stay angry at Roman.

Olivia flicked her hand. "Whatever. I think he was. It was dark out when we got to that dude's house. I called the phone and saw it light up in the backseat. I leaned in and got the phone. When I came back out, I held the phone in the air to show Roman. Real proud like." Olivia lifted her right hand into the air. "You know where he was? Headed toward the house. He rang the goddamned doorbell. I told him let's go. It was late, and the neighbors might hear us. He said, 'Bitch, get in the car.' Just like that." She waved her hand. "I helped him find his phone—the one I'm paying for—and he dismissed me like I don't matter. 'Bitch, get in the car.'" Her eyes hardened. "I don't appreciate being called that."

"I would imagine not."

Olivia looked at the wall.

"Where were you parked?"

She shrugged a single shoulder. "Down the street."

"Did you know he was going to do that? Go up to the house?"

Her face pinched, and she turned to me. "I didn't know what we were going to do. Maybe the phone was inside the house to begin with. I thought we'd figure out where it was, then wait for some of his boys."

"Leon wasn't coming."

She clicked her tongue against the back of her teeth. "Fuck, Leon. He got that new girlfriend of his, and he ain't been worth a shit. Roman's got other boys."

"But they didn't come?"

"He didn't know their numbers. He only knew Leon's. We were sort of stuck."

"So Roman went up to the house?"

She nodded.

"What happened when the door opened?"

"Roman stepped inside so quick I didn't see nothing. I stayed right where I was—out by that car. I promise I never went in."

"How long was he in there?"

"I dunno. Maybe five seconds at the most. When he came out, he got mad because I didn't leave the yard. He grabbed my arm and yanked me to get going. He said, 'Bitch, what'd I tell you?'"

Glenn shifted his stance. "You don't like being called bitch."

"That's right." Olivia smacked the table. "That's right!"

"Did you hear anything from inside the house?" I asked. "Any yelling or screaming?"

Olivia shook her head. "Nothing."

"What about blood?" I asked. "Was there any on Roman?"

"He had some on his right hand, but he was careful not to touch me with it."

"Where was his knife?"

Her brow furrowed. "In his pocket. I learned that later."

"What did you do when you got back to the car?"

"I drove. What do you think I did? Roman couldn't find anything to wipe his hand on, so he wiped it on his pants. Then he took his phone from me and broke it apart." She looked at Glenn again. "I was like, 'What the fuck are you doing? I paid for that,' but he wouldn't say anything to me except 'Drive up to Francis.' He just kept snapping the phone into pieces."

Francis Avenue was the most heavily traveled east-west arterial in north Spokane.

"When I got up there," she continued, "he made me roll down his window. He didn't want to touch the car with his hand even though he got most of the blood off. Then he started tossing pieces into the road."

"Which way were you headed?" I asked.

"Toward Division."

Heading toward Division Street meant she was traveling eastbound. I hurriedly made notes. It was a long shot that any piece of the phone lingered in the street after more than a week. Even if a piece could be located, it would need Roman's fingerprint to be anything more than circumstantial. A bloody fingerprint could be the nail in his proverbial coffin. We would spend some time looking for it.

When I finished writing, I looked up.

"Did you see what he did with the knife?"

"He threw it into some dude's trash can."

I cocked my head.

She nodded as if acknowledging my confusion. "We drove until we found a neighborhood that had their garbage cans out. You know? For pick-up in the morning? He got out, lifted the lid, and dropped the knife inside." She mimed the whole action. "Then I took him home, and he washed up. I washed his clothes, and then he threw them away."

"Did he talk to you about murdering Victor Bachman?"

"We didn't know his name, but yeah, he bragged about it."

I wondered if Roman had really told her or if she'd put it together because she'd heard him say something like it on the closed-circuit monitor a few minutes earlier.

"Did he brag to you, or did he brag to Leon, and you overheard it?"

"He bragged to me. He wanted to be the big man because of what he did. Maybe Roman told Leon the next day, but he was sort of pissed at his cousin for not stepping up."

"Roman said you killed Victor Bachman."

"I had nothing to do with it." She shook her head. "I guess I drove him to the guy's house, so I'm gonna get in trouble for that, but you gotta believe me, I thought we were only getting the phone back. I had no idea he was going to do something stupid."

"When you found out he killed someone, why didn't you call the police?"

"And get myself in trouble?" Olivia's nose twitched, and she rubbed it with the palm of her hand. "But Roman did me dirty. I'm gonna make him pay."

I tore the top page off my notepad and slipped it into my file. I set the pen on top of the notepad in front of her. "I want you to write a statement."

"Why for?" She pointed up to the little red light. "You got everything on camera."

"If you really want to get Roman, it's got to be in writing with your signature. There are no takebacks then."

Olivia's head bobbed. "Well, fine. How many words? You want me to write a novel? I'll write you a fucking book if it means he pays for all the shit he said about me. I let him do things to me no other man has done, and he repays me like that?" She smirked. "Well, fuck him. He's going to jail, and I'm gonna sleep with his boys. Especially Leon, that'll kill him."

She grabbed the pen and started writing.

"We'll give you some time. Come outside when you're done." I flicked off the camera and stood.

Olivia raised her free hand but didn't look up. She was too busy planning her retribution.

Glenn and I left the room.

***

"You're booking *me*?" Roman McCurdy asked. "I told you it was Olivia."

Roman's hands were cuffed behind his back. Kurt Botzon walked on the left side of the man. I was on his right. Ahead of us loomed the monolithic structure of the Spokane County Jail.

Glenn stayed behind with Olivia while she finished writing her statement. She wasn't kidding when she offered to write a novel.

"Listen," Roman said. "What else can I say to make you believe me?"

"Nothing."

"There's gotta be something. What about the Titans?"

I shrugged. "You killed a man."

"That was Olivia." He tried to stomp in emphasis, but Botzon tugged on his elbow. Roman lost his footing and stumbled. "Listen to me!"

Sergeant Trevor Hackworth crossed the parking lot. He made a straight line toward the jail's entrance. I hadn't called him but suggested Botzon did. I thought the man might like to be present while we booked Roman.

Hackworth marched like a military man about to receive an award. He walked with his head held high, chin thrust out, and shoulders pulled back. He didn't smile, however. The moment was too serious for that.

Roman noticed Hackworth approaching. "The fuck is this?" he muttered.

"He's joining us."

"Why?"

"I thought he might like to see you get booked."

"You all are doing this because of his daughter!" Roman stopped walking, but Botzon yanked him forward. He stumbled toward Hackworth. "You're setting me up!"

We stopped in front of the jail's entrance. I pressed the buzzer and looked up at the camera affixed above the door.

"I'm innocent!" Roman yelled. "I didn't do nothing!"

A voice came over a tinny speaker. *"Yeah?"*

"City," I said. I motioned with my head toward Roman. "One for booking."

"*He looks uncooperative.*"

Roman kicked the metal entry door. "You bastards are all the same!"

"*We can work with that.*"

The door buzzed. I started to open it, but Roman kicked it closed.

Botzon and Hackworth jerked Roman away.

After the door buzzed a second time, I opened it.

The SIU officers escorted Roman inside, and I pulled the door closed behind us.

***

Andrew Parker stopped by my desk. Jessie Johnson, his partner, was with him.

Parker was in one of the black suits he always wore. They never fit the guy right. I blamed his physique. The bodybuilding had to make it hard to find a correct fitting suit. Jessie looked more stylish. Even though he spent a considerable amount of time in the gym, his body shape was different—leaner, more flexible. His suits looked fancier, as if he might have spent extra money to have them tailored.

"Heard you guys caught your killer," Parker said.

I leaned back in my chair and glanced at my partner. "It was a team effort."

Glenn nodded but didn't say anything.

"You guys heading out?" I asked.

Parker nodded. "We caught a ripe one."

"Floater," Johnson said. "Over near the T.J. Meenach Bridge. You guys want it?"

I waved them off. "We're good."

"You two old timers could use the fresh air," Parker said. He looked at Glenn. "Get some sun on that pasty skin."

Glenn smirked. "The only sunshine you get is from a tanning bed."

Parker motioned at his crotch. "The wife likes the boys golden brown. You should try it. Might improve your love life."

"I do fine."

"I heard. Librarians, right?" Parker suggestively raised his eyebrows. "What is it about them? Is it their brains or the fact they smell like books?"

Glenn turned to his computer. "Parker, you're like herpes—a little goes a long way."

Johnson laughed and patted his partner's shoulder. "See you outside."

Parker lifted his chin in acknowledgment. He turned to me. "Thanks for coming by this weekend."

I nodded.

"Brooke really enjoyed meeting you. And I appreciated our talk, too." He knocked on the edge of my desk. "Congrats on catching your guy."

Parker walked off.

Glenn spun in his chair. "What is it with that guy?"

I shrugged a single shoulder. "If I could tell you, I would."

"Are you friends now?"

"We had dinner."

"I still can't believe you went over to Parker's. What's it like?"

"His wife makes a mean apple pie."

Glenn leaned forward. "Apple pie?"

"Pretty darn good, too."

"I like apple pie." He looked in the direction Parker had walked off. "How do I get invited?"

"Probably don't compare him to herpes."

"Me? You punched him in the hallway once."

"What do I know? Maybe that's how he makes friends." I turned to my computer. "Now, leave me alone. I need to finish this booking affidavit."

20

"You're sure they know we're coming?"

It was the third time Marlene had asked the question.

"Yes, mom," Sadie said with little girl exasperation. "Dallas said they know."

"Over there," I said and pointed to the curb.

Marlene pulled the car to the side of the road and stopped. Sadie was out first. Even with a broken arm, the kid was hard to corral.

"I feel like I should have made something," Marlene said.

I waved Sadie toward the front of the house. "They ordered pizza. They said just to bring ourselves."

"We could have brought a bottle of wine."

"It's my brother," I said. "He's going to show us pictures of his trip."

The door to the house opened as we walked up the sidewalk.

My brother, Dean, stepped out and smiled. "You made it."

Sadie presented her broken arm. "Want to sign my cast?"

***

"Sadie had a nice time tonight," Marlene whispered.

We'd finally got her to bed, and now the two of us stood at the front door of Marlene's house.

"Thank you for inviting us," she continued. "Their pictures were lovely."

"Yeah."

Marlene had hit it off with Dean and his wife, Arlene. The two women laughed at how their names rhymed. The rest of the night, they tried to rhyme whenever they could. They really had a blast together.

"You're lucky to have them in your life," Marlene said.

I nodded.

She reached out and touched my hand. "It means a lot for you to introduce us to your family."

"I liked having you guys there. It was nice."

Marlene's fingers wrapped around mine, and she stepped closer. Her lips brushed my cheek. "I love you, Dallas." She let go of my hand to touch my face. "I'll talk to you tomorrow."

She winked once and stepped back into the house.

The door slowly closed.

***

It was after eleven when I stood in the silent entryway of my home. The refrigerator wasn't running. The neighborhood was also quiet.

I was tired and wanted to go to sleep. It had been a long day.

But Bobbie was there in the silence. We stayed together for several minutes.

I replayed moments from our life together. Times spent laughing, the moments I lay in bed listening to her softly snoring, those times when we sat quietly side by side as we read our books. The love we had was made in simple times, not big moments.

I closed my eyes and tried to drink all those memories in.

Then the refrigerator started and broke the moment. It was time for bed.

Did You Enjoy the Book?

Thank you for reading *The Fate of Our Years* and visiting the 509! I hope you enjoyed meeting some of the recurring characters. This is a continuing series with other characters occasionally stepping into the lead role. There are two parallel series to the 509 Crime Stories—the Flip-Flop Detective and the John Cutler mysteries. I hope you'll check them out.

I'm always grateful when a reader takes time out of their day to comment on one of my novels. If you do write a review, please email me, and let me know.

I'd love to say thanks!

About the Author

Colin Conway is the creator of the 509 Crime Stories, a series of novels set in Eastern Washington with revolving lead characters. They are standalone tales and can be read in any order.

He also created the Cozy Up series which pushes the envelope of the cozy genre. Libby Klein, author of the Poppy McAllister series, says *Cozy Up to Death* is "Not your grandma's cozy."

Colin co-authored the Charlie-316 series. The first novel in the series, *Charlie-316*, is a political/crime thriller that has been described as "riveting and compulsively readable," "the real deal," and "the ultimate ride-along."

He served in the U.S. Army and later as an officer of the Spokane Police Department. He has owned a laundromat, invested in a bar, and run a karate school. Besides writing crime fiction, he is a commercial real estate broker.

Colin lives with his beautiful girlfriend, three wonderful children, and a codependent Vizsla that rules their world.

Find out more at colinconway.com.

Also by Colin Conway

THE 509 UNIVERSE

The 509 Crime Stories

The Side Hustle
The Long Cold Winter
The Blind Trust
The Suit
The Value in Our Lies
The Mean Street
Murder by Any Other Name
Black and Blue in the Lilac City
The Only Death That Matters
The After-Hours War
The Fate of Our Years
The Night of the Dead Boys
The Path of Progress
When the Wicked Rest

The John Cutler Mysteries

Cutler's Return
Cutler's Chase
Cutler's Friend
Cutler's Cases
Cutler's Bargain
Cutler's Legacy

The Flip-Flop Detective

Strait Over Tackle
Strait to Hell
Strait Out of Nowhere

OTHER SERIES

The Cozy Up Series

Cozy Up to Death
Cozy Up to Murder
Cozy Up to Blood
Cozy Up to Trouble
Cozy Up to Christmas
Cozy Up to Danger
Cozy Up to Terror

**The Charlie-316 Series
(with Frank Zafiro)**

Charlie-316
Never the Crime
Badge Heavy
Code Four
The Ride-Along

OTHER WORKS

Some Degree of Murder (with Frank Zafiro)
Tales from the Road (with Bill Bancroft)